# THE
# VALKYRIE
# DIRECTIVE

# THE
# VALKYRIE
# DIRECTIVE

*Peter MacAlan*

W.H. ALLEN · LONDON
1987

Copyright © Peter MacAlan, 1987

Printed and bound in Great Britain by
Adlard & Son Ltd, The Garden City Press
for the Publishers, W.H. Allen & Co. Plc
44 Hill Street, London W1X 8LB

British Library Cataloguing in Publication Data

MacAlan, Peter
    The valkyrie directive.
    I. Title
    823'.914[F]        PR6063.A11/

    ISBN 0–491–03007–X

The most important things are not always to be found in the records.

– *J.W. von Goethe (1749–1832)*

*Valkyrie*, n. (Scandinavian myth) any one of the minor goddesses who conduct the slain from the battlefield to Valhalla. (Old Norse *Valkyrja* – *valr*, the slain, and the root of *kjosa* – to choose.

*Oxford English Dictionary*

# ACKNOWLEDGMENTS

The basis of this story was first told me some years ago by a man I shall now call 'Kaare'. He told it to while away the hours of a night-time Channel crossing as we huddled in the bar of the ferry *St Germain*, trying to fortify ourselves against the cold and the restless black sea outside. 'Kaare' was in a position to have an intimate knowledge of some of the details. Although he is now dead, my promise not to reveal his identity is sacrosanct. Without 'Kaare' this story would not be told. However, I would like to remind readers that this is essentially a work of fiction, an adventure story written for the purpose of entertainment.

In my researches for this book I would like to place on record my thanks to the officials of the Forsvarmuseet (The Norwegian Defence Museum); Norges Hjemmefrontmuseum (Norwegian Resistance Museum); the Kongsvinger Festning Museum; the Aamotgarden Museum of Kongsvinger; the Imperial War Museum, London; and the Public Records Office, London. I would also like to thank Anne G. Ulset, press and information officer of the Royal Norwegian Embassy, London.

Among the many newspapers, magazines and books consulted in the British Museum, as part of essential background material, I would like to single out the following: *I Saw it Happen in Norway*, Carl Joachim Hambro, Hodder & Stoughton, 1940; *The Invasion of Norway*, Herman K. Lehmkuhl, Hutchinson, 1940; *Narvik and After*, Lord Strabolgi RN, Hutchinson, 1940; *Norway, Neutral and Invaded*, Halvdan Koht, Hutchinson, 1941; *Norway Revolts Against the Nazis*, Jakob S. Worm–Müller, Lindsay Drummond, New York, 1941; *Narvik*, Captain Donald Macintyre RN, Evans Brothers, 1959; *The Campaign in Norway*, T.K. Derry, Allen & Unwin, 1952; *A History of Norway*, T.K. Derry, Clarendon Press, Oxford, 1973; and *The Life of Neville Chamberlain*, Sir Keith G. Freiling, Macmillan 1946 (reprinted 1973).

Finally, I would like to pay a special acknowledgment to Dr

Piotr Klafkowski, now of Solberg, Norway, for his invaluable help and enthusiasm in assisting me with my research in Norway. Where I might have given up, he pressed on and delivered the goods! So, to Piotr, and to his wife Paki Klafkowski MD, I humbly dedicate this book as a small token of my thanks.

*Peter MacAlan*
LONDON, 1987

# PART ONE
*Tuesday, 9 April 1940*

# CHAPTER ONE

There is, in the moments between sleeping and waking, a brief period in which one's mind reaches out and incorporates the sounds of reality into the remnants of the dream state. In those last few seconds before he was fully awake, Lars Sweeny dreamt that he was lying at the bottom of a ship's hold and that large, heavy crates were hurtling down towards his prone figure, landing with great splintering explosions. He had had this particular dream before. It was a fairly regular one and its origin did not require Freudian or Jungian symbolism to interpret its meaning. He had once narrowly escaped being crushed by a falling box while supervising the loading of a hold. The event, although pushed to the back of his conscious mind, often haunted his subconscious. It had become his sleeping fear. But this time a new dimension was added: the reverberating sounds of the contact of the boxes with the steel plates of the deck. Then Lars Sweeny was awake and sweating in his narrow bunk in the darkness of his cabin.

He lay for a moment blinking up at the small round portion of early morning sky which filtered through the porthole by his head. He was confused, for the sounds of explosions were no longer part of his dream. They were a reality in the semi-gloom of the dawn. Across the hill of Byghaugen, towards the southern end of the port of Stavanger, came the dull boom of an explosion followed by two more in rapid succession. For another split second he remained huddled in his warm, sweaty blankets, wondering how he should interpret the noise. Then the staccato rattle of a machine-gun made him jerk forward, ripping aside the blankets. He could see through the porthole a line of tracer curving into the sky, yellow and red against the dull clouds. A line of fairy-lights strung out towards the black shapes that moved relentlessly above.

His cabin door burst open and an elderly man, white hair uncombed and wild, stood on the threshold. He had hauled on oil-stained dungarees which matched a dirty woollen fisherman's jumper.

'Get dressed, Lars!' the old man cried in a voice that was filled with emotion.

Sweeny gazed at him in bewilderment. 'What the hell is happening, Uncle Tenvig?'

'They are bombing Sola airfield.'

'They?'

'The Germans. Who else?'

For the last two days, since they had arrived back in Stavanger from one of their regular trips up the coast to Narvik, they had heard nothing but rumours – rumours of a possible invasion of Norway by the forces of the Third Reich. Sweeny had not paid much attention to them. After all, Norway was a neutral country. It had no quarrel with anyone. It had survived the last war with its neutrality intact and it would survive this new war which had erupted in Europe during the previous autumn when Poland had been invaded. Only two days before, on April 7, the Foreign Minister, Professor Halvdan Koht, had stated: 'We cannot think of any war that Norway might enter except one into which we were forced to defend our independence and freedom.' Why would any of the belligerents want to invade Norway, a small, non-aligned nation with no standing army? Besides, the President of the Norwegian Parliament, whose authority ranked second only to the King, Haakon VII, was also President of the League of Nations and Norway's neutrality was respected throughout the world. The Führer of the Third Reich would not dare to deal with Norway as he had with Czechoslovakia and Poland.

'Get dressed, Lars,' urged Tenvig, turning from the cabin.

Sweeny glanced at the chronometer on the cabin wall. It was a quarter after five o'clock. As he drew on his clothes he could hear the anti-aircraft guns out at Sola Airfield, beyond the headland, throwing everything they had at the circling aircraft above them.

Lars Sweeny was in his mid-thirties; a tall, broad-shouldered and well-muscled man with that curiously deceptive awkwardness of movement which many tall men seem to have. His face was square-shaped, with a deeply cleft chin and a slightly hooked nose. He had a shock of red hair which was permanently unruly and tousled. His eyes were light-coloured but as changeable as the sea. The firm compression of his lips indicated a stubborn attitude which would allow him to admit neither defeat nor mistake. There was something else, too; the face was a mask which did not permit his emotions to surface. It was as if he had been hurt badly at some time and was determined not to allow such hurt to repeat itself.

Sweeny was the son of an Irish father and a Norwegian mother and had been born in Boston, Massachusetts, where he had lived until he was sixteen. His parents had died within a year of each other and Sweeny, who had already fallen in love with the sea, haunting the Boston dockyards, had signed on with a Norwegian iron-ore ship, eventually making his way to Stavanger. Stavanger was one of Norway's oldest towns and most important seaports and it was here that his mother's brother Tenvig lived. Uncle Tenvig had welcomed young Sweeny into his family and given him a home when the boy was ashore. Uncle Tenvig and his wife had had their own child late in life. The birth of their daughter, Freya, had caused Tenvig's wife complications and she had died soon after the child was born. Tenvig had been doing his best to bring up the girl, who was five years old when Sweeny arrived. If the truth were known, it seemed that Tenvig saw in Sweeny the son he would never have.

With his new home and family in Stavanger, Sweeny had served four seasons on the whaling ships and four more on merchant vessels plying between Norway and South America. Uncle Tenvig himself was skipper of a small coaster. One day uncle and nephew had decided to pool their resources and buy a vessel between them, becoming co-owners of an ageing fishing smack. It was seventy-five feet long and had a single-cylinder engine with a speed of eight knots. They called it *Gunnlöd* after the mythological giant Suttung's daughter, who was seduced by the god of war, Odin, in order to obtain a magic mead which she guarded. Now the old smack, *Gunnlöd* traded in the fjords of western Norway, running supplies and small cargoes to the far north, to the remote Arctic townships such as Narvik, Tromso and Hammerfest. It was a good life and old Tenvig and Sweeny made an adequate living. They could usually handle the vessel themselves but since Freya, now an attractive twenty-four-year-old, had married a local seaman, Erik Hartvig, they numbered him as a third crewman.

'For Christ's sake, Lars!' Sweeny heard Tenvig yelling from the deck. 'Aren't you dressed yet?'

Stirring guiltily, Sweeny clambered onto the deck, hauling his fisherman's peajacket on.

The *Gunnlöd* was moored along the old town's Strandkaien Quay among numerous other boats. The air was filled with shouting and the sounds of confusion. He saw that there were a few fires on the outskirts of town where bombs aimed for the airfield had fallen by mistake. People in all manner of dress were tumbling into the tiny ancient streets around the old harbour. On the quayside several men from other ships and boats were standing in groups staring around them in bewilderment, apparently unable to comprehend what was happening. Against the lightening sky Sweeny suddenly saw innumerable black shapes floating. Parachutists, seeming unreal as they jerked like marionettes on the ends of wires. The drone of aircraft engines had become a constant background roar.

Uncle Tenvig was grinding his teeth as he stood beside Sweeny.

'Parachute troops going for the airfield.'

Sweeny nodded slowly.

'Sola is one of the best military airfields in the south,' Tenvig went on unnecessarily. 'I hope the boys and their aircraft have managed to get off and make a fight of it.'

Sweeny's mouth twitched cynically. He knew that the entire Norwegian airforce could count little more than one hundred aircraft. The local newspaper, the *Stavanger Aftenblad*, had pointed out this fact only a few days before when stressing the importance of maintaining an armed neutrality. He could remember the figures. The army had 83 aircraft while the navy had 32, with the majority of the aeroplanes being out-dated scouts. Sola had one squadron of nine ancient MF II scout planes to defend it, plus one Heinkel used for coastal patrol. Not much to make a fight with.

Out in the harbour a ship's siren began its banshee wail. The two men turned to peer out beyond the harbour entrance into the fjord to where the low dark outline of a warship could be seen. Sweeny knew it was the 510-ton Norwegian destroyer *Sleipner*, named after the eight-legged warhorse of the god Odin. The ship had anchored there the previous evening, and now she had steam up, for clouds of smoke were belching from her funnel stacks. She was beginning to move, her sirens still screaming angrily.

'Where the hell is she going?' grumbled old Tenvig as he peered forward. 'She'd do better to stay here and protect the harbour with her guns.'

Even as he spoke, they heard the crack of an explosion and

flame spat from the *Sleipner*'s for'ard guns. They heard the whine of the shell across the fjord.

Sweeny hurried into the wheelhouse and grabbed the glasses there, focusing in the direction in which the destroyer had fired and catching the plume of spray made by her falling shot. A little way beyond the fall of the shell was a dark silhouette moving into the fjord. From its outline it appeared to be an armed merchantman. Sweeny saw an answering flash and heard a dull boom as a gun from the mysterious vessel replied. Adjusting the glasses, Sweeny caught sight of a red and black flag fluttering in the cold morning light from the jackstaff of the ship.

'Germans!' he hissed.

The *Sleipner* was ploughing through the calm waters of the fjord towards the German vessel, sirens still screaming their challenge.

'Go get her, skipper!' yelled old Tenvig, pounding the wood of the wheelhouse with his gnarled fist.

There was another belch of flame from the destroyer and the sound of an explosion as her for'ard gun opened up again. Neither Sweeny nor Tenvig were prepared for the result. There was a mighty explosion. The German vessel seemed enveloped in a column of flame and then there was nothing but smoke and debris on the waters of the fjord.

The *Sleipner*'s siren wailed exultantly.

Sweeny put down the glasses. There was a moment of silence. It seemed so strange and unreal, but somewhere it registered in his mind that he had witnessed the death of a ship and its crew. Alive one moment. Blasted into oblivion the next. It was hard to grasp the reality. This was war.

'We'd better get the *Gunnlöd* to a safer anchorage, Uncle Tenvig,' he said soberly. The terrible explosion had reminded him with sharp vividness that they were due to take a cargo of dynamite to the mines at Hammerfest that day, sailing on the midday tide. If the Germans began to bomb the shipping in the harbour . . .

'We'll have to get clearance from the Harbour Master,' his uncle replied, biting his lip as he realized the meaning behind Sweeny's suggestion.

They decided to go together because the *Hafenkapitan*'s office was only a hundred yards away along the quayside. When they reached it they found it already crowded with officers from numerous ships shouting questions at the Harbour Master, a

[15]

little man looking woebegone and slightly ridiculous with his uniform jacket pulled over his pyjamas. He was trying to still the hubbub by waving his hands distractedly in the air.

'It's an all-out invasion of Norway,' he was shouting above the noise. 'The Germans are invading Norway. That is official. Reports are coming in from Oslo, Kristiansand, Bergen, Trondheim and Narvik of attempted landings. It seems that they are trying to seize the main ports and the airfields.'

A ginger-bearded skipper from an English freighter thrust forward. 'Should we attempt to put to sea?'

The *Hafenkapitan* shrugged.

'Gentlemen, it is up to you to do what you think best for the safety of your ships.'

'What about that merchantman blown up in the fjord just now?' demanded an Italian seaman. 'How can we be sure your destroyers aren't trigger happy? They may attack us.'

The *Hafenkapitan* shot the man an angry glance.

'The ship sunk by our destroyer, the *Sleipner*, was a German vessel. I have received a message from the captain of the *Sleipner*. The vessel was identified as the *Roda*. She was challenged several times before she was sunk. The *Sleipner* reports that she has had messages from Oslo that a large German fleet has entered Oslo Fjord. Several of our ships have been sunk but the gun batteries at Oscarborg are holding the Germans back. I am told that the German Ambassador has delivered an ultimatum to our King demanding surrender to the forces of the Third Reich. There is word of a general mobilization of our forces. That is all I know, gentlemen. I can't tell you any more.'

'What about the safety of Stavanger?' asked a Swedish officer. 'We can see parachute troops landing behind the town.'

'German aircraft are bombing the military field at Sola,' the Harbour Master replied. His voice was bitter. 'German troops are apparently landing in an attempt to capture the field. Our troops, members of the Rogaland Regiment, are trying to hold them back with some machine-gun batteries. I am told that several of our aircraft have been destroyed on the ground. I have had a telephone call from General Steffens, who is commanding the 3rd Army Division at Stetesdal, asking for volunteers to report to the nearest military headquarters immediately.'

The Harbour Master hesitated, frowning. He had become aware of a sound, faint at first, which rapidly grew in volume and fury into the terrifying scream of an aero-engine. Those crowded

[16]

into the tiny office flung themselves down, flinching before the awesome banshee wail which caused their hair to bristle. Then from nearby came the sound of half-a-dozen rapid explosions, followed by a strange quiet. The men climbed to their feet somewhat sheepishly, dusting themselves down, as they realized that the explosions had been some way off.

A sleepy-eyed mate from a Polish vessel was standing by the door, looking out.

'JU 87s,' he muttered. Then he turned round. 'Stuka dive-bombers. I saw them used in Poland last September.'

The *Hafenkapitan* joined him at the door.

'Christ!' he swore. 'They're beginning to bomb the harbour installations. Gentlemen, I suggest you do what you can to protect your ships.'

The captains and other officers began to run from the office, hastening back to their ships. Sweeny turned to Tenvig.

'You'd better get back aboard the *Gunnlöd*, Uncle, and get the engine warmed up. We'll take the old tub across the fjord through the islands to Nedstrand. I'll go and find Erik and Freya . . .' he hesitated. 'I think Freya will be safer with us than remaining in the town.'

Tenvig nodded approval.

'Don't be long. If things get hot I might have to move the *Gunnlöd*. If I do I'll try to stand off in the East Harbour and wait for you there.'

Sweeny gave a wave of his hand and turned to hurry towards the Torget, the old market place that stood at the foot of the quays. People were everywhere now, some running, others simply standing in bewilderment.

As he hurried along, his rubber seaboots clumping on the cobbles, Sweeny thought, inconsequentially, that he would have to apologize to Freya now. Freya had been continually warning about the possibility of an invasion and the dangers from Norway's own Fascist Party, the Nasjonal Samling. For Sweeny, the Nasjonal Samling, and their ridiculous, egocentric leader, Major Vidkun Quisling, were merely a joke – a minority which no one took seriously. Yet Freya should have been taken seriously, he reflected. After all, she was now a reporter on one of Oslo's leading newspapers, the *Dagbladet*, and was in a position to know such things. But for Sweeny, Freya was too close, too much a part of the family, to be taken seriously. On more than

[17]

one occasion she had lost her temper with him when he laughed at the idea of danger emanating from the comically uniformed Hird, the Norwegian fascist stormtroopers, named after the royal bodyguard of Viking times.

'They are the enemy within and could betray Norway, given half a chance!' she had stormed. 'Behind their comic parades and utterances are powerful, influential people.'

'Betray?' Sweeny had chuckled. 'To whom? Are you still claiming that Hitler means to invade Norway? That's nonsense. Why, Norway is neutral. Hitler wouldn't dare invade.'

'Tell that to the Czechoslovaks and the Poles.'

'Norway is different.'

Sweeny bit his lip, embarrassed by his stupidity, as he hurried along the streets to where Freya and Erik had their apartment. Norway *wasn't* different. The mocking sounds of explosions and gunfire told him that now. He should have taken Freya seriously.

It would have taken a discerning eye to spot the firming of the muscles in Sweeny's face. Sweeny had been in love with Freya, was still in love with her. It had been a bitter shock when she had married Erik Hartvig during the previous year. Not that Freya had ever suspected the depth of feeling which Sweeny had for her. He had never been able to fully explain it to her. True, he had tried to tell her of his love some years before. That was when she had been nineteen.

Freya had laughed. Of course Lars Sweeny loved her. Why not? After all, weren't they practically brother and sister? Blushing, Sweeny had not pushed the matter further, hiding his emotions and worshipping the girl from afar. When she had left school and gone to work on the local newspaper, the *Stavanger Aftenblad*, he had shared his uncle's enormous sense of pride. Then, last year, when she had gone to Oslo to join the famous *Dagbladet*, he had rejoiced in her success.

The shock had come soon after, when she had gaily announced that she would marry Erik Hartvig, a local seaman. In spite of the fact that Erik was a likeable, although slightly impecunious man, Sweeny had found it difficult to control the unreasonable hatred he felt for him. Yet he had suffered the marriage in silence, hiding his feelings behind a mask. Suffered in silence, even when old Tenvig had taken Erik onto the *Gunnlöd* as the third member of their crew.

Freya and Erik had a small apartment in a narrow side street. Freya spent most of her time in Oslo but came down to

Stavanger for long weekends, especially when she knew that the *Gunnlöd* would be in harbour. The apartment which she and Erik rented was a couple of rooms on the top floor of an ancient building, up four flights of bare wooden stairs.

Sweeny clambered up them as fast as he could, hoping that Erik had not already left to find the *Gunnlöd*. He was slightly out of breath by the time he reached the top landing. The door of the apartment was marked with the number 9, but the top of the number was loose, and as a result it hung upside down, making it look like a 6. Sweeny banged on the door and found, to his surprise, that it swung inwards at his touch.

'Freya!' he called as he pushed in.

The apartment seemed oppressively silent. It felt as if no one was there. The door opened directly into a small kitchen. Freya kept it very tidy, with a neat red-chequered tablecloth on the small wooden dining table, a pattern which matched the curtains at the window.

'Freya! Erik! It's me, Lars!' shouted Sweeny as he stepped inside.

There was still no answer. He took a step towards the door which he knew opened into the lounge, hesitated before it and then thrust it open. His eyes widened.

The first thing he saw inside was the body of Erik Hartvig. Erik lay on his back, his head was resting awkwardly against the corner of the settee. The eyes were slightly open, with a curious expression as if in disbelief at the last sight which had met them. Blood had trickled into the corner of his mouth and coagulated. There was a reddish-black round mark in the centre of the forehead and a stain on the young man's blue jersey above the heart.

'Erik!' whispered Sweeny, standing for a moment in shock before kneeling and searching for a pulse. There was none and the flesh was already cold.

'Freya?' A panic seized Sweeny as he peered round. There was no sign of the girl. He moved across to the half-open door which led into the bedroom and pushed it open.

He closed his eyes momentarily and a low animal noise came rumbling from his throat.

Freya was sprawled across the chintz cover of the bed. The bed was unmade and she was still clad in her nightdress and gown. They were both red with blood. The girl's lips were pale and parted as if in surprise, but her eyes were shut tight. One hand was flung backwards while the other seemed to be reaching

[19]

out, almost imploring.

'Freya!' The word was a choking sob.

Even as he moved forward, catching sight of the mass of red congealing blood around the girl's neck and shoulders, Sweeny knew that the girl was dead. That her throat had been cut.

# CHAPTER TWO

How long he stood by her body, swaying and groaning like an animal in pain, Sweeny did not know. He stood there murmuring her name over and over again. It was only the wail of the dive-bombers and the crashing of breaking glass in the bedroom window that jolted him back to reality.

He wiped his eyes and stared down, trying to control his facial muscles. Who could have done this? What was the reason behind these pointless killings? Erik had been shot. Shot twice. Once through the head and once through the heart. But Freya . . . Freya's throat had been cut; she had been slaughtered like some animal. But by whom? And why?

He realized that he must get the police. He turned and clattered down the stairs, out into the cobbled street. He knew there was a café on the corner which had a telephone. The glass of the front window of the café had been blown out by the blast of an explosion. The door was also open but there seemed to be no one about. He hurried in, went to the counter on which the telephone stood and took up the receiver. It seemed an age before the frightened voice of the operator answered him.

'Only priority calls allowed,' she began.

'This is an emergency,' snapped Sweeny. 'Get me the police.'

There was a hesitation and then a clicking sound.

'Police!' came a harassed voice.

'There's been a murder . . .' Sweeny began.

The voice cut him short, irritably.

'There's been thousands of murders! Clear the line at once. We need all telephone lines open for purposes of national defence. Don't you realize that the Germans are invading?'

'But you don't understand,' yelled Sweeny. 'There's been . . .'

'Clear the line!' snapped the voice before a silence told Sweeny that the policeman had hung up.

Swearing under his breath, Sweeny turned and ran back to the apartment, pushing his way through panic-stricken groups of people who were scurrying this way and that to escape the thunderous explosions. Yet the invasion seemed somehow unimportant to Sweeny as he stood in the apartment gazing at the bodies of Freya and Erik.

He wondered if he should put Freya's body into a more dignified position. No; no, the police would want to investigate later, later when they had time. He should touch nothing. Then the thought crossed his mind. What if the police never investigated the crime? What if the Germans succeeded in occupying Stavanger? Why would they bother to investigate the murders?

He hovered in indecision. Even with his mind in such a turmoil, some small voice of sanity in its deep recesses reminded him that he should get back to the *Gunnlöd*. Uncle Tenvig was waiting for him. He had to help the old man get the ship and its dangerous cargo across the fjord to a safer anchorage. Uncle Tenvig! How could he tell Tenvig that his daughter had been murdered? That his son-in-law had been killed? He couldn't. Not yet. He would tell him later. There was nothing Tenvig nor he could do. Nothing until this madness stopped.

He was about to turn away from the terrible scene in the bedroom when he noticed something clutched in the fingers of Freya's left hand. Frowning, he bent forward. It was a small piece of cloth, a piece of blue serge, frayed where it had been torn away. He compressed his mouth and carefully prised it gently from the dead girl's grasp. There was something small and metallic attached to the cloth. A button-hole badge. He peered at it curiously. It was a Nasjonal Samling badge. He turned it over in his hands. There was a stamp on the back; small markings which were almost a blur to the naked eye but Sweeny had fairly good eyesight. 5684 PL. What did that mean? Had Freya torn it from the lapel of the person who had killed her? His fist hardened around the piece of metal.

Another explosion caused the entire building to sway crazily, sending Sweeny crashing back into a doorpost, almost losing his grip on the tiny badge. He thrust it into his jacket pocket. He must go – go to join Uncle Tenvig. He moved forward decisively to the bed and bent down, brushing the dead girl's forehead with his lips.

'I'll find the swine who did this, Freya,' he whispered. 'I'll make them pay.'

He turned, dry-eyed, and moved from the apartment like a man in a dream.

The *Gunnlöd* was still waiting at the quayside as Sweeny came running up. Tenvig peered from the wheelhouse with a worried expression.

'Where's Erik? Where's Freya?'

'I couldn't find them,' lied Sweeny. He had formulated the lie as he hurried back through the cobbled streets to the harbour. 'There was no sign of them.' There was no point in telling old Tenvig now, not until they had placed the *Gunnlöd* out of danger. 'They must be taking shelter with some friends. I thought it best to get back and get the old tub across the fjord to safety.'

Tenvig nodded reluctantly. 'We'll come back for them when the air raid is over.'

Sweeny was already casting off the bow line.

'You get the stern line, uncle,' he yelled. 'I'll take the wheel.'

Several large ships were still getting steam-up as they left the quayside. Sweeny opened the throttle and swung hard at the wheel. The single-cylinder engine began to chug furiously as they swung out into the Vågen, the harbour inlet, dodging a freighter and rocking furiously in its wake.

Tenvig was lighting his pipe. He always lit his pipe when they left harbour. It was a ritual. Sweeny felt strangely comforted by the fact that the old man could still perform the ritual in these exceptional circumstances.

'Easy on the wheel, Lars,' the old man admonished him as he came into the wheel house. 'You're gripping it like you were drowning and it was a life buoy.'

Sweeny grimaced and forced himself to relax. His mind was still a whirlpool of thoughts, none of which he felt able to articulate to the old man.

They rounded the Holmen Peninsula which separated the old harbour from the east harbour. Sweeny realized suddenly that the grey shape of the destroyer was missing from its station at the harbour entrance.

'Where's the *Sleipner*?' he asked.

Tenvig leant out of the side window of the wheelhouse and spat.

'About half-an-hour ago she set off for the entrance to the fjord. We heard some gunfire from that direction and she hasn't been back since.'

Sweeny shook his head, wondering how he could have gone to sleep in his bunk a few hours ago and awoken to this nightmare

[23]

world. He kept seeing the bloodstained form of Freya in front of his eyes and found himself swallowing hard to prevent his face dissolving into a mask of anguish.

'Where are you heading her, Lars?'

Tenvig must have asked the question more than once because his voice was now raised and he was frowning.

'Due north.' Sweeny tried to bring his mind back to focus on the immediate problems. 'I'll take her through the islands and across the fjord to Nedstrand. We can put in there and wait to see what happens.'

Tenvig nodded, puffing slowly at his pipe.

'I'll make us some coffee,' he said. 'I could do with some bread and cheese. How about you?'

They had not eaten anything that morning, but Sweeny felt revolted at the idea of food. The image of Freya was too sharp in his mind.

'Just coffee,' he forced himself to say.

A light mist was rolling back from the waters of the fjord where it had risen as soon as the sun began to shed its warmth on the cold waters. Soon the growing strength of the sun would chase the mist away. Visibility was already moderately good. Sweeny tried to coax the throttle to push the *Gunnlöd* towards her maximum speed of eight knots. Then he reached forward, opened the nearest side window and stood letting the bloom of sea spray settle on his face. He felt nauseated but was able to control himself.

Tenvig came back into the wheelhouse with two tin mugs of coffee.

Neither of them said anything. They could still hear the distant boom of explosions and the rattle of machine-gun fire from the direction of Stavanger. They were passing through the little group of islands that lay in the Boknafjord just north of the harbour. Beyond the islands stood Nedstrand and the hills and mountains of the northern shore of the Boknafjord.

Tenvig suddenly extended his arm to port. 'Look!' Sweeny swung his gaze round and felt himself growing cold.

A long grey shape was ploughing through the sea towards them, its bow high like that of a speedboat. There was no mistaking the Swastika flag fluttering from its jackstaff.

'It's a German Motor Torpedo Boat,' muttered Tenvig unnecessarily.

Sweeny was already swinging the wheel to starboard, knowing

even as he did so that it was ridiculous to think that the sluggish and ancient *Gunnlöd* could avoid the faster warship which was capable of three or four times her speed. The sleek dart of the gunboat came roaring across her path, its stern Spandau machine gun firing a warning shot across her bows.

'Bastards!' swore Tenvig, dropping his mug of coffee and scrabbling at the chart locker. He took out an old Smith and Wesson revolver and broke it open. It was a relic from his days on the South American run.

'What the hell do you think you can do with that?' yelled Sweeny as he spun the wheel to port, watching the MTB as it circled lazily around. The German skipper was obviously manoeuvring to come up alongside. Sweeny sighed and eased back on the throttle. There was no escape. They were about five hundred yards offshore, a little to the west of Nedstrand. There was no way of avoiding the attentions of the German ship.

'You're not going to let them take the *Gunnlöd*?' Tenvig shouted.

'Not much else we can do,' Sweeny replied resignedly.

Before he realized it, old Tenvig had moved out on the deck and fired two shots at the closing gunboat.

A machine gun rattled in reply.

Sweeny felt a moment of shock and then he was screaming something incomprehensible as the old man was flung against the wheelhouse bulwarks.

The shots fired by Tenvig had evidently frightened the gunboat skipper momentarily, for the MTB veered away. Some instinct took over in Sweeny's mind, and he threw the throttle forward, sending the old smack towards the distant shore. His sane mind would have recognized the futility of trying to escape but he was no longer capable of quiet, rational thinking. He pushed out of the wheelhouse and dropped to one knee by Tenvig. The machine-gun bullets had formed a bloody pattern across the old man's chest. Now he would not have the burden of telling the old man about the death of Freya. Now they were together. Sweeny grabbed the old man's Smith and Wesson and thrust it into his belt.

He heard the gunboat edging closer. A voice echoed across the water. '*Ubergeben!*' Then in Norwegian: 'Surrender yourselves!'

Sweeny felt as if his movements were compelled by someone other than himself. It was as if he were standing watching another person in his body. He ran to the stern hatch and kicked it open. Below were the boxes of dynamite which he and Tenvig were to have delivered to the mines at Hammerfest. He plunged inside and, using the butt of Tenvig's revolver, he knocked open the nearest box. The explosive was primitive, porous silica saturated with nitro-glycerine. He searched desperately among the boxes and found some lengths of fuse wire. Thrusting the revolver into his waistband, he took out his seaman's clasp-knife, cut a short length and twisted it into the explosive. Sweeny had worked with primitive explosives during his years with the whaling fleet where explosive harpoons had often been used. It took him only a moment to ready the charge and light the fuse, pausing a second to see it spluttering fiercely before clambering out of the hold.

He felt no emotion, no sense of urgency as he stood on the afterdeck and watched the gunboat edging closer towards the *Gunnlöd*. He simply kicked off his seaboots, almost casually, knotted the string to hang them together around his neck, then mentally measured the distance towards the shoreline. About two hundred yards now. Ignoring the shouts from the German MTB, he moved swiftly forward and dove into the cold waters, plunging down deeply before striking out for the surface.

He struck out with firm measured strokes. He thought he heard gunfire but no bullets struck near him. Above the lapping of the waters he could hear the throaty chug of the gunboat's engine as it nestled alongside the ancient fishing smack. He heard voices calling harshly and the crack of a rifle. This time he was aware of something smacking the water ahead of him. He ignored it, swimming with a steady and powerful stroke.

There came a tremendous roar behind him. Even then he did not look back but kept swimming until he came close to the shore and reached his own depth. He stood up and waded forward, stumbling through the icy cold shallows and over a rocky bank before reaching cover behind a boulder. Then he stared back. A pall of black smoke was rising from where the German MTB and the remains of the *Gunnlöd* were sinking. He knelt shivering, his lips still compressed in pain and anger.

A burst of machine-gun fire caused him to start. Racing out of the smoke, which was lying heavily across the fjord, came another long grey shape. A second Motor Torpedo Boat. A bullet whined nearby and a rock a few yards away splintered with a cracking noise.

Sweeny tore at the string with which he had tied his seaboots together and hauled them on. He jerked into motion, turning to the hillside behind him. There was little cover on the hillside, only a few boulders protruding from its slopes here and there. But further down was a gully, a smooth slope with a few bushes growing in it, leading up to a clump of birch trees. The MTB was curving swiftly towards the shore. The Germans were obviously intent on avenging their colleagues. A Spandau was chattering without pause. Sweeny took a deep breath and began to climb up the gully, his heavy rubber seaboots making him feel that he was running through treacle. He pushed upwards, finding the earth in the gully soft and sliding.

He heard the deep throated roar of the MTB engine throttle back, and above the chugging sound of its idling he could hear shouting. He glanced back and saw that a dinghy was being launched and some sailors, with steel helmets and rifles, were springing into it.

Chest heaving, he pushed on, snatching breaths like a drowning man. Then his strength gave out and he flung himself down behind a boulder. Almost as he did so, a shot smashed into the earth near his head.

He dragged out old Tenvig's revolver and peered down the slope. An officer and two ratings were moving up the gully towards him. They made their way up with confidence. Obviously they thought he must be unarmed, or else they were not experienced. Sweeny pressed his lips together and sighted on the officer. He squeezed the trigger. The pistol clicked. Damn! He had forgotten about its immersion in water. He broke open the chamber and ejected two damp cartridges. The third seemed reasonably dry. He aimed again at the officer, now considerably nearer, so near he could almost hear the rasp of the man's breath. He fired. The man flung up his hands, a red stain appeared on his face, and he went slithering backwards. The two ratings flung themselves down as the body of their officer rolled by them and continued on down the slope to the shoreline. For a few moments it was strangely quiet. Then the Spandau from the MTB opened up.

Sweeny waited until there was a pause and began to clamber up the gully again, urging his strength from some hidden source, struggling in desperation in his heavy seaboots. He had half a mind to discard them but some instinct made him realize that barefoot he would stand no chance at all. He shivered as bullets struck nearby, feeling that any moment he would experience the sensation of a searing pain in his back. His breath was choking and a tremendous weariness was overcoming him. He wanted to stop, to pause, to sit down and rest . . .

Then he was over the brow of the hill and among the birch trees. He flung himself down in the undergrowth and sobbed great gulps of fresh air.

The gunfire stopped and, after a few moments, he dragged himself back to the edge of the hill and peered down at the fjord below. There was no sign of the two ratings who had been following him. Then he saw the dinghy being rowed back to the MTB, a body lying in it and its oars being handled by two sailors. They were obviously returning to their ship. The MTB's engines were roaring impatiently now and the skipper hardly allowed his men time to get aboard before he veered his vessel away and tore off across the blue waters. Smoke still hung in the sky marking the spot where the first MTB and the old *Gunnlöd* had gone down. Soon the smoke would clear and there would be nothing, nothing of the *Gunnlöd* nor of old Tenvig. Freya and Erik were also dead. Sweeny had a deep sense of loneliness. There was nothing left of the last twenty years of his life, the twenty years he had spent in Norway. It had all been destroyed within a few hours. He had never experienced such bitter isolation, even when his own parents had died. Now he was truly alone.

He stared with cold eyes at the grey lines of the German ships entering the fjord, steaming towards Stavanger. There was an expression of controlled hatred on his face. To the south he could see fires rising above the old harbour town and see the clusters of black dots in the sky where German airborne troops continued to reinforce their comrades intent on the capture of Sola Airfield.

Something more than the invasion of Norway had happened this Tuesday morning. Sweeny's entire life had been destroyed and there was left to him now only one reason for survival – vengeance. He would dedicate himself to avenging old Uncle Tenvig, avenging his cousin Freya and Erik Hartvig. Somehow, he did not know exactly, he would find out who owned the Nasjonal Samling button-badge 5684 PL. He would have his revenge.

Sweeny moved back into the shelter of the birch trees, stood up, pocketed the revolver and brushed himself down. The Germans would, by now, probably be in Haugensund, the nearest northern coastal town, he reasoned. He would strike off to the northeast, across the peninsula where he now was towards Vikedal. Perhaps there was a chance of getting a ship or joining up with the Norwegian army. They must be fighting somewhere. He glanced momentarily back towards the smoke rising from Stavanger. For a moment he shut his eyes and bowed his head, almost in an attitude of prayer. It was a prayer; a quiet vow of vengeance. Afterward he straightened himself and began to swing hurriedly through the woods towards the north.

# PART TWO

*Tuesday, 23 April – Wednesday, 1 May, 1940*

# CHAPTER THREE

Michael Woods braked a little too sharply and sent his Lagonda Tourer into a skid from which it took all his energy at the wheel to recover. He came to a halt and swore violently, cursing the blackout and those who had devised it. As the momentary shock wore off, he peered cautiously into the gloom of the street and caught sight of the shadowy figure of the man on the bicycle, who had caused his skid and whom he had contrived to miss by a narrow margin.

'Are you all right?' he called.

'Strewth, mister, that was a near one and no mistake.'

'I didn't see you until I was almost on top of you,' Woods replied belligerently as he realized that the man had not been hurt. 'It's the fault of the damned blackout.'

The cyclist mounted his cycle with an air of patient suffering and wobbled off into the gloom while Woods engaged gear and continued his right hand turn from Lambeth Palace Road onto Lambeth Bridge. It was eight o'clock in the evening and there was little traffic about as he continued along Horseferry Road towards Victoria Street. He had had a hard day and felt exhausted. Usually he would have gone across to the Black Lion for a pint of beer and a read of the newspaper, and perhaps a chat with any of his colleagues who happened to be in the pub, before departing homewards. Tonight, however, he just wanted to get home, have a meal and go to bed. He had to face another early morning shift the next day and he wanted to be fit.

He turned his car left into Victoria Street and drove along the almost deserted thoroughfare before entering Ashley Place, where he rented a small flat on the third floor of a mansion block. He parked the vehicle, climbed out and stretched. Then he removed his black case from the rear seat, locked the car and made his way up the six short flights of stairs to his door.

He was fumbling with his key when he became aware of the slight shadow in the gloom of the landing. He turned with a frown as a female voice asked, 'Are you Doctor Woods? Doctor Michael Woods?'

Woods noted the breathless voice and the soft attractive accent.

'What can I do for you?' he acknowledged.

The girl emerged into the dim light of the heavily shaded bulb which lit the landing. It was too gloomy to make out her features but Woods had the impression that she was young and reasonably attractive. Her form was slight although it was muffled in a heavy raincoat and she had a tammy hat on her head. For a moment he thought he recognized her but realized, with a quick smile, that he was remembering the character portrayed by Marlene Dietrich in 'The Blue Angel'. The girl certainly looked a ringer for her so far as he could tell.

'You are the Doctor Woods who is a surgeon at St Thomas's Hospital?'

Woods grimaced. 'I work at St Thomas's but I'm only a humble houseman.'

The girl frowned and pressed forward insistently. 'But you *are* the Doctor Woods who studied under Professor Stenersen at the Riks-Hospitalet in Oslo, aren't you?'

Now he recognized her soft accent to be Norwegian.

'Perhaps you'd better tell me who you are?' he countered cautiously.

'I am Inge Stenersen. The professor is my uncle.'

'I see . . .' Woods hesitated. He saw nothing, but took refuge in the formula. 'Look, perhaps you'd better come in and tell me what this is about . . .'

He turned and opened the door of his flat. He was about to step inside when the distant wail of an air-raid siren began to sound. Another siren took up the wail from close by and in a few seconds the cacophony spread across the city. Woods sighed.

'I suppose we should go down to the shelter,' he said.

He hated the communal shelter in the basement of the building. He never went down there during the air raids. Maybe it was irresponsible but there was nothing to go down for. It was usually a false alarm. When the Luftwaffe did come over it was to drop propaganda leaflets.

'I would prefer to stay here, if that's all right with you,' replied the girl.

'Very well,' Woods said. 'Stay by the door.'

He crossed the room towards the pale square of light on the far

[34]

side. Reaching forward, he fumbled with the blackout curtain and drew it across with a rasping sound, plunging the room into total darkness. Then, more by luck than instinct, he made his way back to the door and clicked on the light switch.

The girl stood hesitantly on the threshold, blinking uncertainly in the light.

Woods regarded her appreciatively. Inge Stenersen was tall and slim, perhaps a little too slim. Her hair was a tumble of golden curls, a deep shade with highlights of burnished copper. Her pale skin was dashed with freckles. Her eyes were a catlike green and almost almond shaped. Her mouth was full-lipped and smiled readily. She had high cheekbones and the line of her jaw was firm, a 'no nonsense' jaw which spoke of strength of character. Woods sighed cynically. She was obviously what was known as an independent young woman. If he were truthful, Woods would confess that he was slightly nervous of them. He was inclined to be old fashioned and chauvinistic in such matters.

'May I take your coat?' he asked, as he drew her in and shut the door.

The girl came in hesitantly and glanced round the room. Woods was not house proud. The room was a dull-looking lounge with ancient, browning wallpaper and filled with a heavy dark oak sideboard, a table and a couple of chairs plus a very heavy brown leather couch. She glanced at the gas fire and Woods, seeing the glance, smiled.

'It is a bit cold,' he acknowledged. 'Hang on. I'll light the fire.'

He lit the gas with a loud 'plop' and stood up.

She had taken off her heavy raincoat and tammy hat and dropped them over the back of a chair. He had been right, he mused. Her figure was slight but well proportioned. She was wearing a simple tweed skirt and a green woollen jumper.

'Sit down,' he invited. 'Can I get you a drink? Something alcoholic or even a tea, perhaps?'

She smiled briefly, nervously. 'Nothing, thanks,' she replied.

Woods removed his own coat while she perched herself, almost uncomfortably, on the edge of a chair. He took out a pack of Players and lit one before realizing his lack of manners and proferring the cigarettes to the girl. She shook her head.

'So you are Professor Stenersen's niece?' he began, realizing that it was up to him to break the awkward silence which had fallen. 'I have not seen him since I left Norway nearly two years ago. How is he? Did he send you here?'

The girl shook her head quickly. 'Uncle Didrik is still in Oslo.'

He detected a slight quaver to her voice. The German invasion of Norway continued to be front page news.

'I see,' Woods said inadequately. 'I'm sorry.'

The girl's green eyes met his and then dropped.

'Uncle Didrik often spoke of you. He said that you were the best of his students.'

Woods reclined in his chair and blew a thoughtful smoke ring.

'I spent three years in the Riks-Hospitalet studying surgical technique under your uncle,' he said. 'He is regarded as one of the best cancer surgeons in Europe.'

'What made you go to Norway to study?' the girl asked. 'You could have studied here in London.'

'Oh, my father had business connections in Norway and he used to take me on climbing holidays there when I was a boy. I left university and decided to become a surgeon. I trained at St Thomas and then applied to study advanced surgical technique under Professor Stenersen in Oslo.'

'You speak Norwegian?'

'I am able to get by in Nynorsk,' replied Woods, dropping easily into the language. 'And I studied Boksmal. There is not a great deal of difference between them, so I am able to get by.'

'You speak very well,' the girl nodded approvingly.

'And you speak excellent English,' returned Woods, switching back.

'I have been in London for two years now,' Inge Stenersen said, smiling almost sadly. 'I am a research chemist at Bart's.'

There was an awkward silence between them. The girl's eyes suddenly fell on the newspaper which Woods had dropped on the table when he had drawn his cigarettes from his pocket. It was the *Daily Telegraph* with its headline banner clearly visible: 'British Successes in Norway – Official'. The girl's face was bitter.

'Successes!' she grated the word. 'The Norwegian forces and the Allies are only just hanging on to central and northern Norway. There is talk that the country may fall. The Germans are in complete control of the southern part of the country.'

Woods gazed thoughtfully at her.

'Why have you come to see me, Miss Stenersen?' he prompted.

'Uncle Didrik is in Oslo. If it were possible to get him out of the city, either to unoccupied Norway or back here to England, would you be prepared to help?'

[36]

Wood's jaw dropped. The girl was serious, her jaw aggressively firm, her eyes steady.

Woods forced himself to smile and said, 'I admired your uncle tremendously, Miss Stenersen. It was a rare privilege to study under him and, of course, I would do anything to ensure his freedom and safety. However, if you are trying to round up volunteers to form a rescue posse then you've come to the wrong person. What you need is the Secret Service or something.'

The girl nodded moodily.

'I have made several telephone calls to the Norwegian Embassy here and to various medical bodies seeking help to get my uncle out of Oslo. I am not suggesting a private . . . what was it you said? Posse?'

'*Posse comitatus*,' Woods explained somewhat pedantically. 'The force of the county, men called out by the sheriff to aid in enforcing the law.'

The girl nodded slightly and reached into a handbag to draw out a sheaf of papers.

'I have a petition which I am asking people in the medical profession who know, or know of, my uncle and his work, to sign in order to put pressure on the authorities to bring Uncle Didrik out of Norway.'

Woods relaxed with a smile.

'Oh! Of course. I'd be only too happy to sign. I thought you were asking for volunteers to head off to Norway on a rescue mission.'

The girl glanced at him with a frown.

'If I were?' she asked thoughtfully.

Woods grinned and shrugged.

'There are quite a lot of Norwegians in England right now who are better qualified than I am.'

'None as uniquely qualified as you are, Doctor Woods,' she replied.

He shook his head, reaching for his pen, and drew the petition towards him. The girl had collected a lot of distinguished signatures among the medical profession. Professor Stenersen's work was well known throughout the world.

She watched him sign and gazed pensively at him as if considering something.

'Uncle Didrik believed that you were someone upon whom he could rely.'

'I'm glad to hear it,' Woods replied as he passed back the

papers. 'And I wish you the best of luck with your petition. As I said, I respect and admire your uncle. If there is anything in my power that I can usefully do to help him I will do it.'

Inge Stenersen rose and put on her coat and hat.

'Goodnight, Doctor Woods,' her voice was abrupt and decisive. 'Thank you for talking with me.'

Woods felt a little foolish as the door of his flat banged shut behind her slight form.

The sirens were wailing the 'all clear' now and he let out a deep sigh. It was a long time before he stopped thinking about Inge Stenersen and feeling slightly sorry for the girl. It was obvious that she was deeply attached to the old professor. It was too bad he had been caught up in the invasion. The poor kid must be pretty desperate to come up with the idea of trying to petition her own Government or the British to spirit the professor out of Oslo in the middle of a war. Well, she probably needed a latter-day Scarlet Pimpernel and he was no Sir Percy Blakeney. He suddenly grinned. The girl would have made a lovely Marguerite Blakeney. He daydreamed for a while before shaking himself mentally. The entire continent of Europe had gone crazy during the last six months. Damned crazy. He was suddenly annoyed with himself. He should have asked Inge Stenersen for her address. He would have to do some hunting to find it tomorrow. He was already making plans for a quiet dinner date, somewhere secluded but inexpensive. He finally went to bed quite happy with the prospect.

# CHAPTER FOUR

Commander Edward Wallace RN entered his office on the third floor of the Admiralty Building at precisely 8:30 am. His secretary, a plump and smiling WRNS officer, had been known to boast that she could set her watch by the appearance of her superior at the office door each morning. Wallace would enter looking as immaculate as if he had just stepped off a parade ground.

'Good morning, sir,' greeted the Wren as he entered.

'Morning, Bracegirdle.' Wallace inclined his head moodily. 'Any signals?' In the navy all messages were referred to as 'signals' even on a shore establishment.

'I have put the file on your desk, sir,' replied the secretary. 'Nothing urgent, except . . .' Her face grew serious. Wallace frowned at her hesitation. Usually Bracegirdle was entirely unflappable. He waited. 'The First Lord rang down personally for you fifteen minutes ago, sir. He would like you in his office at ten hundred hours.'

Wallace involuntarily raised an eyebrow. It was his only outward sign that the telephone request from the First Lord of the Admiralty came in any way as a surprise.

'Right,' he said after a moment. 'Carry on.'

He turned into the inner sanctum where he worked and closed the door behind him. Carefully, meticulously, he removed his overcoat and his cap and moved to his desk. He sat down, placing his hands palm downwards on the desk top on either side of a buff-coloured file marked 'Eyes Only' with his code number in the corner. The door opened and Bracegirdle entered with a mug of steaming tea. It was the usual morning ritual. He paid no attention to her as she deposited it on his desk and left silently.

Edward Wallace was in his fifties, his black hair silvering over the temples and in little streaks here and there. He had a heavy jowl and needed to shave twice a day in order not to appear unkempt. His eyes were black and almost fathomless. His face did not seem the type to break into a smile. It seemed too serious; too humourless. He was a dour man. Everything about his features seemed compressed, especially the lips.

Wallace had begun his service during the First World War as a young midshipman on Lord Beatty's flagship, the *Lion*, seeing action at Dogger Bank. After the war he had displayed a flair for administration and during the early 1930s had served as a naval attaché in Oslo. He had come to know Norway very well. Then he had joined Naval Intelligence and played a role in helping track the *Altmark*, the supply ship of the German pocket-battleship *Graf Spee*, which had been finally located in Norwegian territorial waters, hiding in the protection of Jossingfjord. In spite of Norwegian neutrality, knowing there to be three hundred British prisoners on board, the Royal Navy had sent in HMS *Cossack*. *Altmark* had attempted to ram her but the crew of the *Cossack* had boarded the Nazi ship with fixed bayonets and succeeded in releasing the prisoners. Soon after this incident, Wallace had found himself head of the Norwegian Bureau of Naval Intelligence.

He sipped at his tea as he opened the buff folder and read through the latest messages and requests. There was nothing of outstanding importance. The messages were mainly updates on the situation in Norway, which looked far from good. Wallace closed the file and sat back, turning his mind to the summons from the First Lord. He presumed that there was some aspect of the Norwegian situation which needed explanation, but what? He stood up and went to a cupboard from which he took a file marked 'Norway – General' and returned to his desk, flicking through the reports to refresh his memory. It was not a situation which gave any comfort to the Allied cause.

It was true that Adolf Hitler's plan to occupy Norway had not gone as he had expected, for the Norwegian Parliament, meeting at 7:00 on the morning of the invasion, had voted unanimously against capitulation and rejected the ultimatum of the Third Reich demanding that Norway place itself 'under its protection'. The Norwegian King, Haakon VII, and the royal family, with the entire Norwegian Parliament and the Allied ambassadors, had managed to evacuate Oslo before the German troops entered the city. By 9:30 am twenty motor trucks laden with gold from the Bank of Norway and three more piled with secret Foreign Office papers had also escaped.

Norway had no large standing army to defend itself, only six small army divisions, composed mainly of volunteers, and a pathetically small navy and airforce. The Third Reich had put 25,000 troops ashore during the morning of the invasion, backed by a powerful naval and air cover. To create confusion there had been well-organized Nazi underground gangs acting as a fifth column as well as the Norwegian fascists of the Nasjonal Samling led by Major Vidkun Quisling. Quisling had been the enemy within who had dealt a savage blow to Norwegian morale. He was a graduate of the Norwegian Military Academy, a regular officer who had once been decorated by the British Government as well as his own. From 1931–33 he had been Norwegian Minister of Defence and was spoken of as an aspiring Prime Minister. Then he had broken with his party in May, 1933, to form his Nasjonal Samling, or National Union, in imitation of the other fascist parties which had sprung up throughout Europe in the wake of Hitler's success in Germany.

The Norwegians should have kept a more careful eye on the activities of Quisling, sighed Wallace as he stretched towards the file to refresh his memory. In the last election they had managed to get only 1.83 per cent of the entire vote, and that had been a fall from the previous election result of 2.23 per cent when they had secured a single seat in the Parliament for Opland. Quisling himself had never been able to enter the Parliament on behalf of his party. Yes, it had been easy to dismiss the Norwegian fascists as an insignificant minority, but the Norwegians had not taken account of the fact that Quisling's followers occupied key places within the army. Colonel Konrad Sundlo, for example, had surrendered Narvik to the Germans without firing a shot in its defence. Sundlo was an ardent disciple of Quisling.

On the morning of the invasion, even as the King and his Government were evacuating Oslo, Quisling and his storm-troopers, the Hird, had taken over the Hotel Continental and moved on to occupy the State Radio station and other key points in the city. Quisling made a broadcast naming himself head of government and demanding that the Norwegian people welcome the Nazis as liberators. The German ambassador, Dr Kurt Bauer, had gone north to see King Haakon to request that he recognize Quisling's Government. Haakon refused to do any such thing. A few days later Quisling sent his own emissary, Captain Irgens, to urge the monarch to return to Oslo where Quisling promised to serve him loyally. The emissary was dismissed from the King's presence with harsh words.

[41]

Instead of capitulation, a new commander-in-chief of the Norwegian armed forces, General Otto Ruge, was appointed and rallied the confused Norwegian forces. They began to fight back. The Norwegian Government called for Allied military aid. The German commander, General Nikolaus von Falkenhorst, realizing that no accommodation could be reached with King Haakon nor his Government, gave orders for the capture or destruction by bombing of the royal party and Government. They had to withdraw even further north to escape the Luftwaffe airstrikes, leaving Nybergsynd, the village where they had been staying, a burning ruin. The centre of Norwegian resistance was moved up along the rugged Gudbrands Valley, through the mountains to Andalsnes.

Wallace had been roused with the news of the invasion early in the morning of April 9 and found, by the time he reached the Admiralty, that the Chiefs-of-Staff were already in deliberation. The Allied forces had put together an expeditionary force of 57,000 men to help Finland repulse the invasion of the Soviet Union which had begun on November 30, 1939. A strike force of 15,000 troops had been prepared to move if permission for the force to reach Finland via Norway and Sweden could be obtained from those Governments. But before this could happen, the Finns had signed an armistice with the Soviet Union on March 12. This expeditionary force was still in existence and the strike force still on the transport ships. Winston Churchill, who was not only First Lord of the Admiralty, but on April 4 had been appointed chairman of the Military Coordination Committee, gave the order that they should be moved to Norway. The ships and men were despatched the same day and, following counter-attacks by the Royal Navy on the German invasion fleet, began to land an army of three battalions of British troops, four battalions of Poles and five battalions of French plus two battalions of the French Foreign Legion. The Allied reinforcements were landed in central and northern Norway.

One of the main problems was the Luftwaffe's complete mastery of the air. Casualties were enormously high because of this. The Royal Air Force had no long-range fighters with which to challenge the Germans, who were now installed on the former Norwegian airfields. The Norwegian airforce had been totally obliterated. The Royal Navy had only one carrier, *Furious*, which had been sent into Norwegian waters without any fighters on board, only a collection of obsolete torpedo aircraft. The carriers *Glorious* and *Ark Royal* were hastening from the Mediterranean, but the immediate outlook was bleak. Wallace was well aware that the British army commander, Major-General Carton de Wiart, had grimly apprised London that unless the Luftwaffe air power in Norway could be destroyed there was little hope of his troops holding on. The evacuation of Norway seemed the only possibility.

Wallace knew that Churchill understood the need to smash the Luftwaffe and had personally approved of an attempt by the cruiser *Suffolk* to close in on Stavanger and attempt to shell Sola Airfield, which was now being used as the main Luftwaffe fighter base. But the Luftwaffe had crippled the cruiser, leaving her with seventy serious casualties. Only a few days ago had the *Suffolk* managed to limp back to Scapa Flow, the naval base in Orkney, with her quarter deck awash and 25,000 tons of sea water in her.

His intercom buzzed. Bracegirdle's voice said: 'Oh-Nine-Fifty, sir. May I remind you of your appointment?'

'On my way, Bracegirdle,' Wallace replied.

He stood up, replaced the general file, tidied his collar and tie, smoothed his tunic and took up his cap. Then he left his office and began to walk through the corridors of the Admiralty Building, ascending to the top floor where the First Lord of the Admiralty, Winston Churchill, had his office.

The First Lord was seated at his desk, his aggressive yet cherubic face thrust forward, looking astonishingly like the cartoon caricatures of himself which appeared in the daily newspapers. He held a large Havana cigar in one pudgy hand and barely glanced at Wallace as the commander came to a halt in front of the desk.

'Let's get straight down to business, commander,' grunted Churchill, waving him to an armchair. 'I know what the situation is like in Norway. I've read all the despatches from the three service chiefs. Just how do you interpret the situation?'

Wallace shifted uncomfortably. He knew that Churchill was a man who wanted to know the truth, however unpalatable.

'I think our forces will have to withdraw, sir,' he said quietly.

Churchill's bright eyes came up suddenly, meeting Wallace's dark ones. They narrowed.

'You concur with the despatch from Major-General Carton de Wiart?'

'I do, sir.'

The First Lord pushed himself back in his chair, a speculative gaze on his features as he examined Wallace.

'Do we have the capacity to mount an intelligence operation behind the German lines?'

'Behind their lines, sir?'

'Yes, in Oslo.'

Wallace pursed his lips as he considered the problem.

'It depends on exactly what you have in mind, sir,' he countered. 'To be truthful, the intelligence situation is a new one in this theatre of operations. Before the Germans invaded we had our agents there, of course. They fed us information from our embassy in Oslo. But because the Norwegians were a friendly power there was no need to build up a network as we have done in other countries. It is still a matter of days since the German invasion and we are trying to hammer something together. We certainly have plenty of material, Norwegians escaping from the Nazis, Norwegian servicemen who want to strike back and so forth. Most such people we hand over to the Norwegian authorities to recruit, but we are picking up some individuals who are willing to go back behind the German lines with the idea of starting an underground, a resistance movement. Can you give me anything specific, sir?'

Churchill hesitated and then chose his words carefully.

'Do we have the capability of sending a small team to Oslo whose task would be to bring out certain personages, either through the Allies' lines in the north or through neutral Sweden, and escort them to London?'

Wallace's mind was racing. Certain personages?

'I thought the Norwegian royal family and, in fact, every member of the Norwegian Parliament had managed to get to the north of the country, sir?'

The First Lord's face crinkled in a scowl.

'Don't speculate, commander. Just answer the question,' he snapped petulantly.

'I believe we have that capability, sir,' replied Wallace, flushing slightly. 'Naturally, I would have reservations until I knew more details.'

Churchill continued to stare at him for a few moments, drumming his fingers on the top of the desk. Then the First Lord seemed to notice that his cigar had gone out. He laid it carefully in an ashtray, stretched back and folded his hands, fingers interlocking, over his waistcoat.

'There is a group of seven people in Oslo who must be brought out of Norway to England at all costs,' he said slowly. 'At all costs.'

Wallace tried to disguise the surprise on his face. At all costs? The First Lord was not one to use such melodramatic wording in the privacy of his discussions with his staff.

'May I ask who these people are, sir?' Wallace asked.

The First Lord did not reply but instead reached forward and pressed a buzzer on his desk. A few moments of silence passed before a side door opened and a short, compactly built man in his late sixties entered the room. He was in civilian clothes, well-dressed, with a flower in the buttonhole of his expensive-looking suit. Churchill waved him to come forward but he made no attempt to introduce the man.

'Thank you for waiting so patiently, my lord,' he grunted. 'This naval officer is in charge of our Norwegian Bureau at the Admiralty. I would be grateful if you would explain the facts to him.'

The elderly man nodded to Wallace, the hint of a humorous grin on his lips, and sat down in a chair opposite.

It took Wallace a few moments to place the man's familiar features. Thomas Jeeves, first Baron Horder of Ashford, was well-known to newspaper photographers. He was a famous physician, consulting to some or other ministry. Wallace frowned; yes, he was also physician to His Majesty the King. He turned his attention to the man with curiosity.

'There is in this country a prominent personality, a political personality I should say, who is most seriously ill. Without going into details let me say that this . . . personality . . . will die in about six months unless an operation can be performed soon.'

Wallace stared at the physician for a moment and then said: 'My lord, I am aware that you are physician to the King. Is it . . .?'

Churchill interrupted with a grunt.

'No! It is not His Majesty.'

'May I know who this personality is?' pressed Wallace.

'No!' snapped Churchill. 'It is quite sufficient for you to know that the man's health and continuance in public office is, at this particular juncture, of the utmost importance to the Allied war effort, not to mention the well-being of this nation. While no one is irreplaceable in the long term, his death could have a very disastrous affect on the morale of our people as well as on our allies. Heaven knows, there are enough appeasers within this

[45]

nation, enough people in high places trying to press for a deal with that ridiculous little jumped-up house-painter who runs Germany. The repercussions of . . . of this man's death might swing the balance of the war effort. Do I make myself clear?'

Wallace nodded, wondering for a moment whether Churchill could be speaking about himself.

'Continue, my lord.'

Horder turned to Wallace. 'The condition from which . . . our subject . . . suffers is a malignant tumorous growth . . .'

'Cancer?'

'Of a malignant intestinal order,' agreed Horder. 'You may be aware, since you have recognized me, commander, that I am not only Consulting Physician to St Bartholomew's Hospital but Consulting Physician to the Cancer Hospital of Fulham. As chairman of the British Empire Cancer Campaign I am considered an expert diagnostician in this field.'

Wallace waited while Horder paused.

'I know of only three surgeons in Europe with whom I would say my patient has more than a fifty-fifty chance of survival. Two of them are German surgeons, which naturally precludes them. The third is a Norwegian.'

So that was it! Wallace smiled wanly.

'And you want to bring the Norwegian to London?'

'Exactly so,' grunted the First Lord.

'May I know who he is?'

'Professor Didrik Stenersen. He is one of Europe's leading abdominal surgeons and a specialist in tumours.'

'Would he be willing or unwilling to come to London if contacted?'

'I am told that he would be willing.'

Wallace rubbed the bridge of his nose reflectively.

'You spoke of a group of *seven* people . . .' he said, glancing at Churchill.

'We want to bring out Professor Stenersen's entire medical team.'

'Seven people in all?' pressed Wallace.

Lord Horder nodded.

'Do we have any contact with this Professor Stenersen?'

Lord Horder glanced at Churchill before replying, 'Not directly. He and his team were working at the Riks-Hospitalet in Oslo when the Germans invaded. So far as our knowledge goes, they are still there. All telephone links with Norway have been cut by the Germans. By coincidence, I was contacted earlier this week by a relative of Professor Stenersen who is currently studying bio-chemistry in London and asked me to do my best to help bring her uncle out of Norway . . .'

'Her?' Wallace picked up the feminine pronoun.

'Yes. Inge Stenersen, the professor's niece. She's twenty-five, a good-looker and quite a determined young woman.'

'She could be of invaluable help,' observed Wallace.

Horder took out his wallet and handed over a small card.

'I thought you might say that, commander. This is her address. Naturally, she knows nothing about the situation so far as my patient goes.'

Wallace glanced to the First Lord with a query in his eyes. Churchill sniffed.

'Thank you, my lord,' he said. 'We will take the matter from here.'

Lord Horder rose to his feet, and with a brief smile towards Wallace, left the room.

'I give you full authority on this, commander,' Churchill grunted as soon as the door closed on the eminent physician. 'I want this operation mounted and I want this man Stenersen and his team in London by the beginning of next month.'

'Very well, sir,' said Wallace, rising to his feet.

Churchill gazed up belligerently for a moment.

'This operation is to be absolutely top secret, understand? It has the highest priority. The highest.'

'I understand, sir.'

Wallace saluted and began to turn away, but Churchill's voice brought him back sharply. He was slightly surprised. It was the first time he had seen something akin to embarrassment on the grim features of the First Lord of the Admiralty.

'Commander, I'd like you to do me a personal favour in your capacity as head of the Norwegian Bureau.'

'If I am able, sir,' he said, phrasing his words carefully.

Churchill sighed.

'My nephew, Giles Romilly . . . he was in Narvik when the Germans captured it on April 9. He was sent there by his newspaper, the *Daily Express*. The *Express* received a 'phone call from him on Monday, that was April 8, and he was instructed to go by sea down the coast to Bergen. He was supposed to leave the next morning about eight o'clock . . . then the Germans . . . Well, he hasn't been heard of since.'

Wallace bit his lip.

'A lot of our lads were captured in Narvik,' he said gently. 'Merchant seamen, crews off the *Blythmore*, *Massington Court*, *North Cornwall*, *Riverton*, *Romanby* . . . the British consul and his staff.'

Churchill grimaced awkwardly as if troubled at bringing his personal problems into the open.

'If you do get any news about Giles, I'd appreciate it.'

'I'll do my best, sir,' Wallace replied.

Churchill nodded and then his features resumed their customary scowl.

'Keep me posted on the operation. I want Stenersen here as soon as possible. Good morning, commander.'

# CHAPTER FIVE

Back in his office, Wallace sent for his chief of planning, a tousle-headed, scrappy-looking RNVR lieutenant named Bill Gibson. He outlined the situation to him in brief terms. Gibson, in spite of his vagueness and his slapdash attitude to his personal appearance, had an extraordinary mind when it came to strategic planning. He had been a chess master at the age of twelve and, at the outbreak of war, his unusual talents had been quickly seized upon by Naval Intelligence.

'The team should be a small one and composed of people with local knowledge, preferably Norwegians,' he offered.

'That means we'll have to start from scratch, Bill,' Wallace sighed. 'We don't have anyone in this department who is tried or trusted in field operations.'

'Well, sir,' Gibson replied as he perched himself on the edge of Wallace's desk, a habit of his which irritated his superior, 'we can start with this relative of Professor Stenersen's.'

Wallace pulled a face.

'Inge Stenersen is a woman.'

Gibson grinned.

'I didn't know you were old-fashioned that way, sir. It's the age of female emancipation. Norway gave women the vote in local elections back in 1901 and full and equal suffrage with men in 1913. Anyway, some of our best operatives in the last war were women.'

Wallace looked at his junior with a disapproving stare.

'The girl is twenty-five years old, a bio-chemist, and while she has been trying to get her uncle out of Oslo, that doesn't mean she's prepared or capable of going there to fetch him.'

'We could try,' insisted Gibson.

'Very well. Say the girl was part of the team, who else?'

'We'd need someone with a certain amount of audacity and inventiveness . . .' Gibson paused and clicked his fingers. 'The very man!'

[49]

Wallace glanced up curiously. 'Who?'

'The character who arrived in a German seaplane last week . . . what's his name? Sweeny. Lars Sweeny.'

Wallace's face brightened. He remembered seeing the report from Naval Intelligence at Scapa Flow. The previous week a Royal Navy destroyer had come across a German Arado seaplane floating in the watery wastes east of the Orkney Islands. When they approached it they found two Norwegians in it. One was a Norwegian navy pilot who had flown the machine until lack of fuel forced him to land on a thankfully smooth sea, while the other man was a civilian. The two had met in the confusion of the invasion and were trying to make their way to the Allied positions. They had discovered the Arado moored in a fjord with its two-man crew carrying out some minor repair to the engine. The men had surprised the German pilots, disposed of them (Wallace's mouth quirked as he remembered the phraseology of the report) and took off, following a westerly route toward the north of Scotland. Both men were eager to join the Norwegian fighting forces.

'Get me the report on Sweeny, Bill,' Wallace said.

Gibson swung off the desk and moved to a filing cabinet, found a report and returned. Wallace ran his eye over it.

The Norwegian pilot had been transferred immediately to a fighting unit. As a civilian, Lars Sweeny had presented a few problems. First, he had to be cleared by his own security. It was conceivable that the Germans were sending infiltrators among the numerous refugees flooding into Britain from Norway. Second, it was hard to place a man of Sweeny's abilities. Wallace's infant department had noted that Sweeny had impressed the interrogators of Naval Intelligence. The man appeared to be a born leader possessed of what the Jews called *chutzpah*, an audacity which was much needed in field operatives.

'Has Norwegian security cleared Sweeny?'

Gibson nodded. 'Apparently he's at Hatston airbase in the Orkney Islands, creating a fine old stink at not being allowed to join some fighting unit.'

'Good. Have him flown down here immediately.'

Gibson grunted acknowledgment. 'We ought to have a third member of the team . . . that is, if the girl and Sweeny agree to go. I am thinking that the girl is the weakest link and if anything happens to her it might be difficult to persuade Professor

Stenersen to come to London. We need someone else who knows Stenersen.'

'Then let's hope Miss Stenersen is able to help us with that. We'll get her in for a chat first. In the meantime, make sure Sweeny is flown down here by this evening. I want the plan sorted out before I go home tonight because we only have a few days to get them into Norway. It'll mean a parachute drop.'

'I doubt whether they'll know anything about parachuting, sir,' Gibson pointed out.

'They'll have to learn as they go,' responded Wallace.

'That's a hell of a tough order, sir,' whistled Gibson.

'It's a hell of a tough war,' retorted Wallace.


Lars Sweeny entered the drab nissen hut and frowned at the young lieutenant of the Royal Norwegian Navy who came forward to greet him. The young man, scarcely twenty years old, looked flustered and nervous.

'Well?' demanded Sweeny as he lowered his bulk onto a wooden chair before the solitary desk in the hut. 'Have I proven myself to be a loyal Norwegian citizen? Am I now allowed to fight for my country?'

The young lieutenant moved his arms awkwardly.

'If you will wait here a moment,' he said as he crossed to an inter-connecting door within the hut.

Sweeny let out an exasperated sigh. Since the British navy had landed him here in Scapa Flow, the main base of their fleet, he had spent several days being interviewed and interrogated by officers of both the Royal Navy and the Royal Norwegian Navy. He had expected some such questioning because of the numerous refugees, both civil and military, who were flocking into Britain. But now he was tired of being passed from one bureaucrat to another. He had escaped from Norway in order to join up and fight against the Germans. Didn't they want volunteers?

'Ah, Lars Sweeny?'

A broad-shouldered man had entered the room, closing the door softly behind him. He had a deeply etched, weather-beaten face and a shock of white hair, rebellious strands of which fell over his broad forehead. He had pale grey eyes, grey and cold, which gazed unblinkingly at the younger man. He wore the uniform of a commander of the Royal Norwegian Navy, with a white polo-necked jumper of the type submariners affected.

Sweeny did not bother to get up. He stared insolently at the officer.

'More questions?'

The commander's lips quirked in what might have been a suppressed smile.

'No. The authorities are satisfied that you are who you say you are. You have been cleared.'

Sweeny sat up and stared at the man.

'About time. When can I join up?'

The officer regarded him thoughtfully as he lowered himself into the chair on the other side of the desk.

'You want to get back to Norway very urgently.'

Sweeny took the observation as a question.

'Doesn't every loyal Norwegian?'

'And yet you are half American. You don't have to fight Norway's battles. You were raised in America and America is neutral.'

Sweeny snorted.

'I am sure that you have read my file. It's been twenty years since I went to live in my mother's country with her family. I am a citizen of Norway. I have seen my uncle and my cousins killed during this invasion. Don't tell me that this is none of my affair.'

The commander stared at the suppressed intensity of the red-haired man's expression and noted the controlled anger and the lines of determination around his mouth.

'When can I join up?' Sweeny repeated.

The commander leant back in his chair. 'Cigarette?'

Sweeny took one and leant forward across the desk to accept a light.

'You will be flying down to London in an hour's time,' the officer said abruptly.

Sweeny raised an eyebrow. 'To join up?'

'The British Royal Navy have requested that you be transferred to them.'

'The British?' frowned Sweeny. 'I don't understand.'

The commander blew a smoke ring and smiled faintly.

'Doubtless our friends, the British, will explain to you in their own good time. However, through our goods links with the Admiralty I can tell you this: the British are thinking of sending a small mission into Oslo.'

'Why?' Sweeny felt an odd stirring, a quickening of his pulse.

'Alas, we have no idea. All we in . . .' the officer hesitated and shrugged. 'All we know is that British intelligence are mounting some small-scale intelligence operation which involves people being sent to Oslo.'

Sweeny stared at the officer. 'You are from intelligence, right?'

'In war there are many jobs that have to be done,' replied the officer. 'We Norwegians haven't been involved in a war since Napoleonic times. We have to learn a whole new science but, at least, we are quick to learn. Let us say, yes, I represent an intelligence department.'

Sweeny stubbed out his cigarette and regarded the officer with curiosity. 'So? The British are going to send me to Oslo? I have no objections as to how I fight the Nazis so long as I am doing something to drive them out of Norway.'

'That is good,' replied the commander approvingly. 'From our point of view, we have no objections to you accepting this job with the British provided we are sure that your first loyalty is to Norway.'

'Is there a doubt?' Sweeny spat out the words. The officer raised his hand to still the outburst that hovered in his flushed, angry face.

'No doubt, my friend. The point is that we want you to work primarily for us. We want you to use the cover of the mission on which the British are sending you to undertake a task for us . . . for Norway.'

Sweeny stared at the man's cold grey eyes.

'My first duty is to Norway and Norway's liberation,' he said softly.

'Very well. Tell me, Sweeny, how much of the events at home have you followed in recent days?'

'Not a great deal,' confessed Sweeny. 'I have tried to keep up with the reports from the war front.'

The officer shook his head.

'I was thinking more of the political developments. The political developments within the occupied territories.'

Sweeny shrugged. There had not been much to learn from the newspapers which he had seen.

'I know that Major Quisling claims that he is the head of the Norwegian Government and those idiots of the Nasjonal Samling and their stormtroopers, the Hird, are fawning over the Germans in Oslo.'

The officer nodded slowly.

'I am pleased to say that Major Quisling has not lasted long in his attempt to establish a pro-German fascist regime in Oslo. Half of the men named by Quisling to serve in his Government as ministers have been too frightened to take up their posts and have sent their personal messages of support to the King and his elected Government. Quisling has become a character out of a farce and now he is a liability to the Germans. They wanted to establish a pro-Nazi Norwegian regime . . . but one that had some credibility. Quisling has become a bad joke. I am not saying that Quisling and his Hird stormtroopers are not dangerous. They are. But what the Germans wanted at this point in history was a credible collaborationist regime.'

He paused.

'The Germans, in fact, dismissed Quisling on April 15 and the next day established a Norwegian Council of Administration for the occupied territories.'

'Who would serve in it if the Germans have thrown out Quisling? No respectable Norwegian would have any truck with the Germans.'

'In that, my friend, you are wrong. The Council now exists under the presidency of Chief Justice Paal Olav Berg, the president of the Norwegian Supreme Court. It consists of several leading Norwegian citizens such as Bishop Eivind Berggrav, the head of the Lutheran Church of Norway, and Doctor Didrik Seip, the Rector of Oslo University.'

Sweeny whistled softly.

'These men have become collaborationists?'

'It would appear so. For whatever reasons, Paal Berg and his associates have set themselves up to act as the civilian administration under the Germans. This is more worrying to us than the pantomime clowns of the Nasjonal Samling. This council consists of respectable and prominent citizens and gives the Germans some semblance of legal authority in Norway.'

'I thought Paal Berg was a Leftist,' Sweeny said.

'He was a member of the *Venstrepartiet* and as such was social minister in Gunnar Knudsen's second government and minister of justice in Mowinckel's first government.'

'That's right. He's chairman of the International Labour Organization based in Geneva. How can a man like that collaborate with the Nazis?'

'A lot of people are doing some strange things these days,' replied the commander.

'What is this to do with me, anyway?' Sweeny wanted to know.

The officer's face was a bland mask as he gazed at him; only the cold grey eyes seemed to have any animation.

'You will soon be in Oslo, thanks to the thoughtfulness of our British allies. You may well be in a position in the next few days to strike a blow which will deter any collaborationists or would-be traitors from acting against the King and the legally elected Norwegian Government. The Germans are anxious to establish a puppet regime in Oslo. We must demonstrate publicly and immediately that any Norwegian traitor seeking to co-operate with the Germans may expect no mercy.'

It suddenly became clear to Sweeny what this man was implying.

'Are you saying that you want the members of this Council of Administration assassinated?'

The officer's mouth formed a thin smile.

'Let us put it this way, Sweeny. It would be to the advantage of the Norwegian Government and it would contribute to the eventual liberation of our country if the Germans found no respectable citizens to serve their cause, however unwitting or misguided those people may be in their motivations.'

Sweeny shuddered slightly. There was a dreadfully cold logic to what the man was saying, he thought. Any Norwegian who willingly served the Nazis was a traitor, and there was only one punishment for such betrayal. He thought about the bloody body of poor old Tenvig as he collapsed against the wheelhouse. He suddenly saw the bodies of Freya – dear, beautiful Freya – and Erik. His hand closed over the small buttonhole badge he still carried with him – the Nasjonal Samling Badge with its membership number . . . 5684 PL. He wanted revenge on the killers. He had no compunctions about killing those who were responsible. And the traitors who betrayed the Norwegian people were endorsing the murder of Freya, weren't they? Freya and Erik and poor Uncle Tenvig.

The commander sat back watching the expressions chasing each other across the red-haired man's face. He himself remained expressionless. He knew Lars Sweeny from the numerous interrogations which were on file; knew the man and was certain of the outcome.

'While you are in Oslo, Sweeny, you will seek out and eliminate Paal Olav Berg. He is the cornerstone of the Council of Administration. His name is respected throughout Norway. His elimination will shock the people, especially those who toy with

[55]

the idea of serving the Germans, into a realization of what this war really means.'

Sweeny gazed silently into the man's hard features for a while and then he sighed.

'Are you certain that the British intend to send me to Oslo on some errand for them?'

'We are absolutely certain,' the officer assured him gravely.

'What must I do?'

The commander permitted himself a fleeting smile of satisfaction.

'We can give you few specific instructions. When you are in Oslo you will simply seek out and eliminate Paal Berg. You will act as, and when, the opportunity presents itself. That is all.'

Sweeny pursed his lips.

'I am new to this sort of thing,' he said slowly. 'Shouldn't I have some authority . . . some written instruction?'

The officer chuckled.

'We are not fighting a Boy Scouts' war, Sweeny. Go and find out what our British allies want; use them to get to Oslo. When you have an opportunity, contact my department either through the embassy in London or headquarters here in Orkney. You will ask to speak to Hlodver and your code-name will be Sigurd.'

'Are you Commander Hlodver?' frowned Sweeny.

The officer smiled tightly.

'You should remember your history, Sweeny. Hlodver was a great Viking *jarl* and Sigurd was Hlodver's son. Should you wish to confirm the authenticity of any message from us, we will address you as Sigurd and sign ourselves Hlodver. Do you have a good memory, Sweeny?'

'I think so. Why?'

'I am going to recite some lines from *Njal's Saga* which, with the codenames Sigurd and Hlodver, will be proof of genuine contact. All right?'

Sweeny nodded.

'Good. Remember these lines:

*'Sigurd fell in battle's blast,*
*From his wounds there sprang hot gore.*
*Brian fell, but won at last.'*

Sweeny repeated the lines.

'Excellent,' said the officer, nodding in approval. He stood up and turned for the door without proffering his hand. 'Be ready to leave for London within the hour. Good luck, Sweeny.'

# CHAPTER SIX

Michael Woods entered his flat with a large package under his arm and felt his way in the blackness to the table, where he set it down. Then he felt his way to the window and secured the blackout curtain before moving back to the door and switching on the light. He closed the door and returned to the table, picking up the parcel and tearing away the paper packaging. After a moment he stood holding a streamlined bakelite object and regarding it with a certain amount of pride. It was the very latest thing in wireless sets and had cost him 16½ guineas. The Pye International 8, it was claimed, was capable of picking up any station in Europe. He checked the cord and plug which had been fitted in the shop for him and then connected it, switched on and began tuning. He had been promising himself a new radio for a year or more and had been saving towards this day.

He found the BBC Home Service and caught the tail end of a current affairs programme. A solemn-voiced man was talking about the Budget which had been introduced in the House of Commons the previous day. Apparently, if the neutral-sounding statement was right, there was some opposition to the Chancellor of the Exchequer's new tax on purchases which meant increases on tobacco, spirits, beer, petrol and telephone charges. Woods grimaced. It seemed all the news was bad. He tuned to the Light Programme, found some dance-band music being played by Peter Fielding and his Orchestra, and went into the kitchen to prepare his evening meal.

Just then he heard knocking on the door, a heavy, officious type of knocking.

Frowning, Woods went to the door. Two men in grey trilbys and belted raincoats stood there. The word 'police' flashed through his mind.

'Doctor Michael Woods?' asked one of the men.

'Yes.'

'May we come in?'

Woods assumed they were police. They certainly had the attitude of 'Busies'. Woods enjoyed a good Edgar Wallace thriller and knew the argot off by heart.

'Have I parked my car in the wrong place?' he asked as they pushed into the apartment.

'No, sir.'

Woods closed the door behind them and stood gazing at them uncertainly.

'What is it?'

'You must come with us, I'm afraid, sir.'

'What for?'

'You will be told on arrival, sir.'

'Arrival where?' Woods was growing annoyed now. 'Look, I've had a busy day at the hospital. If it isn't about the car, what is it about?'

He suddenly realized that he had not even asked them for their warrant cards and cursed himself for an idiot. 'Where are your identity cards?'

The first man smiled thinly.

'No need to worry about that, sir. Just come along with us.'

Woods was immediately suspicious.

'I don't believe you are policemen.'

'We never said we were, sir,' the man replied calmly. 'Please don't cause us any trouble, there's a good fellow.'

Woods made a sudden lunge for the door but the second man had slipped a squat, black little object out of his pocket which brought Woods up with a start.

'That's better, sir. We don't want any trouble, so please move slowly down to our car and don't be rash.'

Incredulously, Woods found himself being propelled out of his flat and down the stairs to the street below. Unfortunately, it was deserted and there was nothing to do but precede the two men towards a dark Humber Snipe which stood waiting outside the apartment block with its engine running. One of the men slipped into the back seat while the second man pushed him inside. Nothing was said to a third man, seated behind the wheel, but the car suddenly shot forward, turned into Victoria Street and proceeded at a brisk pace towards Parliament Square.

'I demand to know what is going on!' Woods tried to summon some air of dignity.

The muzzle of the gun dug sharply into his side.

'Please, sir,' sighed the gunman.

Woods shut up. The car sped up Whitehall and into Trafalgar Square and round under the Admiralty Arch into the Mall, then swung off into a courtyard with high gates enclosing it. The driver did not pause, but drove across the courtyard and into a garage. Then the man with the gun was pulling him from the vehicle. In total silence Woods was propelled up a short flight of stairs and into a well-lit corridor. With the two men at his elbows he was guided to a lift. The lift deposited them in another corridor, along which he was marched to a door which one of the men knocked on and swung open.

To Woods's astonishment a man in his late forties, wearing a smart naval commander's uniform, was seated within the room behind a desk. The room was a pleasantly furnished office with panelled walls and a carpeted floor. There were several leather upholstered chairs. The blackout curtain was drawn across the window and a heavy brass reading lamp cast a circle of harsh light on the top of the massive mahogany desk.

'Come in, Doctor Woods,' invited the naval officer. His voice was soft and formal.

'Who the hell are you? Why have I been kidnapped?' Woods entered, his voice strident.

The officer glanced at the two men who had brought him, his eyes falling on the automatic carried by one of them.

'Trouble?'

'A little reluctance to accompany us, sir.'

'All right. Outside.'

The two men removed themselves and closed the door.

'Sorry about the unorthodox method of bringing you here, doctor. Sit down. Have a cigarette.'

A packet of Players was pushed across the desk. Woods shook his head. His anger did not abate.

'I am waiting for an explanation and it had better be a good one.'

'Doctor, my name is Wallace. Please have a little patience. We are at war and in wartime expedience takes precedence over social niceties. Now, take a seat.'

There was something commanding about the man's soft tone. Woods hesitated and then sat down.

'Doctor Woods, the situation is simple. I am – how shall I put it? – involved with intelligence. We want you to volunteer for a special job.'

Woods stared, open-mouthed.

'Am I dreaming this?' he muttered.

'You are acquainted with Miss Inge Stenersen, I believe?' The doctor's eyes widened further.

'Inge Stenersen? Good Lord, yes. She came to see me last night with some sort of petition, and . . .'

'Miss Stenersen is under the impression that you would be willing to volunteer to help get her uncle out of Nazi-occupied Norway.'

Woods began to chuckle and shake his head.

'This has to be some sort of practical joke.'

'It's no joke, believe me, doctor.'

'Then it's absolutely ridiculous. I'm a doctor . . .'

Commander Wallace smiled tightly.

'We know all about your professional background, doctor. That is why we agree with Miss Stenersen that you are a man who is extraordinarily fitted to our urgent requirements.'

'Nothing doing,' Woods grinned. He began rising from the chair.

'Sit down!' snapped Wallace, causing Woods to drop back into his seat in surprise at the sharpness in the officer's voice. 'I think we are misunderstanding each other, doctor. We are sending a team into Norway to arrange to get Professor Didrik Stenersen and his surgical team out of that country. For reasons which I will explain later, it is absolutely essential that the professor and his team are in London within a matter of weeks. We need a person who knows Oslo, knows Stenersen and is young and fit enough to accompany our little mission.'

'I'm not your boy, commander. I'm not a death-or-glory merchant,' replied Woods. 'Why don't you ask Miss Stenersen to volunteer?' he sneered as an afterthought. 'From my impression I would think she is very keen to do so.'

'Indeed, she is,' agreed Wallace. 'In fact, Miss Stenersen is one of the team of three that we propose to send in.'

'Well, bully for her,' retorted Woods, not at all abashed. 'But so far as I'm concerned, I'm not prepared to be one of your little team.'

Wallace regarded Woods bleakly for a moment. He stubbed out his cigarette.

'Very well, Woods, let us level with each other, as I believe our American cousins say. The situation is this: you are going to volunteer because, like it or not, we need you. If you don't volunteer then I can guarantee that within three weeks you will be in an army uniform in the far from pleasant conditions of the Maginot Line.'

Woods gazed at him, appalled.

'You . . . you can't do that!' he protested.

'You may recall that conscription was brought in last year as a war contingency. We are at war, doctor, and we need men.'

'But I'm a doctor. I'm in a reserved job,' Woods protested vehemently.

'The front line needs doctors. You will be entitled to make your protests when you write home from your unit . . . in a few months' time.'

Woods sat shaking his head.

'I don't believe this is happening.'

'I assure you, doctor, that it is,' Wallace said tightly. He glanced at his wristwatch. 'Now, I don't have much time. There is an aircraft that will leave Northolt in two hours' time. We want you to be aboard it.'

'This is blackmail.' Woods stared aghast.

'Yes.'

Woods hesitated.

'What about my job? My flat? My car?'

Wallace smiled.

'We will look after those for you. And you may rest assured that your job at St Thomas's will be waiting for you on your return from Norway.'

'*If* I return,' muttered Woods bitterly.

'Does that mean that you will volunteer?'

'You've made it obvious that I have no choice in the matter.'

'That's right,' nodded the commander. He pushed forward a piece of paper. 'Just something for you to sign, the Official Secrets Act and all that nonsense. Then we can go and meet your companions in this venture.'

As Michael Woods followed Commander Wallace into the adjoining room, Inge Stenersen rose and came toward the doctor with an outstretched hand and a happy smile.

'I told them that you would volunteer to help my uncle,' she said warmly. 'Thank you. Thank you so much.'

Woods caught Wallace's cynical glance and flushed.

'I'll do whatever I can, Miss Stenersen,' he said stiffly, avoiding the girl's green eyes.

Wallace had closed the door and turned to the other occupant of the room – a tall, broad shouldered, red-haired man who was regarding Woods through slightly narrowed eyes.

'This is Lars Sweeny. Sweeny, Doctor Michael Woods will be the third member of the team.'

Woods felt the firm handshake and observed the aggressive stance of the tall man. He was surprised when Sweeny greeted him in English with a pronounced American accent.

Sweeny was weighing Woods up. His first thought was 'a dandified doctor'. He wondered if the man could be relied on in a tight spot. The more he thought about matters, the more it seemed that he had been lumbered with the task of playing nursemaid to a young girl and a foppish doctor.

'Right,' Wallace was saying. 'You all know the purpose of this mission. Professor Stenersen and his surgical team must be brought out of Norway and escorted to London as quickly as possible. How this is to be accomplished will be left entirely to your discretion. The circumstances in Oslo will dictate your course of action. We can't tie you down. Let me impress upon you one thing and one thing only: I have had it from a very high source that it is imperative that the professor should be in this country within the next week or two. He is, so I am told, the only man who can perform a particular piece of surgery which may save the life of a prominent person. That is all I can say.'

Woods became genuinely interested in their mission for the first time.

'Stenersen is an abdominal surgeon, specializing in cancerous growths.'

Wallace glanced at him and nodded.

'Can't you tell us more?' pressed Woods.

'No. I'm sorry.'

'What about the practicalities of this little trip?' Sweeny interrupted. He didn't particularly care who Stenersen was nor what he was wanted in London for. He was faced with a problem which wanted a solution. 'You say that you are putting us in Norway and leaving it up to us to find Stenersen and his team and spirit them out. Any advice on how this should be done? I mean, how we *can* get these people out?'

'The war front in Norway remains pretty fluid at this time,' replied Wallace. 'The Allies are holding a line around Lillehammer, and one possible method would be to contact them in that area, get transport to Andalesnes or another port controlled by us and come back that way. The alternative would be to get across the Swedish border and make contact with our embassy in

Stockholm. The embassy will make arrangements for your transportation to London.'

'Bureaucrats are the same everywhere,' pointed out Sweeny. 'How do we convince your embassy people that we are genuinely working for British Intelligence?'

Wallace's lips thinned.

'Quite simply. The code name for this operation will be "Valkyrie". You will be aware that in Scandinavian mythology a Valkyrie was one of the minor goddesses who conducted the slain from the battlefield to Valhalla. Professor Stenersen will be designated by the code name "Baldur" for a warrior who rose again after he was slain. When you reach Allied territory you will transmit a message to the Admiralty saying "Baldur has risen again" and signing it "Valkyrie". If you reach the Swedish border you will ask the embassy for Captain Jones and use the same message. Everything will then be arranged for you, but only on receipt of that message. Can you all remember that?'

The three of them chorused their affirmatives.

'And just how are we getting to Norway?' asked Sweeny.

Wallace hesitated.

'We need to get you to Oslo fairly quickly. You will be dropped from an RAF aircraft in the region of Dalane, the fairly high wooded country to the north of Kristiansand.'

Woods gazed at the officer in disbelief.

'Now I've heard everything. Did you say "dropped from an RAF aircraft"?'

'By parachute, of course,' replied Wallace humourlessly.

'I've never used a parachute in my life,' protested Woods weakly.

'Nor have I,' broke in Sweeny, gazing at Inge Stenersen. The girl shook her head. 'Surely there is a better way into the country?'

Wallace sighed. 'If there was, we would use it. But there is not in the time allowed. Your method of entry must be by parachute or nothing. If we try to send you by submarine it will take some time and, I'm afraid, the German navy have the southern coastline of Norway pretty well bottled up by now. I'd say that the odds against a submarine landing you safely on the south coast are about one hundred to one.'

'But if none of us have made a parachute descent before . . .?' Woods began.

'In a moment you will be driven to Northolt airfield,' Wallace cut in sharply. 'You will be flown to Manchester, where you will spend the night. Tomorrow morning you will be taken to the Parachute Training School at Ringway, where you will be given some instruction. Tomorrow night you will be flown to Hatston Airfield on the Orkney islands. From there you will be flown to Norway, where you will be dropped just before dawn on Saturday morning. That is the schedule.'

He gazed at them each in turn before going on.

'We have come up with some documents which will provide you, Sweeny, and you, Woods, with new identities. We find it is safer to use as much of the truth as we can, therefore Miss Stenersen will simply be herself, omitting the fact that she has spent the last few years in this country. Sweeny will be Lars Olsen, a seaman who has been working in the whale boats, of which I understand you know a great deal. You are looking for a new berth. We have a seaman's union card in that name. As for you, Woods, you are Bryn Poulsson, a ship's doctor. We have documents for you including a letter from Ingve Haugen, the secretary of the Norwegian Seaman's Union, reminding you of the consequences of not paying your subscriptions.'

Woods pursed his lips.

'That's all very well,' he said, 'but any Norwegian would know that I am not a native.'

'But a German would not. You just have to be careful who you speak to.'

Woods looked pained, but Inge Stenersen shot him a smile of encouragement. 'Don't worry. You'll do fine. We'll be there to help you out.'

Wallace glanced at his wristwatch.

'Right. The car will be here to take you to Northolt. I will see you all in Hatston before you set off. I'll give you a final briefing then. Any comments?'

Woods smiled bitterly.

'Yes. This whole thing is absolutely bloody stupid.'

Inge Stenersen turned a shocked gaze to him, while Sweeny's lips twisted in a sneer.

'Not thinking of pulling out, are you?' Wallace said sharply.

Woods thought about his comfortable flat, his job and his Lagonda Tourer. Then he thought of the grim fortifications of the Maginot Line and gave a deep sigh.

'You asked for comments. All I'm saying is that it's a bloody stupid idea.' He turned to smile at the others. 'However, Com-

[64]

mander Wallace here knows that I am committed to the project.'

Woods's humour was lost on Wallace. The naval commander crossed the room to open the door. 'In that case,' he said, 'I'll see you all tomorrow night at Hatston.'

# CHAPTER SEVEN

The Valkyrie team were roused from their sleep at six o'clock the next morning. There had been little time for them to get to know one another during the drive to Northolt, the flight and the short, bumpy ride to Ringway, south of Manchester. They were taken to an anonymous-looking house outside the military complex, given a meal and a room each. Now a Wren with a brightly scrubbed face drove them through the complex to the far side of the establishment, each of them silently locked in their own thoughts.

Woods was simply bemused, finding himself in some dream from which he believed he would soon awake and discover himself back in his apartment in Ashley Place. The whole thing was just too bizarre to be real. He kept blinking his eyes, half expecting the scenery to change into something more reassuring. But the dream persisted. He fought down a feeling of fear and panic. He wondered what his companions were thinking. Inge Stenersen had been bright and chatty last night. Enthusiastic. How he hated enthusiasm. She was far too pretty to be involved in this ridiculous cloak-and-dagger affair. She should be going to dances and dinners. He let his gaze fall on her fair hair which, while tumbling to her shoulders, did not quite hide her delicate ears with their adornment of tiny ear-rings of beaten silver. He wished he did not find her so attractive. He imagined himself taking her to some hospital dance or some intimate dinner at the Epicure in Gerrard Street, or even the Carlton or the Ritz. The war should have no place in her life nor in his.

Woods glanced sideways at the red haired Norwegian-American, Lars Sweeny, who sat beside him. He had taken an instant dislike to Sweeny. There was something about his quiet pragmatism, his taciturn self-assurance which indicated that he was able to take everything in his stride, and this irritated Woods.

In the front seat of the car Inge Stenersen kept glancing surreptitiously into the driving mirror to examine her companions.

She was caught between excitement and reservations about her comrades. She had been excited and enthusiastic when Commander Wallace had explained the proposition to get Uncle Didrik out of Oslo. Her uncle had been the main influence in her life and she had always been close to him. He had brought her up when her own parents had died. There had been no question about her being reluctant to volunteer for this mission.

She had little reaction to Lars Sweeny. He seemed a little too macho to her. Tall, capable and yet he seemed entirely without feeling, or was he simply able to put on a mask?

Michael Woods, on the other hand, irritated her. The irritation stemmed from the fact that she felt an attraction to the man which she had not been able to understand. He was handsome, that was true. She placed his age at about thirty. She suspected that he knew he was good-looking, for there was an indolent air about him, a vaguely patronizing air when he spoke to her. He was tanned and his build spoke much of the outdoors. She knew from Uncle Didrik that Woods had been an enthusiastic climber and skier during his time in Norway. She also knew that her uncle thought Woods had an excellent career in front of him. Yet she was troubled by the sense of reluctance about the plan to rescue Uncle Didrik that she picked up from him.

In the other corner of the vehicle, Lars Sweeny sprawled his tall body and examined his two companions through lowered lids. He wished that he was going to Oslo alone. He had other things on his mind than the task of playing nursemaid to the girl and the foppish Englishman at his side. Getting the old professor and his party out would not present much of a problem, but the elimination of Judge Paal Berg was going to be a tough one. And there was another task which Sweeny had in mind to do, one which neither Norwegian nor British intelligence knew about. His hand closed on the small buttonhole badge in his pocket. Whoever owned this badge had murdered Freya . . . *his* Freya. His lips tightened as he remembered her sprawled and bloodied body. A life for a life. He must have his vengeance.

The Wren driver stopped the car in front of a tall hangar and they tumbled out to be met by a slimly built army major wearing the shoulder flash of the Parachute Regiment. In spite of the chilly crispness of the early hour, he was dressed as if on a drill parade. He surveyed them with a mournful melancholy.

'I believe your names are Stenersen, Sweeny and Woods?' He seemed to give the indication of sighing without actually doing so, and he gazed at them as if they were some strange species of animal with which he was not quite familiar. 'I am told that you have never jumped before. I have been given exactly one day to show you the ropes.' He sniffed in disapproval. 'Very well. You will be shown the techniques of jumping in our gymnasium with a practice jump from a built-up model of a Whitley. Then you will make two descents. The first one from a delightfully silent balloon known as "Bessie" and the other from an equally delightful but noisy aircraft known as a "Wimpey".'

He paused and his melancholy gaze examined each of them in turn until he finally shook his head in disapproval.

'Usually our pupils stay here for two weeks, making two descents from the balloon and five from the aircraft. This is coupled with numerous lectures, physical training sessions and even little film shows of parachute techniques, of which we are particularly fond. I regret that you will be deprived of all that fun. Instead, you will learn the rudiments of jumping this morning, and I mean rudiments, and after lunch you will make your balloon descent. If you survive that, you will then go straight up and make a descent from the aircraft. Are there any questions?'

For the next two hours the major's new pupils tumbled dutifully on coconut matting to the roar of the physical training instructors. They swung on bars and dropped through holes. They learnt how to fall with both legs kept close together and to roll to the right or the left with both hands in their pockets. They were made to practise this several times. The same exercises were repeated with a parachute harness on, and culminated in a jump from the lofty gallery of the hangar with the control of the fall being maintained by a cable. It reminded Woods of a trapeze act.

In the gymnasium was a mock-up of the fuselage of a Whitley with its hatch about eight feet above a pile of canvas mats. They each in turn had to climb the ladder into this construction, move along to the hatch and sit swinging their legs over. At a signal they jumped down to the mat to the accompaniment of a bull-like roar from the instructor: 'Feet and knees together, for Christ's sake! Tightly now! Elbows tucked into the sides, head forced down. Take the shock on both legs and roll! God damn it! I said, roll!'

The major greeted them unenthusiastically after they emerged from the canteen where they had lunched sparingly. 'Time for your first descent from the balloon. Any questions?'

[68]

They were expected to jump from a small platform attached to a barrage balloon which was winched to a height of 1,000 feet. They survived the experience without spraining or breaking anything and immediately the mournful major gathered them together.

'Now, I'm afraid, you are going for the big one. I would have liked to see you do several more jumps from the balloon but your time schedule prevents it. You'll be taken up in the Whitley and dropped over Tatton Park where I shall be waiting to pick up the pieces. Let me tell you briefly what happens when you jump from an aircraft. As with your descent from the balloon, you will use a static line. It is a length of cable attached to the parachute on your back which tugs out your 'chute automatically and does not leave its manipulation to your fumbling nervousness. Understand?'

Woods smiled thinly. 'No.'

The major raised his eyes to heaven in silent prayer.

'Very well, Mr Woods,' he said sorrowfully. 'When you are in the Whitley you will be wearing a 'chute? Correct? The 'chute is attached by a static line to the aircraft. Correct? When you jump out and fall sixteen feet from the aircraft, the static line begins to draw out the parachute which is packed so that it draws out in a smooth and easy motion. Your parachute is thirty feet in length and when it opens your falling weight will sever the wire, or static line, leaving you free and easy to float safely down to earth like the daring young man on his flying trapeze. Correct?'

The major had edged close to Woods so that his face was now just a few inches from him.

'I suppose so,' muttered Woods.

The major's melancholy face became even more morose.

'You suppose? Well, son, if it does not perform as it should perform you may report the matter to me when you come down.'

Woods joined the others in the dark and noisy interior of the Whitley. They took off and climbed quickly. No one said anything until the young despatcher came crawling back.

'Two minutes to dropping zone!' he yelled, and the bomb doors grated open. Woods felt the icy grip of fear as he linked up the static line under the watchful eye of the despatcher. The man checked each line and stood back to one side of the open hatch.

'One ready!' called Sweeny, sitting down on the edge of the hole, his legs dangling in space.

The despatcher glanced up at the light above the door.

[69]

It flickered and changed from red to green.

'Go!' cried the despatcher as he clapped his hand onto Sweeny's shoulder.

Inge was next and even as Sweeny disappeared she was ready in position.

'Go!' yelled the despatcher again.

Heart thumping fearfully, Woods fumbled into position and closed his eyes.

'Go!' It was more the heavy hand of the despatcher than his own volition that propelled him from the aircraft. The wind howled in his face. He was slung around as it buffeted him. The next thing he knew was that his body was jerking violently and he opened his eyes as he heard the crack of the silk as the parachute spread above him. He hardly had time to adjust to the sensation of floating downwards when the ground came up to meet him rapidly and he scrabbled painfully through a bramble bush, remembering at the last moment to control his contact with the ground.

He was still lying winded when he saw the melancholy major staring distastefully down at him.

'That was bloody awful, my son. Still, you'll probably have beginner's luck when you try the real thing.'

Their aircraft landed at 6:30 pm at Hatston and they were immediately driven to a large, spacious house not far from the airfield. The place stood well back from the road, almost hidden by a wood. At the door they were greeted by the immaculate figure of Commander Wallace. He took them into a lounge where a fire burned brightly and they flung themselves into comfortable armchairs. Wallace took up a position in front of the fireplace and proceeded to fill a pipe.

'Well, Ringwood tells me that you know the rudiments of making a parachute jump. The rest is up to you. You will take off just after midnight. Upstairs, in the rooms to which you will shortly be shown, you will find a change of clothes. You will put the clothes which you are now wearing into the cases in the rooms. Everything, that is. Pants, socks, nylons, the lot. You will then get dressed in the clothes provided. We don't want any enterprising German finding a label from Hector Prowe of Regent Street or,' he glanced at Inge Stenersen's fashionable camel coat, 'a Fenwick label in that.'

Inge stared at the commander and wondered how he knew that

she had just purchased the £5 coat from Fenwick's.

'You will also leave all coins, cigarettes, wallets, documentation and any other articles behind.'

'Make-up?' demanded Inge.

Wallace turned his dark eyes on her and nodded gravely.

'We have provided everything for you. I don't think you will have cause to complain.'

Half-an-hour later Inge agreed with him. She could find nothing lacking in the selection of cosmetics which had been provided in the Norwegian handbag.

Wallace examined their change of clothing with professional approval.

'In addition to your personal effects and documentation, we are providing you with a map of southern Norway, compasses and Norwegian *kroner*. Also, three service automatics and ammunition.'

Woods frowned.

'I've never fired a gun in my life,' he protested.

'I have,' Inge said. 'I used to belong to a *Skytterlag*, a shooting society.'

Wallace glanced at Sweeny with a question in his eyes.

'I can use a gun, commander,' he said shortly.

Wallace turned back to Woods. 'I'm afraid that we don't have time to give you instruction. I hope you won't need to use a gun. The Webley is easy . . . .' He picked up the handgun from the table and thrust it towards Woods. 'You remove the safety-catch here, aim it at whatever you want to hit and pull the trigger.'

Woods took the gun, wondering whether there was an attempt at grim humour in the naval commander's voice.

'Thanks. I'll try to remember,' he said flippantly.

'But before you put it in your pocket,' Wallace added heavily, 'I suggest you push back the safety catch.'

Woods flushed and pushed at the lever.

Inge glanced at him sympathetically. 'When we have a moment, I'll show you how to load and use it.'

'Now,' Wallace was glancing at his watch, 'in a few moments you'll have a meal, put on your flying suits and be leaving. The pilot is under instruction to drop you just north of the village of Bygland, along the banks of the Byglandsfjord. It's about as far as we can get across southern Norway without detection. It's a remote area but from there it should be easy to make your way down to Kristiansand. The journey from Kristiansand to Oslo

[71]

should be straightforward. You all know what is required of you?'

They nodded silently, and Wallace hesitated awkwardly before continuing.

'There is one other thing you ought to know. Increased enemy pressure has necessitated the withdrawal of Allied forces from the positions they previously held at Lillehammer. Our troops have had to withdraw towards the north.'

Wallace did not mention the morale-shattering defeat of British troops at Lillehammer in their first armed conflict of the war with German troops. It was as demoralizing as it was serious. Norwegian resistance, heroic as it was, was crumbling and it was probably a matter of days rather than weeks before the Allies would be forced to agree with Major-General Carton de Wiart that Norway would have to be evacuated from the Allied military point of view.

Sweeny was gazing at Wallace thoughtfully, trying to read behind his bland exterior to his troubled mind.

'Is Andalsnes still an open port to the Allies?' he asked.

'Yes. But the situation is very fluid.'

The commander turned and produced a bottle of brandy and four glasses.

'Pre-war French cognac,' he said solemnly. 'It just remains for me to wish you luck and leave you with another piece of news which, this time, you may find amusing. It has just been announced from Berlin that today, Friday, April 26, eighteen days after the German invasion of Norway, Adolf Hitler has officially declared the Third Reich to be in a state of war against that country.'

Woods smiled cynically. 'The Germans do like to clear up the legal complexities of everything, don't they?'

# CHAPTER EIGHT

Woods, Sweeny and Inge Stenersen sat silently in the fuselage of the Blenheim as the engines revved and the hydraulic brakes whined while the final check of engines and mechanisms was being made. Then, through the tiny windows, they caught sight of a green light flashing from the airfield control tower. There came a sudden roar from the 6,000 horse-power engines and the aircraft surged forward as the brakes were released, gathering speed until it finally rose from the ground and began to climb rapidly into the blackness of the night sky. The RAF despatcher busied himself with incomprehensible tasks in the interior of the aircraft and left them to their own devices. No one spoke; they concentrated their gaze through the windows of the craft as it rose upwards.

The moon was high in the sky, sending a stream of silver over the shadows of the North Sea below. Clouds, bathed in white moonlight, floated above and below them. It was a clear and tranquil night, the sort of night the old Vikings had called 'Odin's Moon' when they put to sea to conduct their war-raids.

It was a while before the three modern Valkyries heard the despatcher speaking to the pilot and he turned to them with a reassuring grin.

'Norwegian coast to port!'

They peered forward. Away in the darkness they caught a glimpse of white breakers far below and the broken dark shadows of an irregular coastline. Then, through the clouds, came the white glow of moonlight on snow capped mountains. White lights flickered here and there, and jewel-like clusters of lights shone from inhabited regions. The Germans had not been able to enforce blackout regulations as yet.

'Ten minutes to target!' cried the despatcher.

Sweeny acknowledged and turned to the others.

'Okay?'

Inge smiled and Woods raised his thumb. They began to

check their harnesses, and then the despatcher made a second check before they climbed towards the hatch. The despatcher bent forward and opened it and an icy blast blew up through the hole. Below them the mountains and dark valleys slid by, jagged, repellent and cold.

'Hook up!'

The despatcher now ensured that each of their parachutes was linked to the static line which would automatically jerk open the thirty-two foot diameter of silk on which their lives depended. Each parachute was capable of bearing a maximum weight of 225 pounds.

Sweeny was the first to jump. He adjusted his equipment, swung his legs over the side of the hole and held himself ready. Below he could see the contours of the mountains and valleys and then a broad stretch of water lit by the moon. Byglandsfjord! Sweeny glanced up to the despatcher's face. The man's eyes were on the little light above the hatch, which was still showing red. The aircraft was following the banks of the fjord now, weaving a little, rising and sinking with the force of the wind. The light blinked from red to green.

'Go!' screamed the despatcher, at the same time slapping Sweeny on the shoulder.

Sweeny flung himself forward and began to drop, the wind howling in his face. He felt himself stopped short in a sudden jerk. He was buffeted by the wind, but above him the dark canopy was open and he was floating gently downwards. He adjusted his straps, easing himself in the harness, and examined his surroundings. He could hear the drone of the Blenheim moving away, a small dark shadow in the sky. And there were two other shadows. Woods and the girl. They were floating above him but fairly close. Below lay the waters of the fjord reflecting the silvery moonlight. He was drifting towards the lower slopes of the snow-capped mountains, near to the edge of a dense fir forest.

He looked round, searching the dark terrain for a good landing place.

The roar of an aero engine caused him to stare up in astonishment. What was the Blenheim pilot doing? The fool! Flying back over the dropping zone would draw attention to them. But the dark shape of the aircraft which sped close by was not that of the Blenheim. Sweeny went cold as he recognized the silhouette of a Heinkel and then realized that it was climbing

[74]

swiftly after the disappearing Blenheim. He heard the staccato chatter of its guns, and before he could even register the meaning of it in his mind there was a loud explosion above the far side of the fjord, a sudden burst of flame in the sky and then the Blenheim, from which they had dropped only moments before, was plunging earthward in several flaming pieces. The dark silhouette of the Heinkel, now framed by the moon, was performing a climbing turn towards them.

Sweeny supposed the others had seen it too. He hung helplessly in his harness watching the black shape reach the apex of its turn. It was still a few miles away across the fjord but it would only be a few seconds before . . . He glanced down as something brushed his leg. To his surprise he saw a stand of conifers rushing at him. He had been so busy watching the Heinkel that he had failed to keep an eye on the approaching ground. There was a crash of breaking branches as he hit the trees and went plunging through them with a ripping of parachute silk. He swung violently against the trunk, the impact knocking the breath from his body. A moment later he was cutting away the parachute straps with his knife and slithering down the remaining few feet of the trunk to the foot of the tree.

He was conscious of the roar of the Heinkel now. He slid off his back pack, grabbed his Webley revolver from his flying suit pocket and ran swiftly to the edge of the trees. A few yards away the forest opened onto a clear slope of mountainside which ran down to the shores of the Byglandsfjord. About a hundred yards away he saw Michael Woods struggling to gather in the white canopy of his 'chute.

'Leave it!' Sweeny shouted. 'Take cover!'

The roar of the Heinkel's engine was ominous. Where the hell was the girl?

The third parachute was just landing further along the slope, about fifty yards from where Woods had now given up the struggle with his 'chute.

'Get down!' cried Sweeny, flinging himself back into the cover of the trees as he heard the chatter of the aircraft's machine guns. Even as Sweeny flung himself down he saw Woods take off at a loping run in the direction of the girl, who was struggling to free herself from the 'chute. Bullets created little explosions of dirt across the slope all around Woods. He reached the girl in a diving rugger tackle and they went sprawling. By then the Heinkel had sped overhead. Sweeny saw it climbing for another run.

'Get in the trees!' he yelled. 'This way!'

Woods sprang up and hauled the girl to her feet. Together they began to race up the slope towards Sweeny. The scream of the Heinkel grew louder again. Once more they flung themselves to the ground, almost trying to burrow into the earth. Then the aircraft was gone again. The Heinkel circled and flew over them for a third time, but this time it did not open fire. It climbed and flew southward.

Sweeny rose and brushed himself down.

'Welcome to Norway,' Woods said cynically.

The girl was white-faced as she stood up, gazing across the waters of the fjord to where what seemed to be a small bonfire was burning.

'Should we try to see if they are alive?' she whispered.

'No one would have survived,' snapped Sweeny. 'Besides, we have a job to do.'

'Someone *might* be alive . . .'

'No one is alive. And we won't live long either if we don't move from here very quickly. What do you think our friend in the Heinkel is doing right now, if he has not done so already? He will be on the radio to his base telling them that three parachutists have landed and to send the nearest troops to pick us up. Troops may be on their way already.'

Woods sighed. 'He's right.'

Inge compressed her lips.

'Those poor young men.'

'A lot of poor young men and women, and old men and women, have already died in this goddam war. A lot more will die, no doubt,' Sweeny said.

Woods helped Inge retrieve her 'chute, gathered his own and the remains of Sweeny's, and hid them in the middle of a thorn bush together with their flying suits.

Sweeny glanced at his compass and then at the map. 'I make the village of Bygland a few kilometres south of us. We won't use the main road in case we meet Germans searching for us. We ought to be able to get a bus to Kristiansand from there.'

They took to the forest, keeping roughly parallel to the road to Bygland. The area was one of the principal forest regions of the country and the forest presented plenty of shelter, a thick mixture of conifers, birch, dwarf birch and black alder. Now and again, as they passed through small clearings, they saw a few *fjeldrype*, or field grouse, indulging in breakfast among the bilberries. Sweeny felt a surge of homesickness as he took deep draughts of crystal air scented with the perfume of reindeer moss and fir. It was still April, he reflected. The cod shoals would still be spawning on the coastal banks and the small whales would be following the cod to their grounds off Stavanger. He thought about old Tenvig and all that the old man had taught him about the seas; about the capelin off Finnmaken which could be fished at ease during April and May.

A twig cracked somewhere in front of them and halted them in their tracks.

Sweeny's hand came up with the service Webley clasped in it.

'Who is there?' he demanded sharply.

Something was moving under the shade of a dwarf birch. Sweeny aimed his automatic.

An elk rushed abruptly into the clearing with a rustling of leaves, stared for a moment at the three of them and then bounded away. Woods chuckled. 'We nearly had a fine meal for the cooking.'

Sweeny swore softly.

'Let's move on. It's dawn now and I want to be in Bygland by breakfast.'

It was nearly eight o'clock when they came to the outskirts of the village. Bygland stood by the banks of the fjord at the foot of the Lysheia, a mountain that was nearly 3,000 feet high. It was an old place, occupied even in the misty times of prehistory. Sweeny halted them on the edge of the forest.

'I'll go into the village alone,' he said. 'There might be Germans about. I'll check things and find out about transportation to Kristiansand.'

He was back within half-an-hour.

'There's no Germans about and there's a bus from Austad due shortly which comes across the Storestraum Bridge through Bygland to Evje and then to Arendal. We don't have to go into Kristiansand because we can catch a train from Arendal directly to Oslo.' He glanced at his watch. 'The bus is due to arrive within ten minutes so I'll go down to the Storestraum Bridge first. You two follow me. It'll be best if we travel separately to Arendal.'

They watched Sweeny move off.

'Damned self-opinionated bastard,' breathed Woods.

'You don't like him?' asked Inge.

[77]

'He's certainly not overly sensitive about the feelings of others,' replied Woods. 'We're supposed to be working together. Sweeny has apparently placed himself in command.'

The girl sighed. 'Let's go,' she said, adding, 'personally, I don't care who's in charge so long as we complete this job successfully.'

The village was still fairly deserted as they strolled down the street to the crossroads near the bridge which connected Bygland with the road from Austad on the far side of the fjord. There was a bench there on which they saw Sweeny sitting, apparently relaxed, smoking his pipe. Next to him sat an old woman, who was knitting, and beyond her a middle-aged man.

'*God morgen*,' greeted the man as they came up. The old woman smiled and nodded.

'*God dag*,' returned Inge.

Woods gave a vague nod, sat down and pulled out an old Norwegian magazine which Wallace had supplied and pretended to lose himself in it.

'Nice weather for April,' the man said.

'Very nice,' agreed Inge.

'You are not from these parts?'

Woods glanced at the man suspiciously.

'How can you tell?' Inge smiled. 'I am from Oslo.'

The man smiled. 'Oh, I have an ear for accents. Besides, I know most of the people in these parts. It is not often we get strangers through here except during the hunting season. I knew you were not from here.'

There was an unspoken question directed towards Woods. Inge covered for him.

'You're right. We have been on a trekking holiday in the mountains for the last three weeks.'

The sound of a motor vehicle caused them to glance up.

'Ah, the old bus is on time,' the man said, standing up.

An ancient omnibus came wheezing across the bridge and halted before them. There were a dozen or so people inside, mainly farm workers and a few foresters judging by their clothes. There were also some old women who were obviously taking farm produce to the villages. Woods was thankful that the garrulous middle-aged man had only come to the bus to meet someone, one of the women, and the two went off up the road chatting. The old woman climbed into the bus first, paid her fare to Evje and took the nearest seat.

[78]

Sweeny climbed in next, and while he was getting his ticket Woods whispered to Inge: 'It's best if we travel separately, too. You never know.'

He stood aside and allowed her to climb up. She asked for a ticket to Svenes. She had worked out that at Svenes she would pretend to change her mind and go on to Arendal. She took a seat on the left-hand side of the bus three seats down from the driver. Sweeny had already seated himself in the rear seat. Woods bought a ticket to Arendal and seated himself next to an old farm worker who was dozing in his seat on the right-hand side of the bus.

The vehicle wheezed into motion, skirting the shores of the fjord. It was a fine bright morning now and the sun was quite warm as it shone through the dirty windows of the bus. The heavily wooded slopes of Lysheia looked like a picture-postcard rising above them. They moved southwards through some sections of the roadway which had been blasted from the rock of the mountain as it swept down into the lake. At the southern end of the lake, from which the River Otra began to flow due south into the sea, the small village of Evje constituted the next stop for the bus. It halted by the boatyards and the old woman, with her knitting, alighted while two or three other people climbed on board. Once more the vehicle set off, following the road down the Saeterdal valley and across the wooded heathlands.

Woods was relaxing and nodding slightly. The previous night without sleep and the warmth of the sun was making him very drowsy.

The squeal of brakes and the motion of the bus threw him forward in his seat. The farm worker, in the next seat, had awoken and was scowling through the window.

'*De grønne!*' he spat in annoyance.

Woods frowned, not understanding the man's reference to 'the greens'.

'*Se der, tyskere!*' the man grunted.

Woods peered through the window. A German road block.

# CHAPTER NINE

The door at the front of the bus was swung open and two German soldiers in green uniforms climbed aboard. They carried Schmeisser machine-pistols hung on straps and held casually at their sides, but ready for instant use. Both men carried the single *Gefreiter* chevron on their left arms, denoting them to be military police corporals, and each had a ceremonial dagger hung in a scabbard above his left hip. The farm worker next to Woods cursed under his breath.

The leading corporal gazed down the bus.

'This is a Field Security Police check,' he said in German. '*Ausweiss bitte!*'

No one moved. The corporal's face reddened. Woods, who understood some basic German, knew that a lot of Norwegians had a working knowledge of the language, but no one was responding to the corporal.

'*Geheime Feld Polizei! Ausweiss bitte!*' snapped the man again.

When no one moved he issued another sharp command over his shoulder. Another man climbed into the bus, a thin, lanky youth in a uniform Woods had never seen before. His appearance was greeted with an angry muttering from those on the bus, which died away when the leading German swung his machine-pistol upwards.

'The swine,' whispered Woods' neighbour. 'One of Quisling's Hird traitors.'

Woods glanced down the bus to the young man. So this was one of Quisling's stormtroopers? In ancient times the Hird had been the royal bodyguard of the Viking kings. Quisling had adopted the name for his party's stormtroopers.

'Papers,' snapped the youth. 'All identifications cards and documents.'

One of the Germans remained next to the driver while his companion and the arrogant-looking young Hird man moved down the aisle checking papers. Inge, sitting forward in the bus, had her papers swiftly glanced at and handed back immediately. Woods felt his muscles tighten as the German and his companion came closer. His Norwegian might be good enough to fool a German but if the Hird man asked questions his accent would be spotted within moments.

'Können Sie sich ausweisen?'

Woods found himself gazing into the pale eyes of the policeman. The Hird man was passing some papers back to a woman on the other side of the aisle and Woods prayed he would be asked no questions as he pressed his identification card into the German's hand.

'Doktor Bryn Poulsson,' read the German. 'Welche Staatsangehörigkeit besitzen Sie? Norwegish?'

'Ja. Ich bin norwegisch,' replied Woods, thankful he knew enough German to answer the man in kind.

The Hird man suddenly turned and scowled across the shoulder of his German companion.

'Hva heter du?'

Woods summoned his best accent: 'Jeg er skipslege. Jeg skal til Oslo for å skaffe meg hyre.'

'You are not a local man, doctor,' pressed the Hird man. 'No.'

'From where do you come?' demanded the Hird man suspiciously.

'From Alta near Hammerfest,' lied Woods, trying to think of the most remote part of Norway he could. 'I've been abroad a lot working on ships.'

'You are no Norwegian!' the young fascist yelled abruptly.

The German soldier's Schmeisser came up to cover Woods as the Norwegian repeated it in German.

'Aus welchem Lande kommen Sie?' snapped the soldier.

'I am a Norwegian. A ship's doctor,' Woods insisted.

'Lügner! Sind Sie Fallschirmjäger!'

'Of course I am not parachutist.'

There were some sympathetic murmurings from the people on the bus. Inge was white-faced. Woods couldn't see Sweeny at the rear of the bus. All he saw now was the taut mask of the German soldier's face. The man was nervous. Abruptly he grabbed Woods by the front of the jacket and yanked him upright.

'Raus!'

There was nothing for it. Woods could not endanger his two companions. He allowed himself to be pushed down the aisle of the bus. The soldier gave him a sharp thrust which sent him staggering down the steps of the vehicle into the roadway. Two more green-uniformed *Geheime Feld Polizei* stood covering the bus with their Schmeissers. The Hird man followed the two Germans from the bus, smiling maliciously.

'I think the man is English from the way he pronounces Norwegian,' he told the German with undisguised glee in his voice.

The soldier who had questioned him told him to raise his hands and move to the side of the road. Another of the Germans moved to a small wooden sentry hut where Woods could see a field telephone. He bit his lip. He knew the whole venture had been so bizarre that it was not surprising that it should end like this. He hoped the Germans would allow the bus to move on; be content with his capture and let Inge and Sweeny alone. He must not betray them. The German military policeman stood staring at him unblinking, the Schmeisser levelled at his chest.

How bloody stupid it all was. A few days ago he hadn't a care in the world. He was a doctor, saving lives. Now he was a spy, a spy caught and probably about to be shot by the side of some godforsaken roadway in Norway. He glanced towards the bus. The pale face of Inge Stenersen was staring through the window at him. He wished she would avert her gaze. She might give herself away.

He didn't know what registered first, the single crack of a rifle or the scream of the German corporal, who was curiously spinning in the roadway, throwing his machine gun from him with both hands outstretched. It seemed to be happening in slow motion. The man spun and then collapsed to the ground with a gash of red across his face. There was another sharp crack and another of the soldiers took a step forward. Woods saw a look of total amazement on his face before he clutched at his stomach and pitched face forward.

The two other soldiers began to run towards the trees at the side of the road. One man let off a long burst of gunfire into the bushes but there were more loud explosions and both of them fell awkwardly by the roadside.

The young man in the Hird uniform gave a bleating cry, almost an animal noise, and dived to the side of the bus, crouching on the ground and covering his head with his hands as if in protection.

Woods stared around him stupidly. He had not even had time

to lower his hands. From the dark pine forests a group of half-a-dozen men were emerging in a curious collection of uniforms. They looked like a group of bandits. A tall young man seemed to be their leader. He was clad in a military battledress jacket, trousers and stout army boots. He carried a knapsack on his back and a rifle in his hand. He had a broad smile on his fresh features as he came up to Woods.

'Looks like we arrived just in time, eh? You are all right?'

Woods nodded, pulling down his hands. Two of the men were hauling the young Hird man to his feet. The former arrogance had gone from the youth. He was trembling and trying to suppress his sobs. Another member of the newly-arrived party was climbing into the bus. 'Everyone all right in here?' he called.

The youthful leader, who wore captain's stars on his shoulder tabs, was examining Woods with interest.

'Who are you?'

Woods saw no point in denying he was English.

'Trying to get through to the Allied lines?'

Woods shook his head and countered: 'Who are you?'

The young man smiled. 'Let's say we are a unit of irregulars operating behind German lines.' He turned, suddenly aware of the young fascist held between two of his men. The young man's eyes narrowed; the pleasant smile was wiped off his face to be replaced by a mask of hate. He moved to the Hird man, tore open the breast pocket of his uniform and took out an identity card, which he examined and thrust into his own pocket. Then he glanced at the two men holding the youth and nodded slowly. They dragged the Hird man towards the trees at the side of the road.

Woods frowned. 'What do you plan to do with him?' he asked.

The young man scowled.

'What do you think? Spank his bottom and send him home?'

Woods saw that one of the men had taken a rope from his knapsack. The Hird youth was sobbing openly now, crying like a child. The two men ignored him. One of them threw a rope over a branch and fashioned a noose.

It was over in a moment, even before Woods had time to take in what was happening. The Hird man's sobbing ended in a choking scream and then his body was twisting grotesquely at the end of the rope which the two men were securing to the trunk of the pine tree from which the man was hanging.

Woods shuddered. His face mirrored his distaste, and the

young man turned to him in annoyance.

'This is a war, Englishman, not a game of cricket. We cannot afford to treat these traitors to trials and codes of fair play. They are the enemy who have betrayed our country. They have plotted and planned the destruction of our people. They deserve no humanity.

'I am a doctor,' Woods said slowly. 'It is hard to witness death.'

'Believe me, doctor, I, too, was brought up to believe that life is sacred. But now, what I want to know is whether you are a refugee or a deserter from the British forces in the north? What *are* you doing here?'

Woods drew his gaze from the terrible sight of the swinging body of the youth to the young guerilla leader.

'I am on a special mission in Norway. I cannot tell you more.'

'I cannot release you without some explanation.'

'Then I'll supply it.'

They swung round to find that Sweeny and Inge Stenersen had left the bus.

'And who are you?' snapped the young man.

Sweeny told him briefly, omitting to explain why they had been sent into Norway.

'We heard that the Germans were looking for parachutists,' the man said. 'This entire road is roadblocked from here to Arendal. Had you managed to get through this roadblock you would have been picked up at another one.'

'Then I suggest that you send the bus on its way and we all remove ourselves from the scene of this little ambush before the Germans arrive here in force,' replied Sweeny.

The young leader hesitated, but there was something impressively commanding in Sweeny's voice.

'Very well,' he said reluctantly. 'The bus continues on. But you and your companions will come with us and satisfy our curiosity. I am not content with your explanation.'

He moved to the bus and climbed inside.

'Listen to me, my friends,' he called to the passengers. 'The next stop is Haegeland. You have had no incidents on the way. None at all. You have had a pleasant and uneventful journey and have seen nothing. No Germans, no partisans, no one. Neither were there three passengers who left the bus at this point.

The driver spoke for them all. 'It is understood.'

The young man climbed down and waved the bus onwards.

They stood watching it disappear down the road. Then the

[84]

young leader gathered his men together.

'We'll be making a fast pace up the mountains,' he informed his three new comrades. 'We know a cave there on the far side, about two hours' journey. I hope you will keep up.'

Without another word they set off, marching in single file through the dark conifer trees. As Woods passed the hanging body of the Hird youth he noticed that someone had pinned a placard to the boy's breast. It simply said, 'A Norwegian Traitor!' No one had made any attempt to hide the bodies of the four dead German soldiers.

# CHAPTER TEN

Hauptmann Karl Eschig of the *Amtsgruppe Auslandsnachrichten und Abwehr*, usually known simply as the Abwehr, the German foreign intelligence and counter-espionage service, sat back in his chair and gazed thoughtfully around his office. It was a high-ceilinged, oak-panelled room in what had been a Norwegian Government office building in Akersgate, overlooking the impressive building that had housed the Norwegian Storting or parliament. It was a pleasant enough office, tastefully furnished with antique pieces that blended with the oak panelling. Several gilt-framed, oil-painted images of Norwegian dignitaries stared down in disapproval at the German captain. Eschig smiled complacently back at the dour faces of men like Christian Michelsen, who had presided over the dissolution of the union of Norway and Sweden; Fridtjof Nansen, who had been Norway's first delegate to the League of Nations; and Ivar Aasen, who had set out to revive Norway's national language in the 19th Century.

Eschig was forty-five, a copper-haired man with blue, almost metallic eyes. His features were broad, his face not unpleasant though certainly not a handsome one. The face betrayed his shrewdness which was sometimes disguised by his slow, rolling Bavarian accent. It was a lean, hard face with tiny lines at the corner of the eyes. Eschig was a regular army officer who had initially entered the service of his Fatherland in 1914. He had left the army for a while in 1919 with the rank of *leutnant* and two decorations for gallantry, including the Iron Cross (Second Class), after having survived the perils of trench warfare. It was due to the entrenched class structure of the German army that Eschig had not risen to a higher office. In the mid-1920s he had returned to the army, but had been unable to get promotion until Hitler came to power in 1933 and there was a need for trained men to help in the expansion of the armed forces. Not that Eschig was a Party member. He still wasn't, even though it had been suggested that his rate of promotion would be a lot quicker if he joined.

Eschig was not interested at all in politics. But he had a policeman's mind and this had helped bring about his transfer to the reorganized Abwehr in 1934 under Colonel Hans Oster, the chief assistant to the Abwehr's boss, Admiral Wilhelm Canaris. When the Führer gave the formal directive for the *Weseruebung*, or Weser Exercise, the code name for the invasion of Denmark and Norway, Eschig had been attached to General von Falkenhorst's staff with orders to set up an immediate counterespionage system as soon as Oslo fell into German hands. Any attempts to organize resistance or underground movements were to be firmly crushed.

For Eschig it was a matter of military tactics, like playing chess, a game he was particularly good at. He had a mania for *Grünlichkeit* – thoroughness, or as some would have it, the art of taking pains. He had tenacity as well. He could doggedly pursue a problem, wearing away at it until he had finally solved it. He enjoyed his job in so far as it involved the working-out of a problem, but he had never been able to come to terms with the inevitable consequence of his success – a lonely wooden stake in front of a brick wall, a blindfolded figure and the crack of a firing squad's rifles in the cold grey of dawn.

The door to his office opened and his assistant, Feldwebel Weiss, entered with a tray bearing a cup of coffee and a snack of black bread and sausage. Under his arm the sergeant carried a bulky folder.

'*Guten morgen, Herr Hauptmann,*' Weiss said with a click of his heels.

Eschig nodded as he reached for his coffee.

'What's this, Weiss?' he asked as the sergeant laid the bulky folder before him.

'Local intelligence reports for the southern sector, Herr Hauptmann.'

Eschig sighed. It was part of his duties to go through the local intelligence reports of the occupied sectors of the country to monitor any activities which might indicate the formation of resistance groups.

Eschig spent several hours reading through the reports. One item in the batch did strike his attention. Earlier that morning four members of the Field Security Police and a member of the Norwegian Hird had been killed at a roadside near Evje. The incident was nothing much in itself. Indeed, such incidents were common in occupied territory and those who collaborated with the German troops often put their lives at risk. The local military police commander had stopped a bus which had been passing along the road about the same time as the killings occurred. By a stroke of luck there was a collaborator travelling on the bus at the time who was able to give the local commander a full account of what had happened.

A detailed description of two men and a girl, who had joined the terrorists who had done the killing, was available. One of the men was definitely an Englishman. The other was a well-built man with red hair. His description intrigued Eschig. There were not many Norwegians who answered that description.

The local commander, in accordance with General Von Falkenhorst's general directive of April 12, designed to prevent terrorism, had seized a number of people from the bus and shot them as a reprisal.

Eschig sat back, his eyes hooded. An Englishman, a girl and another man who was tall, well-built and had red hair. He pursed his lips and reached for his telephone to put through a call to the local commander, who told him that there was no sign of the terrorists.

'The swine have burrowed down into some hole up in the mountains. My men have combed the area without a trace of them,' the officer assured him.

Eschig replaced the receiver and leant back, his hands before him, fingertips to fingertips, a frown on his forehead.

He did not know why he was so intrigued by the description of the red-haired man, nor why this incident should occupy his mind more than the hundreds of other incidents which he was supposed to check through. He only knew that he experienced a *fingerspitzengefuehl*, a mysterious intuitive feeling in his fingertips which is the German equivalent of a sixth sense. He took a plain folder, wrote in bold capitals on its cover 'Red-Haired Man', and occupied the next half-hour making some cross-reference notes from the local military police commander's report.

The cave was high up in the mountains, but still below the upper limit of the conifers and dwarf birch which grew in profusion in this area. Since the incident on the roadway, the young leader of the partisans had maintained a silence. His men moved swiftly after him up a small mountain track on a route which left Woods both dizzy and breathless. It was two years since he had been in the mountains and he was clearly out of condition. Inge and Sweeny made no complaint, but Woods could see that they, too, were unused to the exertion. The group made no pause for refreshment, but several times they had an enforced rest while a German scout plane circled lazily above them as they hid beneath the trees.

It was not until mid-afternoon that they finally came to the cave, a well-hidden complex which could not be found by a casual observer. It was only then that a primus stove was produced and water boiled. Cans of soup were opened and emptied into a large saucepan to simmer. Sentries were posted, but the rest of the small group threw aside their backpacks and guns and lay down to rest.

'And now,' the young leader said, as the three newcomers stood watching the proceedings, 'I must have some information.'

'Information for information then,' Sweeny replied. 'Who are you?'

'I am Captain Arne Branting, formerly of the Rogaland Regiment.'

'I am Lars Sweeny, that is Inge Stenersen and this is Doctor Michael Woods,' Sweeny replied in kind.

'From?'

'We parachuted here this morning from England.'

'Can you prove this?'

'Of course not. You don't expect us to have papers that would incriminate us if we were searched by the Germans, do you? The only things we carry are three Webley service revolvers.'

Branting shrugged.

'Those you could pick up anywhere. I must have something more to satisfy myself that you are who you say you are.'

'We came down north of Bygland,' Sweeny said after a pause. 'Our aircraft was pounced on by a German fighter just after we bailed out. It was a Blenheim. It was shot down on the mountains on the west bank of the fjord.'

Branting looked at him steadily.

'I could check that out.'

'I intended you to do so.'

'Granted, for the moment, that you parachuted into Norway this morning . . . Why? What is your mission here?'

'We can't tell you that. I've told you before. All we can tell you is that we are on our way to Oslo.'

'It's a great deal to take on trust.'

Woods suddenly swore. 'Do you think we are German spies or something? Do you think the Germans were pretending to drag me off that bus?'

Branting gazed at Woods thoughtfully and then smiled.

'No, I don't think you can be German. No German agent would be sent into Norway with such an appalling English accent. You are English, of that there is no doubt.'

'Thanks,' Woods replied sarcastically.

Branting suddenly turned to the saucepan of simmering soup and ladled out two servings, giving one to Inge and the other to Woods. Then he dipped out two more and handed one to Sweeny.

'Take a seat and get some food into you. You see, we are unused to war. Two weeks of war have not made us veterans but served merely to create many confusions.'

They sat down, realizing that they were very hungry. Branting put his soup down on the ground beside him and nodded reflectively.

'The Germans have overrun the southern half of our country while our troops still hold out, with Allied help, in the north. Those of us who remain in the occupied areas are trying to form some kind of resistance . . . not only to the Germans but to the followers of Quisling. Those who support the Nasjonal Samling are crawling out of the woodwork everywhere, like the parasites they are.'

He gazed at the other three thoughtfully.

'You must appreciate that it is difficult to know whom to trust and whom not to trust.'

Woods nodded. 'I can understand that, Branting. But all you have to do is confirm what we say about our aircraft. You'll even find our parachutes in the woods on the east bank of the fjord.'

'It won't mean much. We know already, as I've told you, that the Germans are looking for parachutists. It does not mean that you are those parachutists.'

'Look,' Sweeny leant forward. 'We are not interested in you or your group, Branting. All we want is to get to Oslo.'

Branting shrugged. 'And how are you planning to go? To Kristiansand or Arendal and then the railway from there?'

'That was the idea,' Woods agreed.

'The Germans have cut off Kristiansand for the moment. They have placed restrictions on all coastal movement because the German warships are now using it as a base and the Germans have taken over the batteries of Odderoy. We know the Germans have a flotilla of MTBs there, but they are letting no one near the ports, and railway traffic along the coast railway is restricted to German troops.'

'Damn!' Sweeny muttered. 'Is there a safe alternative route to Oslo?'

'Perhaps,' smiled Branting. 'But first I must see if your story checks out.'

'And if you can't check it out?' asked Inge.

Arne Branting pursed his lips and shrugged in an eloquent fashion.

# CHAPTER ELEVEN

'What the hell are all these, Weiss?' demanded Hauptmann Eschig as the Feldwebel placed a pile of reports on his desk. It was Sunday and he was irritable. He had been looking forward to a day of relaxation, of getting down to writing a long letter to his wife, Liselotte. She had been worried because their eldest son Joachim had applied to join the Luftwaffe for training as a pilot. Now Eschig was faced with a mountain of reports to check through.

Feldwebel Weiss shifted his weight uncomfortably. He was, at fifty, a slow speaking Westphalian, ponderous but thorough.

'The Norwegian police have passed them over to us, Herr Hauptmann,' he said. 'They think that we might be able to help them.'

'We are the Abwehr, not the damned Kripo,' replied Eschig in annoyance.

Weiss blinked. He had once been a member of the *Kriminalpolizei*, the Kripo, before joining the Abwehr, and was proud of his service with them.

'Even so, Herr Hauptmann,' he said carefully, 'the Norwegians think that our field security police may have encountered some criminal elements which they are looking for. Normal channels have broken down between the police regions.' Weiss hesitated and then indicated a signature on the file's cover. 'The chief-of-staff has passed the files on to this office to deal with,' he added softly.

Eschig caught sight of the signature and ground his teeth in annoyance. Another waste of time. As if the Abwehr had time to indulge in catching petty thieves and sheep-stealers.

'Very well,' he muttered. 'Leave the file with me. I'll check through it and ensure that copies are sent to the field security commanders.'

'*Zum Befehl, Herr Hauptmann.*'

It was not until late in the afternoon that Eschig found time to glance at the papers. They were mainly concerned with a number of people who were suspected of murder in various parts of the country. Eschig found it a curiosity that, in the middle of a war, with thousands being killed, people could still occupy their energies tracking down the killers of tramps, prostitutes and the like. He was about to shuffle the reports into a folder for Weiss to copy to the local commanders of the *Geheime Feld Polizei* when his eye fell on a report from the Stavanger police authority. Something to do with a tall, well-built, red-haired man. Eschig frowned.

'Lars Sweeny' he read, 'wanted for questioning in connection with the murder of Erik and Freya Hartvig.'

Eschig went to his cabinet and removed the file he had started on the 'Red-Haired Man' and compared the descriptions. They were certainly similar. Lars Sweeny. It was an odd sounding name. Eschig did not think it sounded exactly Norwegian. He picked up his intercom and asked Weiss to send in the Norwegian liaison officer, an elderly civil servant who had been attached to the Abwehr office. The man came in and stood respectfully before Eschig's desk.

'I want to know if your central criminal records contain any information on a Lars Sweeny, probably from Stavanger.'

The civil servant frowned.

'Sweeny, did you say, sir?'

'I did,' replied Eschig. 'Is there something unusual about the name?'

'Well, . . .' The little man smiled apologetically. 'It's not exactly a Norwegian name.'

Eschig raised an eyebrow. So his suspicion had been right. 'Can you be precise?'

'Why, yes sir.' The little man smiled happily. 'It's actually an Irish name, but of Scandinavian origin. It comes from the name Svein. The Vikings settled in parts of Ireland, you see, sir, and the name came to be adopted in Irish as Suibhne. When the English went to Ireland they Anglicised the name to Sweeny.'

Eschig gazed at the civil servant with a degree of amazement. 'And how do you know this?'

The little man seemed to preen himself.

'It's my hobby, sir. I read all I can on the history of the old Viking kingdoms.'

'I see. Well, go away and check for me if anything is known about this man Lars Sweeny.'

Eschig sat tapping a finger on the file for a while after the little man had left. How many tall, well-built, red-haired men were there in Norway? Lars Sweeny. Once more he had that odd tingle; that *fingerspitzengefuehl* – some sixth sense about this red-haired man.

It was not until late on Sunday that Arne Branting came back to the cave. When Woods, Sweeny and Inge had woken up in the morning he had been missing. The young Norwegian soldiers had offered them no explanation as to where Branting had gone. They were correct in their behaviour towards the three strangers, but not friendly. Any attempt to engage them in conversation resulted in monosyllabic replies. By late afternoon Sweeny was growing restless.

'If Branting does not return by midnight,' he whispered to his companions, 'we'll have to try to escape.'

But it was while they were eating their evening meal – a plate of *fiskekaker*, fish balls, with *rødkal*, boiled red cabbage, and coffee – that the young Norwegian officer returned.

'Our men in the Bygland area have found your parachutes and confirmed that a British Blenheim was shot down opposite Bygland. German troops have been scouring the area.'

Sweeny bit his lip.

'So you will allow us to go on to Oslo?'

Branting smiled. 'Better yet, I will take you there by a route which will be safer than the one you proposed to use.' He started to turn away and then glanced back. 'Just in case you are under any illusions about the nature of the enemy we face, you may like to know that the Germans took six people from the bus on which you were travelling and executed them for a reprisal.'

Sweeny's face remained impassive. Inge shivered slightly, while Woods stared in horrified disbelief.

'The German commander, General von Falkenhorst, has issued orders that prominent people are to be taken as hostages for the good behaviour of the population. If incidents occur, these people are to be shot in order to dissuade resistance. I hope your mission to Oslo is worth the lives of the people who may be placed in danger.'

Woods flushed. 'We didn't ask you to kill the Germans, nor the Hird youth.'

Branting eyed him placidly.

'No? I suppose you would have preferred to have been shot by them or handed over to the Gestapo? I am merely telling you this so that you know the score.'

'We know it,' Sweeny replied tightly. 'When do we leave for Oslo?'

'We'll start before dawn. I'll call you.'

The journey to Oslo was far easier than any of them had imagined. They had to admit that Arne Branting was well organized. The young officer, with another man, led them to a village at the foot of the mountain where they were taken to a local garage. Inside, hidden away, was an ambulance with the name 'Didemark Mental Asylum' prominently displayed on it. Branting grinned. 'This way the Germans aren't usually too curious to search and question the passengers. If they do, you can always feign inability to speak.'

The three of them climbed into the back of the vehicle while Branting and his companion put on white coats and sat in the front. So far as Sweeny could make out, they headed due north and joined the main Haugesund-Oslo road at Brunkeberg. They were stopped several times but no one attempted to look inside the vehicle. The journey was not interrupted until they reached Kongsberg. When Branting opened the doors they were in the shelter of another garage.

'This is as far as we can go with this method of transport,' Branting told them. 'The next stage is by train to Oslo. There are no restrictions imposed as yet on this stretch of line, although there are *Feld Polizei* at all the stations.'

They had an hour's wait before the train left for Oslo, and the owner of the garage brought them a *koldbord*. Branting suggested that they travel in pairs and meet up at the Oslo terminus because groups of people tended to be questioned by the German police.

Inge and Woods were first to leave the garage, which was just off the main market square of the old town which straddled the River Lågen. There was a strong German military presence here because the Nazis had wanted to secure the silvermines of Kongsberg, famous for over three centuries. The station was on the far side of the market square and there were no other people in the waiting room. Several obviously new posters adorned the walls with slogans like 'With the Nasjonal Samling for Norway!' and 'Norwegian Youth for Norway with Quisling!' Inge went to the bored-looking booking clerk and asked for two tickets to

Oslo. The clerk stamped the tickets and handed them over. She rejoined Woods in a corner of the room and they sat quietly, pretending to read newspapers. Several more people entered and then Sweeny and Branting came in, bought tickets, and went to the far side of the room without glancing at Inge or Woods. Just before the whistle of the train was heard, two green-uniformed members of the *Geheime Feld Polizei* entered and glanced round at the people and then left. It seemed that the new Norwegian euphemism for Germans was *'de grønne'* – 'the greens' – because of the military police uniforms.

The journey to Oslo was without incident. There were many people travelling to the capital and several Germans among them, but no one seemed to take any interest in them. In fact, there was an almost studied inattention to the uniformed military. The train rattled along, only halting briefly at Drammen before pushing into Oslo to the Vest Banegaard, the West Station, by the Pipervika Harbour in the old quarter. Branting and the other three walked individually with feigned unconcern, passing the scrutiny of the *Feld Polizei* at the station barrier, and then crossing the concourse into the Radhusplaser where they met as arranged. For Woods there was a strange feeling at being in Oslo again. Little had changed except the numerous German military vehicles which were parked around the Radhusplaser with little groups of men in Wehrmacht grey or *Feld Polizei* green. And there was the occasional ring of marching boots on the cobbles of the roadway.

'Welcome to Oslo,' Branting said with a grimace.

'We appreciate your help,' Sweeny said.

'It is nothing,' replied the young Norwegian. 'We are fighting the same war.' He paused. 'Where will you go now?'

Sweeny glanced at him, wondering whether there was something more than idle curiosity in his voice.

'It is best if we keep our intentions to ourselves,' he replied.

Branting shrugged. 'Perhaps. The resistance is in its infancy but we are organizing quickly. If there is any need to contact us then go to Blom's on Karl Johansgate . . .'

'The artists' and students' cafe?' asked Inge.

'That's it. Ask for Sigurd Enden from Alvdal. That will be the password.'

They shook hands with the young officer and watched him striding away across the Radhusplaser.

'Perhaps we should have taken him into our confidence,'

Woods observed. 'The resistance might have helped us.'

'No,' Sweeny was emphatic. 'The fewer people know why we are here, the better.'

'Then what do we do now?' asked Woods.

'Find a quiet place to stay.'

Inge, during their brief discussions, had already suggested staying at her cousin's apartment in Oslo. She was adamant that he could be trusted.

'Is the apartment far?' asked Woods.

'Walking distance,' affirmed Inge.

'Then we'd better go and stop hanging around here looking conspicuous,' suggested Sweeny.

Inge led the way, turning right at the quayside and moving through the streets lined with warehouses near the docks. The apartment block to which she led them was in a little street off the Huitfeldsgate. On Sweeny's instructions, Inge went on alone to make contact with her cousin while he and Woods found a nearby coffee stall to wait at. It was twenty minutes before Inge rejoined them.

'My cousin is away,' she greeted them breathlessly. 'But don't worry. I have collected the key of his apartment from the concierge, who knows me.'

'Is that safe?' demanded Sweeny with a worried glance.

'Oh yes,' the girl replied. 'The concierge is to be trusted. My cousin Edvard was in a reserve regiment and was called up during the general mobilization on April 9. The concierge's son was in the same regiment, which was part of the division protecting Oslo, the Second Division, I believe. They were pulled out of the city by General Haug and since then there has been no word. The concierge thinks they might have gone north or simply crossed the border into Sweden with General Eriksen. Apparently, rather than surrender to the Germans, he took three thousand troops into Sweden where they've been interned.'

'You are absolutely sure you can trust the concierge?' insisted Sweeny.

'She doesn't know that I have only just come back from England. I made her believe that I have been back for several months. Edvard's apartment is leased for a year, so I merely said that I had promised to look in from time to time and would probably stay a few days with some friends of mine.'

Sweeny was not exactly happy with the arrangement but he had no better plan. Inge took them back to the apartment block and let them in. There was no sign of the concierge and they went straight to the third floor where the apartment was situated. It was a small one, with two rooms, a kitchen and a bathroom.

Woods gave a sigh as he flung himself down on the couch and stretched luxuriously.

'I feel as if I haven't slept in an age,' he moaned.

Sweeny moved quietly thorough the apartment, checking the windows and noting the metal-runged fire-escape which led from the kitchen window at the back of the building. Woods and Inge watched him with a slightly bewildered air while he made the checks.

'Good,' he said, returning to perch himself on the arm of the couch. 'Our first priority is to get some sleep. Tomorrow morning Inge will make contact with Professor Stenersen. It would be best if you go to his house rather than the Riks-Hospitalet.'

Inge nodded. 'It's not far from here. His house is near the Uranienborg Church.'

'Shall I go with Inge?' asked Woods, taking out a packet of cigarettes and lighting one.

'No. We will let Inge make the first contact and see if Stenersen is agreeable to the principle of the plan. If he is then we must work out its details.

Inge smiled. 'And if he is not?'

'Then we will have to work out an alternative plan,' replied Sweeny with a frown. 'But I thought you said he would be willing to leave Oslo.'

Inge grimaced. 'I was trying to introduce some humour . . .'

'It is best never to say things that you don't mean,' snapped Sweeny.

'So we will wait here until Inge returns?' asked Woods, seeing the flash of anger in the girl's face.

'You will wait here,' Sweeny said. 'I have to go out.'

Woods frowned.

'May we know where?'

'No,' replied Sweeny with aplomb. 'I shall be back in the afternoon.' There was a tone of finality in his voice which indicated that it would be futile to press the subject further.

Sweeny stood up and glanced round.

'Inge will take the bedroom. You and I can sleep on the couch and the chairs here.'

'Any spare blankets?' asked Woods hopefully.

They found some in the bedroom. Sweeny tossed a coin and opted for the two armchairs pushed together, while Woods made himself comfortable on the couch.

It took a long time before sleep came to Sweeny. Yet the furthest subject from his mind was the mission involving Professor Didrik Stenersen. He was thinking about his orders to eliminate Judge Paal Berg and he was thinking about Freya . . . poor, dear Freya. His lips compressed harshly as he thought of her. Vengeance was more important than Paal Berg or Professor Stenersen. It was several hours before a sleep of exhaustion overcame him.

# CHAPTER TWELVE

Sweeny was up early, despite his troubled sleep, and left the apartment before Inge and Woods were awake. He strolled through the streets to the Post and Telegraph Building. It seemed so strange. Here was a city under occupation, a few weeks after an invasion, yet people seemed unconcerned, hurrying about their business, going to offices, on trams, on bicycles and in cars, moving about their daily lives as if nothing had happened. Outside the Post and Telegraph Building a military vehicle was parked with half-a-dozen young German soldiers in it. There was a machine gun mounted for action on it. Several young girls were standing round, gazing admiringly at the field-grey uniforms and swapping jokes with the men. The *gefreiter* in charge looked down on his admirers with a superior smile, conscious of his role as a member of the conquering legions.

With a disgusted glance at the girls, Sweeny went into the building. It was fairly deserted, although two German sentries were marching up and down the large hall, slowly, as if deliberately pounding the heels of their boots on the cement floor to make a point; each step echoing loudly and menacingly. The echo of those hobnail boots seemed amazingly eloquent to Sweeny.

He found a booth with a directory of telephone subscribers in it. It was amazingly simple. A telephone number and address was listed against the name BERG, PAAL O. Yet he had to be sure. Sweeny picked up the receiver and asked the operator to connect him. A woman's voice answered.

'Is that the home of Herr Berg?' asked Sweeny.

'It is.'

'Herr Johan Berg the architect?' pressed Sweeny.

'Why, no. This is the residence of Judge Paal Berg.'

'I'm sorry.' Sweeny smiled thinly, replacing the receiver. Now there was no mistake. Before he left the Post and Telegraph

Building he consulted a street map of the city. He decided to walk, for the house was no great distance away. Moving through the streets of Oslo, Sweeny was surprised to find that music and song were being used by the Germans to lull the public into an illusion that all was normal. He had to admit that the Nazis seemed to know a lot about psychology. Here and there German troops were giving impromptu concerts. In Karl Johansgate a twelve-piece military band was parading gaily. The Germans seemed polite and courteous to all Osloans. In one square he came upon a group of young soldiers, arms locked, swinging from side to side as they sang the words of an old German song, 'Going to town', in magnificent harmony, sounding like students at a football match. Outwardly they seemed like a group of carefree young men whose only desire in life was to have fun and serenade the onlookers. Could people really forget that just behind them, in a neat stack, were their kit bags, their rifles and bayonets?

Sweeny fought back his anger. Were the Germans trying to convince the Norwegians that there was nothing serious about the thousands of iron-muscled troops pouring into the capital? Were they trying to convince them that the armoured vehicles and machine guns which daily poured from the transport craft in Oslo docks to enforce the enslavement of their country had no meaning?

It took some while before Sweeny reached the avenue in which Paal Berg's house was situated. It was a large house in its own grounds with a high surrounding wall. Sweeny walked by it as if disinterested, although his eyes swiftly scanned the property and recorded as much detail as possible. He was surprised to note that there were no German sentries outside. He had supposed that the German garrison would supply guards to all prominent citizens who collaborated with them. Yet the house did not appear to be guarded.

Sweeny did not wish to draw attention to himself by walking past the front of the house again. After all, the house was in a quiet residential area and the streets were deserted. He turned and found a smaller boulevard which passed along the back of the house. There were no guards here either, but the gates at the rear of the house were open and a uniformed chauffeur was adjusting them. In the short driveway stood a rather impressive saloon car. Sweeny thought it was an English Rolls-Royce. He caught sight of an elderly man in the rear seat. The chauffeur, having adjusted the gates, climbed back into the vehicle and started it up. Sweeny, his heart thumping as he realized the opportunity, moved his hand to the Webley in his pocket. Even while his mind was turning over the possibility of shooting the judge and making his escape, the sound of motorcycles came to his ears. Two machines turned into the boulevard with *Feld Polizei* astride them, Schmeissers slung on straps from their shoulders. They roared to a halt before the saloon, saluted its occupant and took up outrider positions. The cavalcade moved off down the street without taking any notice of Sweeny.

Sweeny watched them turn the corner and disappear. He hesitated a moment and then stepped through the open gates, his eyes noticing the details of the rear of the house. The drive ended in a little courtyard. A small balcony with french windows opening onto it ran along the back of the house. The wall which enclosed the back of the house was not high, about six feet. It could easily be scaled. Then one could get onto the small balcony and force one of the french windows.

'Hey! What are you doing here?'

An elderly, stern-faced woman in a maid's uniform stood at an open door with hands on her hips, regarding him suspiciously.

'I'm looking for work, my good *Fru*,' Sweeny answered immediately. 'Does your boss need a handyman?'

The woman scowled.

'There's no work here. Be off with you!'

'These are hard times,' Sweeny sighed. 'Can you spare something . . . it doesn't have to be money, perhaps some food?'

The housekeeper hesitated and then darted behind the door, returning in a moment with a large slice of *hvetebrød* topped with *pølse*. Sweeny took a mouthful as if he were starving. The bread and sausage tasted good and reminded him that it was long past midday.

'Now be off with you.'

'Bless you, good *Fru*,' grunted Sweeny and turned away, munching thoughtfully. He was thinking that it was going to be easier than he had imagined to eliminate Judge Paal Berg.

Bracegirdle's voice came over the intercom: 'Commander Espeland of the Royal Norwegian Navy is here to see you, sir.'

Commander Wallace had been waiting with some degree of interest ever since Espeland had telephoned for the appointment.

'Send him through, Bracegirdle,' Wallace grunted. He rose

[102]

from his desk as a wiry, weather-beaten Norwegian naval officer entered and threw him a salute.

'Make yourself at home,' Wallace said, indicating a chair. 'Can I get you a drink?'

The Norwegian officer shook his head with a smile.

'It's too early for me. But perhaps some coffee . . .?'

Wallace passed on the request to Bracegirdle and then sat back and regarded Espeland with interest.

'What can we do for you?'

Espeland removed his cap and dropped it on the desk with a grimace.

'I'll come right to the point. As you know, or may suspect, I represent our Naval Intelligence here in London.'

Wallace inclined his head in acknowledgement of the fact.

'We know that your department have sent a small team into Norway to bring out Professor Stenersen,' Espeland stated matter-of-factly.

Wallace had to fight for control of his features. Luckily, Bracegirdle chose that moment to enter with the tray of coffee and Wallace was able to disguise his facial slip in turning to thank her. When she had gone he turned back with a bland expression, but Espeland was smiling.

'It is no good denying it, Commander Wallace. Lars Sweeny was recruited into our intelligence service before you enrolled him in your little operation.'

Wallace sighed in resignation.

'Very well, Espeland. What do you want of us?'

'I have come here to ask whether there is any way in which you are in contact with Lars Sweeny?'

Wallace raised an eyebrow and smiled cynically.

'You mean that you are not in contact with your own agent?'

'Please, Commander Wallace.'

There was something behind the Norwegian's bluff mask that indicated a state of anxiety which intrigued Wallace.

'I think you should tell me more about your relationship with Sweeny,' Wallace said.

Espeland bit his lip, hesitated and then shrugged.

'Sweeny was enrolled by us for a special mission in Oslo. He was to carry out this mission concurrently with the one he was carrying out for you. It is now imperative that he be contacted so that we can give him alternative orders.'

'May I ask what this mission involved?'

[103]

Again Espeland hesitated before replying.

'I want an assurance that what I am about to say will not go beyond these walls. I speak to you as a brother intelligence officer as well as a brother officer of the Allied forces.'

'Understood.'

'We told Sweeny that it would be in the interests of our country if the head of the Norwegian Administrative Council, running the civil government under the German occupation, was removed and that the removal would serve as an example to our people of what would happen to any collaborationist.'

Wallace struggled to understand the meaning behind the formula of words.

'Speak plainly, commander,' he said shortly. 'Do you mean that Sweeny was ordered to assassinate Judge Paal Berg?'

'Yes.'

'And you now say that it is imperative that Sweeny be given other instructions?'

'Yes. Our earlier decision was taken in the confusion caused by the situation. We have since been in touch with our King and his Government and discovered that Paal Berg is not a collaborationist.'

'How so?'

'The initiative for forming the Council of Administration came from the industrial leaders in Oslo, who realized that the occupied territories needed a more authoritative administration than the one provided by the traitor Quisling. If any semblance of order was to continue under German occupation, however long the occupation is to last, Quisling and his comedians would have to go. The only state authority remaining in Oslo was the Supreme Court of which Paal Berg is head. Apparently Gunnar Schejldrup of the *Kristiania Spigeverk* and Jens Bache Wiig of *Standard Telefon og Kabelfabrik* went to Paal Berg with a proposal. The Germans would be offered an authoritative civil administration run by prominent Norwegian citizens if they dismissed Quisling and his non-representative fanatics.'

Espeland paused and took a sip of his coffee.

'Judge Berg immediately contacted King Haakon and his advisers. It was imperative that civil government should not break down. The King approved the scheme to prevent civil chaos. The Germans had been ignoring civil administration, transport, food supplies and so forth. With His Majesty's approval, Berg appointed Ingolf Christensen, the *fylkesmann* of

[104]

Oslo and Akershus, who was known to be friendly with the Germans, to go to them and offer the council's services. However, it was stipulated that the Administrative Council would not operate until Quisling and his sycophantic followers were removed. General von Falkenhorst, as you know, obviously realized that Quisling had little authority, dismissed him, and the council was established.'

'So the council had the full approval of King Haakon and his Government?' asked Wallace. This was news to him and he was sure that Churchill would want to know it as soon as possible.

Espeland nodded.

'It seems that Judge Berg has acted honourably with the best intentions for the civil populace.' Espeland hesitated and lowered his voice almost theatrically. 'There is more . . . Judge Berg is currently organizing the nucleus of a resistance army to fight behind the German lines.'

Wallace was startled. He sat back with a low whistle.

'And this is the man you've ordered to be assassinated?'

A pained expression crossed Espeland's face.

'Please, commander . . .' He spread his hands helplessly.

'Well, that's the gist of it,' interrupted Wallace gruffly. 'We have no time to wrap things up in diplomatic language. The situation is that you have sent Sweeny to kill a Norwegian patriot.'

'That is why I have come to you. As soon as we had a full understanding from our Government, I came here. Can you get in touch with Sweeny so that this catastrophe can be prevented?'

Wallace shook his head.

'It can't be done.'

The Norwegian's face was grim.

'Can't be done?'

'There is absolutely no way that we are able to contact Sweeny or his companions.'

Inge Stenersen turned into the gate of her uncle's house and rang the bell. It seemed only a few days since she had last done so, not two entire years. A few moments passed before an elderly woman with a matronly appearance and a worried face drew open the door.

'Hello, Mathilde.'

The woman's eyes widened in astonishment.

'My God! Frøken Inge. Why, we thought you were safe in . . .'

'Hush,' smiled Inge as she pushed by the old woman into the hall. As the door closed behind her she turned with a grin and hugged the woman. 'You haven't changed a bit.'

There were tears in the old woman's eyes.

'Neither have you, Frøken Inge. I cannot believe my eyes. He will be pleased to see you . . . and yet . . .'

'Yet what?'

'He had fondly thought you were safe in England. These are bad times for Norway.'

Inge nodded. 'Listen, Mathilde, you are to forget you saw me.'

The woman looked puzzled.

'As far as you know, Mathilde, I am still in England.' Inge turned and glanced across the hall. 'Is he in his study?'

'Yes. Frøken Inge . . . may I touch you again? I just want to make sure you are no vision.'

Inge smiled as the old woman rubbed a hand on her apron and reached forward, stretching to touch the girl's hand, holding her fingers for a moment before releasing her grasp. 'Yes, you are really here, Frøken Inge. It is no dream.'

The girl grinned.

'I am really here, but not for long. I must see my uncle. Tell me, is there anyone else in the house?'

Mathilde shook her head vigorously.

'Only the Herr Professor and myself, Frøken Inge.'

Inge turned across the hall to the study doors. It seemed only yesterday that she was in this house; only yesterday that she was knocking at those doors. Her uncle was bent over a desk. His white hair was tousled as he examined a piece of paper before him.

'Mathilde!' His voice was sharp as he heard the opening door. 'I said that I wasn't to be disturbed.'

He raised his head fully and saw Inge. The look on his lined face was one of total astonishment. Professor Didrik Stenersen was in his late fifties. He was a man of medium build with white hair, a small spade beard and piercing blue eyes. There was something about his manner, an inward vitality and presence, which marked him out from the ordinary.

'Inge!'

The girl went swiftly to him as he rose from his desk. They hugged each other long and hard before he held her at arm's length, shaking his head in bewilderment.

'You were supposed to be safe in London.'

[106]

The girl kissed him gently on the cheek and dropped into a nearby chair. She looked very cool and composed, sitting calmly as if she were merely a patient come to consult him.

'I've come to take you to London, Uncle Didrik.'

Stenersen's mouth went slack.

'What?'

'I was sent by London to get you out of Oslo. You and your surgical team.'

Stenersen sat down abruptly in his chair and stared at her.

'It's quite simple, Uncle,' Inge went on cheerfully. 'The British Government want you in London. You are urgently needed there to perform an operation on someone very important. Don't ask me who because I just don't know. All I know is that the British consider it important to save this man's life.'

Her uncle shook his head in bewilderment.

'How can I go? My surgical team as well . . .?'

The door opened and Mathilde came in with a tray of coffee and a plate of little cakes.

'This is to celebrate Frøken Inge's homecoming, Herr Professor.'

Inge rose and took the tray from her uncle's housekeeper.

'Thank you, Mathilde. You must be sure to tell no one that you have seen me.'

The old woman nodded. 'I will not tell anyone.'

When she had left Inge poured out coffee and handed a cup to her bemused uncle.

'The situation for Norway is pretty desperate, Uncle. You know that it may well be that the King and his Government will have to leave Norway? Then the Germans will be in total control. It is possible that they will go into exile in England.'

'Are you telling me that the British have sent you here to ask me to go to London?'

The girl nodded emphatically.

'Are you willing to go?'

'Of course,' replied Stenersen. 'If it is in the service of our King and his Allies, of course I'll go.'

'What about the members of your surgical team?'

A troubled look crossed Stenersen's face.

'Most of them would adopt the same attitude as I have,' he said.

'But?' prompted Inge.

'These are hard times for Norway. There are many traitors

[107]

among us. There is at least one member of my team who, I believe, is a member of the Nasjonal Samling.'

'Who is that?'

'My anaesthetist, Hersleb. He has several times defended the attitudes of Quisling and the Nasjonal Samling.'

'What about the others?'

'There are two assistant surgeons, Arendt and Birkenes, my chief nurse, Trina, and two other theatre nurses, Kristine and Hilde. I think they are all loyal Norwegians.'

'Tell me what you know of them, Uncle, and also give me details of your work schedule for this week.'

'This week? Do you intend to move so soon?'

'The sooner the better.'

'And are you to accomplish this task on your own?'

'No. I have friends.'

'Who?'

'I can't tell you yet. Don't worry. You'll be told all you need to know when the time is right.'

'You realize that if the Germans discovered this . . .?'

'I know,' the girl cut him short.

Stenersen sighed. 'So far the Germans have been trying to woo us. They initially thought that Quisling could deliver the country to them without a fight. They are becoming increasingly aggressive as our resistance continues. Hitler has appointed a Reichskommissar to take charge of the country who is arriving in Oslo today . . . one of his old SS cronies. I think things will be getting very tough from now on.'

'All the more reason to get you and the others out as quickly as we can.'

Stenersen smiled at the girl.

'You are very brave, Inge, but very foolish to risk your life for an old man. Your father would have been very proud of you. I only wish that you had not come.'

Inge bent over the desk and laid her hand on his.

'Don't worry about anything, Uncle Didrik. You just answer my questions. Let's start with this anaesthetist. Do you know for a fact that he is a member of the Nasjonal Samling?'

# CHAPTER THIRTEEN

Sweeny returned to the city centre and stood on the corner of a street waiting to cross it. His plan was very simple. He would return to the house of Judge Berg later that night, gain entry through one of the French windows and shoot him. Simple plans had the best chance of success. But there was something else which occupied his thoughts as he strolled through the streets. His hand kept toying with the little buttonhole badge which he had carried in his pocket since he had taken it from Freya's hand. He should have obeyed Wallace's instructions to leave all his possessions behind but he would not have parted with the badge come hell or high water. He had to find out who owned it.

Standing on the corner he became aware of the newspaper kiosk which was displaying copies of *Dagbladet*. It was the newspaper that Freya had worked for. The thought struck him immediately. He knew what he should do. The newspaper would have an interest in discovering who had murdered one of its own reporters, especially if there was a political motive involved. He bought a copy and looked for the address of the newspaper. It took him only a short time to reach the offices. There were two Germans patrolling the entrance but he ignored them and marched in. A nervous-looking woman greeted him at the reception desk.

'I want to see the editor.'

She glanced at him in disapproval.

'Have you an appointment?'

Sweeny shook his head.

'The editor is a very busy man. Perhaps if you told me . . .'

'I need to speak to the editor,' snapped Sweeny. The woman started at the sharpness in his voice.

'Just one moment.'

She moved to the far end of the room and talked quietly into a telephone for a few moments. Then she beckoned him.

'There's a reception room here, sir. Would you like to come in and wait? Someone will be with you shortly.'

Sweeny went into the room, sat down and drew out a packet of cigarettes. A moment later a stocky, grey-haired man entered.

'Can I help you?'

'Are you the editor?'

'Not exactly. The editor is a busy man. What can I do for you?'

'Nothing. I need to see the editor. Tell him its about Freya Hartvig.'

The man looked startled.

'Freya? What do you know about Freya Hartvig?'

Sweeny hesitated. 'Tell the editor that I am her cousin.'

The man whistled slowly and perched himself on a corner of a table, swinging one leg.

'To be truthful, the editor is having an . . . an interview with German security at the moment.' He smiled cynically. 'So far, the German censors have been fairly moderate with us but we've been warned that things are going to be a little restrictive from now on. Today, a new Reichskommissar, Josef Terboven, has arrived in Oslo. We are a radical newspaper and the odds are that the Germans will close us down altogether. I was sorry to hear about your cousin. She was a damned good journalist.'

'When will it be possible to see the editor, or someone with whom she was working when she died?' pressed Sweeny.

'To be frank, I don't know. Schanche, the special features editor, was her direct boss.'

'Let me see him.'

'He would be at home right now. Doesn't come into the office until the evening shift.'

Sweeny controlled his anger.

'Where does he live?'

The man hesitated.

'What did you say your name was?'

'I didn't.' Sweeny waited belligerently. The man shrugged and reached for a telephone and asked for a number.

'Schanche,' he said, when the connection had been made, 'Swein from the office. There's a man here who says he is Freya Hartvig's cousin and wants to speak with you? Yes?'

He handed the receiver to Sweeny.

'Schanche,' said a voice. 'What can I do for you.'

'I must see you,' Sweeny said. 'It's about Freya's death.'

There was a slight pause.

'Do you have a pencil and paper?'

'I can remember addresses.'

'Good.' The voice gave him an address. 'I'll see you there in half-an-hour.'

Sweeny replaced the telephone and smiled at the reporter.

'Thanks. You were very helpful. I hope the Germans don't close the paper down.'

The man chuckled mockingly.

'Some chance. *Arbeiderbladet*, the chief Labour newspaper in Oslo, has already been warned. We're next. I've heard that Christian Oftedal of the Stavanger *Aftenblad* is already under arrest for speaking out too freely. But it's not the Germans we need worry about so much as our own fascist informers.'

Sweeny left the building and hurried directly to the address he had been given. It was a pretty detached house on the banks of a canal towards the east of the city. Before Sweeny could knock on the door a small, harassed-looking man opened it and leaned out.

'Are you Schanche?' asked Sweeny.

'Freya's cousin?'

Sweeny nodded. The man stepped out of his house and slammed the door shut behind him.

'We'll walk along the canal,' he said, nodding in its direction. 'There is more security in open spaces these days.'

They walked in silence for a while and then Sweeny said, 'Freya worked for you on special features?'

'Freya's dead,' the man replied flatly.

'I know.'

'She was murdered.' The man, Schanche, wheeled round to face him abruptly. 'Did you murder her, Lars Sweeny?'

Sweeny halted in astonishment.

'The answer is, no, I didn't. And how did you know my name?'

'The Stavanger police believe you murdered her and have issued your description.'

Sweeny was thunderstruck.

'They believe *I* killed Freya? Why?'

'Lover's revenge. They picked up local gossip. It seems they think that you were in love with Freya. Hated Erik Hartvig. Killed him and Freya in a fit of jealousy. Did you?'

'That's utterly stupid!' exploded Sweeny.

'It seems that Freya's father also disappeared about the same time.'

'Freya's father, Tenvig, was killed when the Germans shot up our boat,' replied Sweeny.

Schanche was gazing closely at him.

'I see.' He turned and continued his walk along the canal path. 'Freya was one of my best investigative reporters. She had a great career in front of her. Now . . . well, it seems all our careers appear to be limited thanks to the intervention of the Führer of the Third Reich.'

Sweeny was frowning.

'If you knew who I was before I came here, why haven't you reported me to the police?'

'Did you know the police were after you?'

'Good God, no! I didn't even know that I was supposed to be a suspect. I came to see if I could find out a motive for Freya's death. I believe her murder was political.'

Schanche glanced at him. He pulled out a pack of cigarettes and offered one to Sweeny, took one himself and lit both from a box of matches.

'Why did you disappear from Stavanger the day after she was killed?'

'The Germans, why else?'

'Tell me.'

Sweeny told him the full story of his escape.

The man was bewildered. 'You say you reached England by stealing a German aeroplane? Then how did you come back here?'

'I have been sent here by the British. I cannot tell you anything else. That is why I have not been back to Stavanger since Freya's death.'

Schanche shook his head and whistled.

'It's such a crazy story that it can only be the truth.'

'Was Freya working on a story for you when she was killed?'

Schanche nodded.

'A few months ago we discovered that a number of Quisling's supporters, members of his Hird, were being trained in Germany. We also discovered that Quisling himself had been there and met several top Nazis including the Führer himself. We began to guess that something was in the wind. We decided to start carrying out research on members of the Nasjonal Samling and, more important, the power behind Quisling's comedians. And, believe me, Sweeny, there are some powerful industrialists who were supporting the little Major in his attempt to take over with German help.'

'And Freya? Was she working on that story, too?'

'Yes. Freya had learnt that a certain industrialist had persuaded Quisling to propose a plan to Hitler in which his stormtroops were to seize strategic points in Oslo while the little Major declared himself head of state and invited the Germans in to help him "protect" Norway against Allied aggression. It was to be another Austrian *Anschluss* all over again, with Quisling playing the part of Seyss-Inquart. Naturally, as soon as the basic plan was known we sent what details we could to Doctor Koht's department at the Foreign Office.'

'Freya was involved in this?' Sweeny was remembering all the hints his cousin had dropped during those blithely ignorant days before that fateful April 9. What a cretin she must have thought him as he dismissed her warnings about the Nasjonal Samling and the Nazis as pure fantasies. He ground his teeth as he realized just how ignorant he had really been.

'She was busy trying to get the goods on the industrialist. He was a highly placed man who was a friend of Crown Prince Olav. She discovered that the man had a young mistress who belonged to the Nasjonal Samling and served as his contact with Quisling.'

'Did Freya tell you the names of these people?'

Schanche shook his head.

'She was working on a dossier. She was keeping all her notes and evidence to herself until she knew that she had a water-tight case to present to Doctor Koht. With this man, the industrialist, being a friend of the Crown Prince it would be impossible to accuse him without making sure that every avenue of escape was closed.'

'So you don't know who this man is?'

'Not even the name of his mistress.'

'What about Freya's notes? What about the dossier?'

Schanche shrugged.

'By the time I heard the news of her death, the feature was already out-dated. The Germans were crawling all over the place and the Nasjonal Samling were coming out of the woodwork everywhere. A day or so later I did send a leg man to see the police and check Freya's apartment. There was no dossier to be found.'

'So you did think, *do* think,' Sweeny corrected himself, 'that Freya was killed to prevent the information contained in that dossier becoming public.'

'It was a good theory. Except that the Stavanger police think *you* killed her for entirely different reasons. Also, from the police

[113]

viewpoint it will be argued, why should Freya be killed to hush the matter up when the Germans were within hours of landing in Norway, and the involvement of Quisling and his Nasjonal Samling in the invasion would become public knowledge anyway?'

'Maybe whoever killed Freya had not been let into the secret of the German invasion. Maybe they still thought it was some time in the future and Freya's story could still warn the people of this country.'

'Perhaps. But there is no evidence.'

'Yes there is.' Sweeny drew out the small buttonhole badge. 'When the Stukas started bombing Sola Airfield, my uncle, Freya's father, and I decided to move our ship, the *Gunnlöd*, across the fjord. I went to Freya and Erik's apartment. I found their bodies. Freya was clutching this Nasjonal Samling badge in her hand. It's my belief that the person who owned this badge killed them both.'

Schanche took the badge and held it up.

'Five Six Eight Four P L,' he read slowly.

'I need to trace the owner of that badge. It's obviously a membership number.'

'Obviously,' Schanche agreed. 'But how can you find out, short of breaking into their headquarters and going through the membership records?'

Sweeny's face fell.

'I was hoping you might be able to help me.'

'It would be easier to go over to the Continental Hotel, walk up to Room 430 and ask to speak to Quisling himself. The Nasjonal Samling offices are extremely well guarded by Hird members. As for the power of the Press, we can do very little to help. The Nazis will be closing down radical newspapers such as ours and then they'll be rounding up anyone with an independent mind and incarcerating them in concentration camps. We've seen the pattern before.'

'You can't help me trace the badge owner?'

'I'm sorry. I wish I could. But good luck whatever you do. If you do find out anything, and *Dagbladet* and myself are still in existence, try to contact us. However, I feel our days are limited.'

The man began to turn but Sweeny caught his arm.

'One thing . . . it puzzles me. Why do you believe my story? If I had been in your shoes I would have been very sceptical. In fact, I might even have been onto the police.'

Schanche grinned.

'Not all Norwegians have sold out yet. I have a contact working with Nazi security as a liaison man. He tells me that the Abwehr are very interested in you. They suspect you of parachuting into Norway with two other people and they want to know what you are up to. They have a good description of you, so be careful.'

Sweeny stared at the journalist in astonishment.

'Are you joking?'

'If I were you, Sweeny, I would not stay in Norway any longer than I could help.'

With a wave of his hand, Schanche turned and strode back along the canal path, leaving Sweeny alone.

Woods and Inge were waiting for him when he arrived back at the apartment. Inge had been back for some time; time enough, in fact, to have prepared an evening meal for them. Over the meal she told him about her visit to her uncle's house. Sweeny reflected grimly.

'If Stenersen is unsure of his staff, then we are going to have problems.'

'I don't see why,' Woods countered. 'We'll just have to take those who want to go and leave the others behind.'

Sweeny glanced at him with something akin to pity in his eyes.

'How are you going to ensure that those who are left behind won't blow the whistle on you? Besides, London's orders were to bring back the entire surgical team. We must find a way to do it.'

Inge frowned thoughtfully. 'In that case we will just have to surprise them; not give them any advance warning.'

Sweeny smiled. 'Exactly.'

'So what's the plan?' demanded Woods.

'To sleep on things. We'll turn the possibilities over and discuss it in the morning. I have to go out again this evening . . . to reconnoitre.'

Woods exchanged a look with Inge.

'Shouldn't we go as well?'

Sweeny shook his head. 'It only needs one of us.'

'Well, shouldn't we know where you are going, just in case anything happens?'

The red-haired man chuckled.

'Nothing is going to happen to me. I'll be back later.'

The one thing to his advantage, reflected Sweeny as he left the apartment later that evening, was that the Germans, in their attempt to court the population, had not yet imposed a strict curfew in the city. There were a few people about on the streets and the occasional armoured car or foot patrol, but no one seemed to pay him any heed. It was not long before he reached the boulevard onto which Paal Berg's house backed. The place looked in total darkness. He reached into his pocket and felt for the cold comfort of the Webley.

Pausing for a moment in the shade of the trees, he examined the boulevard and assured himself that it was deserted. Then he left their shadow, walked briskly to the six-foot-high wall and heaved himself over it almost without effort. In a moment he was crouching in the shadow of the wall on the far side. He could see a faint chink of light at one of the French windows but there was no other sign of light from the house. The courtyard was deserted, although the saloon car which he had seen earlier in the day was parked and standing in the darkness.

Sweeny felt little emotion as he slipped across to the balcony which ran across the back of the house and onto which the French windows opened. He glanced round to make sure that he was unobserved before crouching to apply his eye to the chink of light emerging where the curtains had not quite met. He could see a study, and an elderly man bending over a desk. The light from a table lamp illuminated a circle in which the man's bent head and shoulders could be seen as he scribbled away on a sheet of paper. Sweeny could not see if there were any other people in the room. His range of vision was limited by the narrowness of the chink. He reached the conclusion after a few moments that if there were anyone else in the room, the man at the desk would not be concentrating so hard on his writing.

It was a chance Sweeny would have to take.

He looked down and smiled softly as he saw the ancient catch. Unless there was a cunningly fitted alarm system or hidden bolts, entry would be child's play. He reached for his knife and slid it into the soft wood of the door. A moment later he quietly eased the catch up and pulled the French window open. He paused for only a moment, taking a deep breath, and then stepped through the heavy curtains into the study beyond.

The elderly man glanced up as he caught the draught from the open window. He was alone in the room. A man in his late sixties with a broad forehead and grey, receding hair. He had a firm jaw, but the set of his mouth did not disguise the humour behind

[116]

the stern authority of the face. The features were familiar to Sweeny, as they were to most Norwegians. The man's photograph had appeared often in the newspapers. He had won a reputation as an honest and non-partisan arbitrator who, during his deliberations in the Labour Court, enjoyed the respect of both sides, having the full confidence of both workers and employers. His book *Arbeidsrett*, on Labour Law, was considered the most authoritative source work on the subject.

There was neither fear nor anger in the old man's eyes as he beheld Sweeny, just a momentary look of surprise.

'Who are you?' His voice was soft, without a tremor.

Sweeny took a step forward away from the curtained windows.

'Are you Paal Olav Berg, Justice of the Supreme Court?'

The old man pushed himself slightly back from the desk, both hands resting lightly before him.

'I am Berg,' he replied.

Sweeny reached into his pocket and drew out the Webley. There was a soft click as he released the safety catch.

# CHAPTER FOURTEEN

The elderly man gazed up at Sweeny without any sign of
perturbation in his quizzical eyes.

'Is it permitted to know why you are doing this, young man?'
he asked softly, with an almost casual nod to the gun.

Sweeny had not been prepared for such calmness and he found
himself hesitating.

'It is orders, sir.' He wondered why he was calling the man 'sir'.

Sitting there in front of Sweeny's pistol, Paal Berg managed to
emanate an incredible aura of authority.

'I have come from London,' Sweeny added.

Paal Berg's eyes widened slightly.

'From London? Surely there is some mistake?'

'No mistake,' Sweeny replied heavily. 'There is to be no
collaboration with the Nazis. Your death must serve as both
punishment and lesson.'

He raised the Webley. The old man gave a long sigh and shut
his eyes, as if waiting for the bullet. He made no further protest.
Again Sweeny found himself hesitating. It worried him that the
man meekly accepted his fate. A man who would sell out to the
Nazis would surely argue, make excuses, plead for his life. It
would have made the task much easier for Sweeny had the man
done so instead of just sitting there with bowed head. Damn it!
He was being sentimental. He began to squeeze the trigger.

'*Sta stille ellers sa skyter jeg!*' hissed a voice behind him.
Something hard pressed into his backbone and a voice he
recognized added, 'That's right, Sweeny, stay still or you are a
dead man.'

A hand came from behind and took the Webley away from his
relaxed grasp.

Paal Berg opened his eyes and shuddered slightly.

'You took your time, Branting,' he said softly.

Arne Branting moved round in front of Sweeny and ran his
hands over his pockets with professional relish, removing

[118]

Sweeny's clasp knife.

'*Op med hedene!*' he snapped.

Obediently, Sweeny raised his hands to shoulder height. He shook his head slightly in bewilderment.

'I thought you worked for the resistance, Branting?'

'You thought correctly, Sweeny. But I must confess that you had me fooled. How long have you been working for the Nazis?'

'Me?' Sweeny couldn't quite work things out. He was totally bewildered.

Arne Branting glanced towards the elderly judge.

'I was on my way here when I saw him sneaking in through the windows.'

'You've met him before?' asked Berg.

Branting told him of the meeting and the journey to Oslo. 'He had me fooled all the time. Shall I take him out and eliminate him, sir?'

'Wait a moment, Branting,' Berg said, raising a hand to stay the younger man's enthusiasm. 'There is something not quite right here. Let's not make any hasty decisions. Young man,' he continued, turning to Sweeny, 'a few moments ago you said that you had been sent from London. Explain.'

Sweeny shrugged.

'I was sent to kill you because you are a collaborator.'

'Liar!'

Arne Branting caught Sweeny a stinging blow across the side of his face with the flat of his hand. Sweeny stumbled but regained his balance. A trickle of blood oozed from the corner of his mouth.

'That will not change matters,' he muttered.

'Wait, Branting,' the old judge said sharply as the young man moved forward again. 'Violence is no argument. Who sent you from London, young man?' He turned again to Sweeny. 'The British?'

Sweeny shook his head. 'Norwegian intelligence.'

Branting chuckled.

'Now we know he is lying.'

Berg pursed his lips.

'Maybe not. Maybe there has been a genuine mistake.'

Sweeny stood totally confused. The old man looked at him closely.

'I am not a collaborationist, Sweeny . . . is that your name? Everything I have done has been done with the full knowledge and approval of His Majesty and our Government. In fact, I take direct orders from our Foreign Minister, Doctor Halvdan Koht.'

There was something sincere in the man's face. Sweeny found himself wanting to believe him.

'Then why did the Norwegian authorities in England want you killed?' he asked, frowning.

'That is what we must find out.'

Branting scowled angrily.

'Surely you are not going to believe this man, sir?' he said in outrage. 'He can only be a Nazi agent sent to eliminate you because they have found out who you are and what you are really doing . . .'

Berg sighed sharply.

'The Germans would not have to go to the trouble to assassinate me, my fiery young friend. All they would have to do is arrest me and ship me off to Germany, as is happening with so many of our countrymen.' He turned back to Sweeny. 'We will hold you until we have investigated this matter.'

Sweeny stood indifferently.

'Just a moment, sir,' Branting intervened again. 'What about his companions? They might be a danger.'

'Where are your companions, Sweeny?' asked Berg.

'I will not tell you that. They have nothing to do with this mission.'

'We'll soon find them,' Branting said.

Sweeny stared at him a moment and then smiled defiantly. 'Do so, then.'

Berg shook his head almost sorrowfully.

'There is no need to take this attitude if you are telling us the truth, young man.'

'As far as I am concerned, I don't even know if you are telling me the truth. I have only your word that you aren't a Nazi collaborator,' returned Sweeny.

Berg reflected.

'You are right. However, there is nothing I can do to clear matters up at this time. We will both have to be patient. Branting,' he turned to the young Norwegian officer, 'take our guest down to the basement and lock him in. You know the room?'

Arne Branting jerked his revolver at Sweeny.

'Don't give me an excuse to use this, Sweeny.'

Sweeny glanced at the judge.

'What if you cannot make contact with the Government or find out that I have been sent from London? What if you are the one acting some charade and are a collaborator?'

Paal Berg smiled and shrugged. 'That, my friend, will be your problem.'

Michael Woods was woken by someone shaking him vigorously by the shoulder. He groaned for a moment and then, remembering his surroundings, became wide awake and found himself staring at the anxious face of Inge Stenersen.

'What is it?' he hissed, blinking round the gloom of the lounge and easing himself up on the couch where he had been asleep.

'It's Sweeny,' the girl replied. 'It's nearly five o'clock and he's not back yet.'

Woods reached out his arm and confirmed the time from his wrist watch.

'Damn it!' he muttered. 'He should have told us where he was going.'

The girl stood with her arms wrapped around herself. She was clad only in a man's pyjama jacket top and even in the half-light of approaching dawn she looked attractive. Woods had to concentrate to bring his mind onto the matter of Sweeny.

'Something must have happened to him,' the girl was saying.

'Damn the man!' Woods exploded. 'This is what his pig-headed egotism . . .'

The girl frowned. 'Cursing him won't do any good. He may have been arrested.'

Woods sighed angrily. 'That's just it. We don't know. He might be anywhere. We have no way of knowing.'

'If he has been arrested, he may be traced back here. I think that if he has not returned by midday, we must assume the worst and move out.'

'Abort the mission?'

'No!' The girl was emphatic. 'We'll proceed with a plan on our own.'

Woods bit his lip.

'Yeah. The hell with Sweeny! I hate these death-or-glory merchants who are all muscle-flexing virility.'

Inge shook her head.

'You're being unfair to the man. I think he is just a loner.'

'A loner?' Woods chuckled sardonically. 'He's damned indifferent and totally without sympathy. He's just too much of an individualist to be part of a team.'

The girl smiled at him.

'You're something of an individualist yourself.'

Woods shrugged.

'I don't believe in death-or-glory and useless self-sacrifice, if that's what you mean. I wouldn't have become a doctor if I worshipped those qualities. I like life too much.'

Inge Stenersen nodded slowly, wondering why she was so interested in this man, a man who, by some subtle alchemy, made her feel wanted. She was young and healthy and her life in London had been far from solitary. Yet she had never felt attracted to the boys she had dated the way she was to Michael Woods. She reached out a hand to lay on his arm to ease his mind about Sweeny. She didn't quite know how it happened, but the next moment Woods's mouth was hungrily on her own and she was responding. It was some time before she forced herself to break away – as Woods began to fumble with the buttons of her pyjama top.

'Don't spoil it, Michael,' she said as she firmly pushed him away. 'I like you. I think I like you very much but I have to be sure . . .'

For a moment his face was like a petulant schoolboy's, but then he sighed and nodded.

'I understand,' he said.

Her hand closed over his quickly.

'I'm glad you do,' she responded. 'I want to be sure that this is something more than a need which has come out of the strange circumstances in which we find ourselves.'

He smiled softly.

'Will you come out to dinner with me when we get back to London?'

She chuckled.

'Consider it a date,' she said, leaning forward and brushing his forehead softly with her lips.

The elderly judge glanced up as Sweeny was pushed into the room by Arne Branting and brought to a halt before his desk.

'Good morning, young man. I hope you managed to get some sleep?'

Sweeny grimaced.

'Your cellar was not exactly comfortable, sir,' he replied stiffly.

Paal Berg gestured toward a chair.

'Take a seat. It seems that you have told us the truth. There has been a mistake which . . .' the old man's eyes danced with merriment for a moment, 'could have been fatal for one or both of us.'

Sweeny remained impassive.

'London have confirmed that they sent you to kill me in the mistaken belief that I was collaborating. They have now learnt their mistake from our Government in the north.'

'Am I to take your word for this?' asked Sweeny, raising a cynical eyebrow.

Paal Berg smiled.

'You are obviously a cautious young man, Sweeny. I like that.'

He slid a paper across the desk.

It was addressed to 'Sigurd' and bore the lines:

*Sigurd fell in battle's blast,*
*From his wounds there sprang hot gore.*
*Brian fell, but won at last.*

Then came a simple message: 'Abort your mission, Repeat – abort your mission. Information on collaboration mistaken. Hlodver.'

Sweeny pushed the paper back.

'We are new to this game of war, Sweeny,' Berg said. 'We are all amateurs and in such times of confusion mistakes can be made.'

He stood up and opened a small drinks cabinet behind him.

'A cognac? It is not too early? It was probably cold in the cellar?'

'Very cold,' confirmed Sweeny. He glanced behind him to where Arne Branting was still standing leaning against the door, his hands in his pockets. Berg caught the glance and smiled.

'Branting, too, is a cautious man. In these times we all have to learn caution. It is the only way to survive.'

Sweeny took the glass of brandy from the judge's hand.

'How could Norwegian intelligence in England make such a mistake?' he asked.

'It is easy with our country in a turmoil and people not knowing who are the traitors, who are those who have sold us to the Germans and who are not. On the surface I am pretending to go along with the Germans but beneath the surface I am trying, with young men like Branting here, to build up what I call a "Home Army", a secret army of resistance which will operate in the occupied territories.'

[123]

Berg examined the younger man carefully before continuing. 'That resistance could do with men such as yourself, Sweeny.'

'I have another mission to carry out,' Sweeny said.

The judge nodded.

'Ah, yes . . . you and your companions. The ones Branting spoke of.'

He gazed shrewdly at Sweeny. 'It would be better if we cooperated with you on this mission . . . in order to avoid any more mistakes.'

Berg was a persuasive man and Sweeny felt implicit trust in him. He had been relieved to see the message, which had obviously originated in London.

He quickly told Berg the details of the Stenersen mission. The old man nodded thoughtfully.

'I know Stenersen. He is a fine man. We will do all we can to help you fulfil this task.' He raised his eyes to Branting. 'I am going to appoint Branting here as the liaison officer between our organization and your group. He can support you in any way you think best.'

Sweeny turned to Branting. Their eyes met, they gazed steadily at each other for a moment, and then the young officer smiled, moved forward and stretched out his hand.

'All right, Sweeny? No hard feelings about last night?'

Sweeny rubbed his cheek, which was still painful, and grimaced.

'No hard feelings.' He grinned ruefully as he accepted the young man's hand.

'Excellent,' Berg said. 'And now . . .'

Something prompted Sweeny to make a swift decision.

'There is one other thing, sir . . .' He hesitated. 'There is something else which I would like to speak to you about alone.'

Paal Berg stared thoughtfully at him for a few minutes and then turned to Branting and nodded. Branting withdrew.

Sweeny started to tell the old man about the death of his cousin Freya, about the Nasjonal Samling buttonhole badge 5684 PL and the information with which Schanche had supplied him. Paal Berg listened like a priest hearing confession, not interrupting, nodding now and then. He made a few notes on a scrap of paper.

'I have contacts with the Stavanger police, young man. I will make some enquiries to see how they are proceeding.'

'According to Schanche, they think I've killed Freya and

Erik,' muttered Sweeny.

'I'm a pretty good judge of people, young man,' Berg said. 'I believe your story. I will do what is in my power to find out who this badge number Five-Six-Eight-Four PL belongs to.'

Sweeny rose and stretched out his hand to the judge.

'I am glad Branting prevented me from making such a terrible mistake,' he said with a smile. 'And I'm pleased, if slightly amazed, that after such an experience you granted my request to have a few words alone with you.'

Berg chuckled uproariously.

'Apart from being a pretty good judge of men, Sweeny,' he replied, 'I also believe in insurance.'

He handed Sweeny's Webley across the desk.

'I believe this knife is yours as well?'

Sweeny took the weapons with a rueful smile.

He joined Branting outside the study door. The young man looked relieved.

'The old man is quite a character,' observed Sweeny as he pocketed the automatic and his clasp knife.

'Quite a character,' agreed Branting solemnly. 'If anyone has a chance to build up a resistance movement, it is the judge.'

Sweeny suddenly caught sight of the time on the grandfather clock which stood in the hallway.

'Woods and the girl will be worried about me,' he said.

'Then we'd better go and find them before they make any stupid moves,' Branting observed. 'The new Reichskommissar arrived yesterday, bringing with him a number of Gestapo men to keep us in order. I wouldn't fancy anyone's chances if they fell into the hands of those thugs.'

# CHAPTER FIFTEEN

Hauptmann Eschig glanced up from his desk with a frown of annoyance at the sound of raised voices coming from outside his office door. He was about to get up to see what was wrong when the door was unceremoniously thrown open. He saw Feldwebel Weiss's face, looking pale and anxious, behind a young civilian. The man was slimly built with a tanned oval face. His dark hair was perfectly groomed and held in place with a glistening oil. He carried a grey felt hat in his hands and Eschig's eyes wandered swiftly over his well-creased trousers, carefully cut jacket and spotlessly white shirt and black tie. The young man came forward into the office with a degree of arrogance in his every motion. Eschig sighed. It was obvious that the young man was one of the janissaries of the New Order.

'Hauptmann Eschig?' The voice was nasal and its sound irritated Eschig.

Eschig pushed back his chair and stared up at the man. He suddenly noticed that the man's eyes were tinged with shadow and that they were dark, almost without pupils, and flickered from side to side with the greatest rapidity.

'Yes?' Eschig answered curtly.

'*Geheime Staats Polizei.*'

The young man reached into his pocket and drew out an identity card which he thrust in front of Eschig.

Eschig groaned inwardly. He might have known. Gestapo. The Secret State Police. He knew that yesterday Josef Terboven, the former *gauleiter* of the Krupp district of Essen, had arrived in Oslo to take up his appointment as Reichskommissar of Norway. Terboven was a special favourite of the Führer, who had actually been attending Terboven's wedding while issuing instructions which set into motion the fateful 'Night of the Long Knives' in 1934 when Hitler had eliminated all his rivals within the Nazi Party. Wherever Terboven went, there too went his cronies of the Gestapo. Ironically, Eschig had been offered a transfer to the

Gestapo when Goering had created it in April 1933 out of Department 1A of the old Prussian Political Police. Eschig had been thankful he had remained with the Abwehr, especially after the Gestapo was taken over by Heinrich Himmler a year later. In the seven years of their existence, Himmler had made the name of the Gestapo a by-word for fear. It was odd that a name invented by a Berlin post office clerk who simply needed an abbreviation for yet another Government department, had become a word with which German mothers frightened unruly children.

Eschig suddenly realized that the young man was staring insolently down at him.

'My name is Knesebeck, Herr Hauptmann. *Sturmbannführer* Knesebeck.'

Eschig bit his lip at the emphasis on the man's rank and slowly rose to his feet, coming to attention with a click of his heels. A *sturmbannführer* was equivalent to a major and therefore outranked a lowly captain such as himself.

'How can I be of service?' he asked as he inclined his head.

Knesebeck stared at him coldly for a moment and then sat down abruptly in a chair. Eschig resumed his seat.

The young man took a cigarette from a silver case, slipped it into a tortoise-shell holder and lit it.

'I am in charge of an *Einsatzgruppe*, a special task force which is based in Oslo,' he said slowly, blowing a perfect smoke ring into the air above Eschig's desk. 'I have been ordered to arrange for the transfer of certain Norwegian citizens to Germany, citizens whom the Reich feels will be more valuable to the war effort working in the Fatherland than here.'

Eschig raised his eyes in mild surprise.

'Are we talking about the forced deportation of Norwegians?'

Kneseback scowled.

'If they refuse to serve the Greater German Reich voluntarily then I have the power to enforce their removal.'

'Surely this will be a contradiction in policy?' frowned Eschig. 'Doctor Bauer, our ambassador here, delivered the Norwegian Government a note which, if I recall correctly, stated that the German Government had received documents which proved that England was going to extend the war by the occupation of Norwegian seaports for use by her fleet. It was the opinion of the Führer that Norway would not be able to resist such an occupation. Therefore the Third Reich had decided to come to

[127]

the aid of the Norwegians because we would not allow the Norwegian people to be used in such a fashion. We came to save Norway; we did not come here as enemies.'

Knesebeck regarded Eschig dourly.

'You may also recall that ambassador Bauer failed in his mission to convince the Norwegians of our good intentions. Bauer was recalled by the Führer last week and has been retired from the diplomatic service. He is now making reparation for his failure as a soldier on the Western Front. Because of his failure the Third Reich has been compelled to declare war on Norway. The Norwegians were given the chance to be our friends and comrades in this war against international Jewry and Communism. They chose not to be our friends.'

Knesebeck had begun to lean forward, his voice rising in a passable imitation of the Führer.

'They have behaved abominably! The Führer has said so. If they want to be treated like a conquered people then we shall treat them as such!'

Eschig bit his lip to keep himself from smiling. He had met too many ardent young Nazis who indulged in what was called *anschnauzen* or snorting – raising the voice, screaming in order to instil fear or awe into the object of their rages. Well, it merely washed over Eschig. He stared back at Knesebeck and raised his eyebrows.

'Has our policy now changed?'

Knesebeck stopped in mid-flow and then continued in a quiet, cold voice.

'You will soon see many changes here, Eschig. Reichskommissar Terboven is now in charge of administrative matters. Yes, there will certainly be changes.'

'You have not told me, how can I be of service to the Gestapo?'

Knesebeck burrowed into the pocket of his coat and threw a piece of paper onto Eschig's desk.

'There is a list of people who are to be requested to go to Germany. I want to know where they may be found.'

Eschig made no effort to pick up the list.

'I would suggest that you take the list to the third floor of this building. We have a number of Norwegian civil servants who are helping this department. They will find the addresses which you want, Herr Sturmbannführer. Ask Feldwebel Weiss to take you down. Now . . . if there is anything else?'

Knesebeck stood up and retrieved his list in annoyance.

'Nothing, Herr Hauptmann. Doubtless, however, my task force will be liaising in the future with the Abwehr.'

He turned and stalked out of the room without bothering to close the door behind him.

Only Arne Branting seemed totally self-assured as he, Sweeny, Woods and Inge sat around the kitchen table in the apartment.

'It seems a matter of providing transport, that's all,' he said.

'And a question of gathering everyone in one spot without their previous knowledge,' observed Inge. 'How can it be done?'

'Simple,' Branting replied. 'At the Riks-Hospitalet.' He turned to Inge. 'Didn't you say that your uncle was operating there this week? Tomorrow and Friday. We could pick him and his team up directly from the hospital and drive them to Sweden.'

Sweeny nodded. 'Sounds the best idea, but is it possible to drive directly across the Swedish border?'

Branting shook his head.

'No. We'd have to make a detour. The main roads from Oslo to the Swedish border are crawling with Germans. Ever since General Eriksen took his troops across the border the Germans have had the immediate border passes covered. We'd have to take a route further north.'

'What do you intend using for transport, Branting?' asked Woods.

Branting grinned.

'We can work a double switch to throw off any pursuit. A coach from the hospital and then into the old ambulance to get out of the city.'

Sweeny rubbed his nose thoughtfully.

'Then the next step is for Inge to go back to her uncle and find out the precise times when Stenersen and his team will be in the hospital.'

Inge stood up and smiled.

'I'll be on my way immediately. It should be no problem.'

Feldwebel Weiss came into Eschig's office without knocking, his face flushed with excitement. The captain jerked his head up with a frown that was halfway between anger and astonishment. Weiss had always been punctilious in such matters. Yet the sergeant seemed not to notice Eschig's darkening brow as he strode across to his desk.

'It is the red-haired man, Herr Hauptmann!' he said breathlessly. 'A report about the red-haired man that you have been looking for.'

Eschig took the report from his sergeant's hand and glanced at it. It was a copy of a local Norwegian police report which was being passed to the police at Stavanger. A man answering the description of Lars Sweeny, sought by the Stavanger police, had been seen in the area of Akersleva. The sighting had been made because the man had been observed talking to one Schanche, a special features editor of the radical Norwegian newspaper *Dagsbladet* who had been under surveillance due to the subversive nature of his politics.

Eschig pursed his lips. He knew all about the anti-fascist stance of the *Dagsbladet*. But what connection had Sweeny with the newspaper? The policeman conducting the surveillance had not, unfortunately, recognized Sweeny immediately but had only realized who he was after returning to his station and checking through the wanted files. He had immediately sent off his report to Stavanger, a copy of which had automatically come through to Eschig's office to be picked up by Weiss.

Eschig sat tapping his fingers on his desk as he stared at the report. What was the red-haired man, Lars Sweeny, doing in Oslo? Why was he in touch with a known subversive, a journalist on the *Dagsbladet*?

He was aware that Weiss was still standing by his desk.

'You did good work here, Weiss,' he said grimly. 'I want this man Schanche picked up and interrogated.'

'But, Herr Hauptmann . . .' Weiss was nervous. 'Schanche is already under surveillance . . .'

'I said I want him picked up. I want to find out why Sweeny spoke to him. What is his connection with Sweeny? Understand?'

'*Zum Befehl*, Herr Hauptmann!'

Mathilde let Inge Stenersen into the house with a joyful smile of welcome.

'Your uncle is in his study,' she said as she closed the front door behind her. Professor Stenersen was already opening the study door.

'I thought I heard your voice, Inge. Back so soon?'

Inge waited until they were alone together in the study before she spoke.

'We are going to put the plan into operation as soon as we can, Uncle Didrik,' she said. 'I must know the exact times that you

[130]

and your surgical team will be operating in the Riks-Hospitalet.'

Stenersen grimaced. 'Tomorrow, Thursday, and then on Friday. Then we have a schedule for the first three days of next week. Why do you wish to know this?'

Before she could answer there was a loud and imperative knocking on the front door. The sound made Inge jump. Her uncle, his face suddenly grey and pinched, moved to the window whose bay overlooked the door. He drew back with a start.

'Germans!' he said, in a voice which cracked. 'Did they see you come in here?'

'No, I am sure they didn't.'

Stenersen glanced round. They could hear old Mathilde moving across the hallway to open the door.

'It's best if they don't see me, Uncle,' Inge said softly.

Stenersen moved to a side door. The professor had an en suite washroom attached to his study which he used when examining patients privately. He held the door open. Inge slipped through and closed the door behind her.

Stenersen had just reseated himself as his study door was thrown open and a pale-faced young man in a felt hat entered. He was followed by two men in black uniforms. Stenersen had never seen such uniforms before. Both had red swastika armbands. Behind them, Mathilde's indignant face was red.

'Professor, I am sorry . . .'

The civilian turned and shut the door on the angry housekeeper.

'What is the meaning of this?' rumbled Stenersen angrily.

The civilian turned and gazed at the professor with dark, fathomless eyes.

'You are Professor Didrik Stenersen?' His Norwegian was appalling but understandable.

'I am.'

'Good. I am Sturmbannführer Knesebeck, *Geheime Staats Polizei*. You will be ready to leave for Berlin within forty-eight hours.'

# CHAPTER SIXTEEN

Professor Stenersen was speechless for a moment.

'Leave for Berlin?' he echoed. 'What do you mean? Am I under arrest for something?'

Knesebeck smiled thinly.

'My dear professor, what an absurd idea. Your name and reputation as one of Europe's leading surgeons is well known in the Reich. Our most eminent surgeon, Professor Ferdinand Sauerbruch, who, I believe, is an old friend of yours . . .'

Stenersen's mouth pinched.

'I have worked with Professor Sauerbruch,' he acknowledged when Knesebeck paused, inviting a reply.

'And will do so again. The Herr Professor has suggested that you should go to Berlin to teach your surgical techniques to our German surgeons.'

'I have no wish to leave Norway,' Stenersen said, frowning. 'My first duty is to my own country.'

Knesebeck's eyebrows seemed to meet across the bridge of his nose.

'I was not implying that you had a choice in this matter, Herr Professor,' he said softly, his voice ominous. 'You are being accorded the honour of being transferred to the Charité Hospital, our oldest and largest hospital, in the Mitte District of Berlin.'

'I know where the Charité Hospital is.'

'Good. You will be ready to leave within forty-eight hours.'

'I refuse to accept this high-handed attitude,' snapped Stenersen.

Knesebeck shrugged and removed an envelope from his pocket.

'This is a direct order from Reichskommissar Terboven. It is an *order*, Herr Professor. You will be taken to Berlin either willingly or unwillingly.' He turned for the door, hesitated and glanced back. 'You would be well advised to pack what belongings you need for a protracted stay. In the meantime, as a protection against Norwegian dissidents, I am placing these two men with you until you depart for Tempelhof.'

Knesebeck nodded towards the black-uniformed men. Stenersen ground his teeth.

'Then see that they are placed outside and do not disturb me in my work. I have much to do.'

'Of course, Herr Professor,' smiled the Gestapo officer.

Stenersen heard them go into the hallway and then the door slammed. He went to the door to check. The two men had taken up positions in the hall. The professor closed the door and went to the window. Knesebeck was getting into a black Opel saloon which drove off down the street. Stenersen heard the closet door open behind him and wheeled round with his finger against his lips. He hurried across to Inge and whispered, 'You heard?'

She nodded.

Stenersen's face was taut with anxiety.

'It seems that you have arrived too late to help me.'

'We won't give up now,' Inge assured him, keeping her voice low. 'We'll just have to move more quickly, that's all.'

'But the guards?'

'They'll have to be dealt with. If they've given you forty-eight hours we shall have to move sometime tomorrow. What is your schedule?'

Stenersen reached for his diary.

'Tomorrow from ten o'clock until two o'clock we are operating at the Riks-Hospitalet. Theatre Number One. I would say, allowing for any contingency that may arise, our finishing time would be more like four o'clock in the afternoon. After that, I was going on to the Didemark Mental Hospital to see its director, Doctor Gjessing. The next day I was to conduct a clinic at the Riks-Hospitalet.'

Inge inclined her head and then glanced over her shoulder into the en suite washroom.

'Where does that small window lead?'

'The window?' Stenersen frowned. 'To the back yard, which leads to a roadway that runs along the back of the house.'

'Can I get out that way?'

'I think so. It is certainly the only way to avoid the guards.'

Inge smiled. 'After I am gone, close the window but do not put the catch on. I will have to come back and tell you the plan, maybe later tonight.'

Stenersen looked worried as he acknowledged her instructions.

'I'll be working here late tonight. Be careful, Inge.'
He helped her squeeze through the little window and pushed it gently shut behind her.


Feldwebel Weiss observed military protocol this time by knocking on Hauptmann Eschig's door before entering.
'I beg to report that Herr Schanche has been able to make a brief statement to our interrogator.'
Eschig glanced up with a frown but could read nothing in the impassive gaze of the sergeant. His lips turned down cynically.
'I presume Herr Schanche is still alive?'
Weiss's eyes did not waver.
'I believe he has been removed to the military hospital with a respiratory problem, Herr Hauptmann.'
'And did he know anything?'
Weiss placed a piece of paper before the captain.
'That is the report of the interrogator, sir.'
'You have obviously read it, Weiss. Tell me the details.'
'It seems that Lars Sweeny was a cousin to Freya Hartvig, one of the two that the Stavanger police believe him to have murdered. Herr Schanche had never met Sweeny before. Sweeny denied that he killed either Freya or Erik Hartvig. He admitted going to their apartment and finding the bodies. He believes, from evidence that he found, that the murders were political . . .'
'What evidence?' snapped Eschig.
'Sweeny showed Schanche a buttonhole Nasjonal Samling badge which he found in the hand of Freya Hartvig. Sweeny thought that it had been torn from the coat of the assailant. Some material was still attached to it when Sweeny found it.'
Eschig was frowning.
'The finding of a political badge is not evidence that the killings were political. Sweeny must have more evidence than that? Also, why did he go to see Schanche if Schanche did not know him?'
'Freya Hartvig was a journalist, Herr Hauptmann. She was working for Schanche when she was killed. Herr Schanche says that her assignment was to uncover the involvement of certain members of the Nasjonal Samling with the Third Reich's plans to occupy Norway.'
Eschig let out a long, low breath. He sat back and placed his hands together, fingertips to fingertips.

'Did Schanche say anything else?'

'Only that Sweeny had told him that on the morning of the invasion, Freya Hartvig's father had been killed. Sweeny had managed to escape to England. That is all.'

'All?'

'Our interrogator is a most persuasive man, Herr Hauptmann. I am sure that if there had been anything else, Herr Schanche would have revealed it.'

Eschig bit his lip. There *was* something else, there had to be. If Sweeny had escaped to England why had he come back to Norway? Eschig was sure that he was one of the three parachutists who had been reported in the Kristiansand area. Why had he returned? Simply to clear his name and find out who had murdered his cousin and her husband? It seemed very unlikely. Again he felt that unique tingling sensation in his fingertips.

'Could Schanche remember anything about the buttonhole badge? Did it have a number?'

'It did, but Herr Schanche could not recall it beyond the initials PL.'

'I do not suppose Schanche knew where to contact Sweeny or his companions?'

'No, Herr Hauptmann.'

'Very well,' Eschig sighed. 'Put through a call to the headquarters of the Nasjonal Samling.'

'Herr Hauptmann?'

'Perhaps they can help identify this buttonhole badge.'


Sweeny took Inge's news calmly.

'It doesn't leave us much time,' he remarked.

'No time at all,' muttered Woods moodily.

'Still time enough,' Sweeny said, glancing toward Branting. 'Can you organize your transport by tomorrow?'

Branting started, then gave it a moment's thought.

'I think so.'

'Then do so,' said Sweeny, getting to his feet. 'Woods and I are going to the Riks-Hospitalet for a reconnaisance.'

'Me?' Woods was startled.

'You worked at the Riks-Hospitalet for three years. You ought to know your way around it blindfolded.'

'Sure, but . . .' Woods began.

'What about me?' demanded Inge, interrupting.

'You stay here. We'll all meet back here at six o'clock this evening, no later. We'll go over the final plan then and you'll have to go back to your uncle to tell him.'

Woods felt very conspicuous as he accompanied Sweeny out of the apartment. At the end of the street they caught a tram which took them along the Draamensveien and into Karl Johansgate. At the Storting, the parliament building, they changed to another tram which headed north along Akersgate to the Catholic Church of St Olav's, where they alighted to walk the remaining two blocks to the Riks-Hospitalet, Oslo's premier hospital. The large teaching hospital was Norway's most prestigious and its surgery department was one of the best in Europe. The main building itself was a large L-shaped complex with at least a dozen other outbuildings scattered through its extensive grounds.

'Do you think anyone will recognize you after three years?' asked Sweeny as they neared the main gates.

'I can't be sure, but I wouldn't think so. Most of the people I worked with have gone on to other hospitals, and people like Professor Stenersen would hardly give me away.'

There were several German soldiers on guard duty outside the hospital.

'The Germans are everywhere,' Sweeny observed, frowning.

'I'm not surprised,' Woods replied. 'The hospital must be dealing with the German casualties from the war front.'

Indeed, there were several military vehicles in the hospital grounds.

'Where do you want to go?' asked Woods.

'Let's see the operating theatres.'

'The main surgical building is the one which fronts onto the Ullervalsveien,' Woods said, swinging off round a building and nearly colliding with a German soldier.

'*Verdammt!*' muttered the indignant man. '*Eintritt verboten!*' Then, summoning some bad Norwegian, 'This area is forbidden to enter.'

Sweeny smiled. '*Verzeihen Sie Bitte.* We were going to the main surgical block. Can't we go through this way?'

'This area is for wounded German soldiers. Didn't you see the sign?'

Sweeny shook his head and apologized again. The sentry softened a little.

'Well, no harm done. You may go across that way, but follow the path.'

'*Ich bin Ihnen sehr dankbar*,' said Sweeny expansively. He led Woods hurriedly away.

'That was a near thing,' Woods whispered.

'Just watch where you are going,' muttered Sweeny. 'It's not wise to go round bumping into German soldiers in restricted zones.' He glanced around and added: 'If we are stopped, remember that we are builders come to take some measurements.'

Woods nodded, a little chastened.

They came to a large building which fronted onto a road. On the other side of the road, exactly in front of the building, was a large graveyard.

'What's that place?' asked Sweeny.

'*Vår Frelsers Gravlund*,' Woods replied grimly. 'Our Saviour's Cemetery. They used to say that when student surgeons failed with a case it was only a short trip across the road to hide the mistake. Actually, this is the old part of the hospital and there is a morgue just below the theatre complex. From the morgue the bodies would be transported to the basement of the hospital through an underground passage and up into the cemetery.'

Sweeny glanced at the cemetery grounds thoughtfully.

'Is the passage still used?'

Woods shook his head.

'I don't think so. Why?'

'Let's explore the basement first.'

Woods turned toward a side entrance in the building. Although there were plenty of people about, nurses, men in white coats and an assortment of patients and others, no one seemed to pay them a second glance. Woods remembered the way, for he stepped through a door which led down a winding iron stairwell into a small anteroom. Workmen's overalls hung on pegs. It was obviously the changing room for the maintenance staff.

'We are getting all the luck we need,' grinned Sweeny, seizing an overall from its hanger. 'Put on a coat and don't forget we are builders, eh?'

While Woods fitted himself out, Sweeny sorted through a tool box and came up with a tape measure and a note pad on a blockboard.

'The perfect disguise,' he said with satisfaction. 'If you see anyone looking suspiciously at us, just start measuring.'

Woods led the way again, this time through a metal door which led into the basement area. It seemed to run the entire length of the building. Several large dynamos hummed softly, giving the building its lighting and emergency back-up systems for the surgical department. There was also a series of boilers throwing out a stifling heat. The place seemed deserted.

'Do you know where the passageway into the cemetery begins?'

Woods nodded.

'It would have to be on that side of the building.' He moved along a walkway between the humming dynamos. They came upon doors which opened into an elevator.

'That must go up to the morgue,' observed Woods. 'There's an emergency staircase next to it and beyond them . . .'

Beyond were two large iron doors.

'Those must open into the passage.'

Sweeny bent down and examined the doors carefully.

'The bolts don't look as if they have been drawn for some years,' he mused. He glanced at Woods. 'Would it be easy to get Stenersen and his team down here from the theatre without anyone seeing them?'

Woods nodded. 'If you can get Stenersen away from the guards which Inge mentioned.'

'Forget them for the moment. Can it be done?'

Woods pointed to the circular stairs near the elevator.

'They lead up to the roof as an emergency fire escape. There is a fire door from the theatre washroom which leads out on to them.'

'Who are you?' demanded a harsh voice.

They swung round in alarm. A thick-set man in workman's overalls was standing, hands on hips, glaring suspiciously at them.

'Who are we?' Sweeny snapped back. 'That's a question we should be asking you.'

The workman blinked at the tone of authority in Sweeny's voice.

'I . . . I'm an assistant janitor here.' A tone of deference crept into his voice.

'Ah? Name?'

'Holmboe . . . sir.'

'These bolts aren't kept in good condition, are they, Holmboe?'

[138]

Sweeny said, indicating the iron doors.

The man bit his lip nervously.

'The doors of the old passage have not been used in years, sir. But they still work. Why do you ask, sir?'

Sweeny sniffed.

'It may be that we will want to start using the passage again. When you have time put some oil on them. Thank you, Holmboe.'

'Excuse me . . .'

Sweeny was moving away, saying to Woods in a loud voice, 'I'll have to mention the matter to the *Direktor.*'

The assistant janitor watched them go with a frown.

Once through the anteroom door, Sweeny and Woods moved more hurriedly, leaving the overalls where they had found them.

'Damn it,' muttered Sweeny as they moved out of the hospital. 'I would have liked to try the bolts on the door to make sure they work. Let's hope our janitor friend decides to oil and test them before tomorrow.'

'But why?' Woods was frowning. Sweeny did not reply.

Woods followed him out of the hospital building and across the road towards the cemetery. Sweeny did not speak. He inspected the cemetery carefully through the iron railings which surrounded it. There was no gate into it from this side of the perimeter. Sweeny moved off again, following the wall of the cemetery until it turned south again by the Old Akers Church. There they could see the main entrance. Woods shrugged as he followed the taciturn Sweeny into the grounds and through the winding paths among the headstones.

'Where does the passageway come up, Woods?'

Woods nodded to a tall mausoleum structure.

'So far as I remember, it comes up in there.'

Sweeny made towards it without hesitation and examined the rusting iron doors.

'Bolts,' he said. He leant his weight against them and they gave a sharp protesting screech. He eased them out and tried the door. It took some pressure before it swung inwards to reveal a dark and musty interior. After a few stone steps the floor began to slope rapidly down into a yawning black hole.

'Wait here,' Sweeny said, pulling out a box of matches. 'If anyone comes along swing the door shut behind me.'

'Where are you going?' demanded Woods in surprise.

'I want to follow the tunnel back as far as I can to make sure that there are no obstructions.'

With that he was gone into the dark passage. Woods saw the tiny flicker of his match-torch dying away. Rather Sweeny than himself, he thought as he turned and paced up and down, pretending to be interested in deciphering inscriptions on the nearby tombs. It seemed a very long time before Sweeny reappeared and stood with his back against the brick of the mausoleum, breathing in deep draughts of fresh air. Then he drew the iron door shut and slipped back the bolts.

'If all goes well,' he said, smiling tightly, 'this will be our escape route out of the hospital. We can have our transport waiting at the main gates of the cemetery.'

'I still don't see why we need to use the underground passage,' Woods said in puzzlement.

'First, to avoid the SS guards that have been placed to watch Stenersen, and secondly, because we will be moving seven people out of the hospital, of whom one at least will be unwilling to come with us. The less people see of us the better.'

At the apartment Branting was already back and having a coffee with Inge.

'No problems about transport, Sweeny,' the young officer reported, grinning.

'Good.' Sweeny took the cup which Inge was offering him. 'The plan is simple. Inge and Woods will go to the Riks-Hospitalet tomorrow. They must somehow be in the theatre itself as Stenersen and his team are finishing their last operation of the day. Inge, you will have to work that out with your uncle. Do you think you can persuade him to give you and Woods some sort of special pass to observe . . . say to observe surgical techniques?'

Inge nodded. 'I think so.'

'He must also ensure that the SS guards are not allowed in the theatre while he is operating. As soon as the last operation is completed, you will move Stenersen and his team to the washroom.'

'That's normal procedure, anyway,' intervened Woods. 'You scrub up before an operation and afterwards.'

'From the washroom,' went on Sweeny, 'you will take them down into the basement and proceed by an underground passage, which Woods will show you, to the cemetery next door to the hospital. I will be in the cemetery to open the doors of the mausoleum, where the passageway emerges. Branting will have his transport ready and waiting at the cemetery gates. What is the transport, by the way?'

'An old motor coach,' Branting said. 'We'll go from there to a safe house in the eastern quarter and transfer to the ambulance for the journey to the Swedish border.'

There was a silence before Inge observed, 'Perhaps the plan is too simple?'

'The best plans are simple,' Sweeny said. 'That way we can allow for variations.'

'It all depends on the guards,' said Woods. 'What if they insist on being in the theatre?'

'Stenersen must ensure that they are left outside.'

'But,' Inge intervened, 'sooner or later they will become suspicious when Uncle Didrik and his team do not emerge from the theatre or the washroom. They'll break in. I don't think they will give us a long enough lead.'

Sweeny frowned.

'We only need a few minutes. If we can move them through the passage, across the cemetery and into the coach, before we have been discovered, that's all the lead we want.'

He smiled grimly at the girl.

'It is up to you, Inge, to impress on your uncle that you are to be given admission to the theatre and that, as he finishes the last operation, only you two and his team are to be in the theatre. Timing will be of the essence. Neither Branting nor I want to attract any suspicion by being seen hanging about too long at the cemetery, so ask him if he can be precise about the time he will finish operating.'

'I don't think that will be possible,' Inge reflected. 'There are so many unpredictable things that can happen.'

Sweeny sighed.

'Well, do the best you can. And another thing, your uncle is to give no hint to anyone in his team. Nor is he to make any farewells, write any letters, contact anyone at all, or pack clothes or other belongings. So far as he is concerned, tomorrow will be just another normal day at the hospital.'

Michael Woods smiled tightly.

'That is the last thing it will be,' he murmured.

# PART THREE

*Thursday, 2 May – Sunday, 5 May, 1940*

# CHAPTER SEVENTEEN

It was a little after one o'clock the next day, Thursday, when Inge and Woods alighted from the tram opposite St Olav's Church. There were very few people about as they crossed the road and went into the hundred-year-old Catholic shrine. The gloomy interior was deserted. They moved to the darkest corner, by the confessional box, and glanced round to ensure that they were unobserved. Woods opened the small case he had brought and took out the two white coats and stethoscopes which Inge had borrowed from her uncle's house. They put these on, ensuring that the Webley automatics they carried did not show, and slung the stethoscopes around their necks.

They left the church and strolled nonchalantly alongside the wall of the cemetery, before crossing the road and entering the hospital building. Few people gave them a second glance, and Inge now began a long, involved and moderately loud monologue on the problems of hyperglaecoma, punctuated with occasional nods and grunts from Woods.

He led the way to the theatres, where the hurrying nurses and doctors paid little attention to another two doctors in white coats. There was a notice board which listed the theatres and the operations for the day in each one. Professor Stenersen, as he had told Inge, was listed as operating in Theatre No. 1. Woods turned down the corridor towards the theatre. There were two black-uniformed Germans sitting uncomfortably in the corridor outside the theatre anteroom. One was reading the German popular radio magazine *Hör mit mir*. As Inge and Woods approached, the one who wasn't reading stood up.

'Halt!'

They came to a stop in front of the heavy-jowled soldier.

'What business have you here?'

'We are here to witness an operation by Professor Stenersen,' replied Woods, confident that his Norwegian was far superior to the soldier's. He produced the letter which Inge had had her uncle write the previous evening, giving full permission for Doctor Bryn Poulsson and Doctor Inge Ingersson to attend the operating theatre. The soldier glanced at it. It was obvious that he could not read Norwegian very well. He grunted, '*Alles in ordnung.*'

Feeling cold with relief, Woods led Inge into the anteroom to the operating theatre. There were two sets of doors, one set leading directly into the theatre itself while the other set led into the washroom.

'In here we scrub up and put on theatre gowns,' Woods said as he pushed open the washroom doors. It was strange; here he was in his own environment. He felt an assured calm at the familiarity of the place. In the washroom they scrubbed up and donned gowns, caps and gloves.

'Here goes,' said Woods, pushing through the swing doors into the theatre.

There was a concentrated silence in the white-tiled room. A group of people stood clustered under the bright arc lights around the operating table. A theatre nurse glanced up, her brows drawn together in a frown. She began to move towards them.

At the same moment, Stenersen, whom Inge had no difficulty recognizing in spite of his gown and mask, glanced up, sensing that someone had entered the theatre.

'Ah, it's all right, nurse. These are the two observers that I was expecting. Doctors Poulsson and Ingersson. They have come from the Oslo Radium Hospitalet to see my operation on Fru Gronvold. Make yourselves at home, Doctors. I just have to finish sewing up this patient and we will have Fru Gronvold in.'

'That will be the last patient for today, Professor,' said one of the nurses.

'Indeed, Frøken Lanstrad.' Stenersen glanced at the clock on the wall of the theatre. 'If all goes well, we shall be finished about four o'clock.'

Woods glanced toward Inge, realizing that the professor was speaking for their benefit. They took up positions on one side of the room. Actually, Woods became professionally absorbed in what the professor and his team were doing and the time had little meaning for him. Inge, however, was very conscious of the slow, monotonous tick-tocking of the clock. She tried to control her increasing nervousness as the hands made their slow passage across its face. It was five minutes to four o'clock when Stenersen stood back and sighed.

'That's it. Get the ward orderlies to wheel Fru Gronvold to the recovery room.'

One of the nurses moved to the theatre doors and pressed a bell. Two nurses eased the patient's body from the operating table onto a trolly and pushed it towards the doors. As they reached them, two more nurses came from the anteroom and took the trolly away.

'Best bit of sewing I've seen for some time, professor,' one of the doctors was saying jokingly.

Stenersen, however, was gazing across at Inge.

'That's it for today,' he said with meaningful softness.

The girl glanced at Woods. Woods moved swiftly through to the doors of the anteroom and threw the bolt, then came back into the theatre and bolted its own doors quickly and decisively. As he turned, he was aware that Inge had drawn her automatic and was covering the startled surgical team. Only Stenersen seemed unconcerned.

'Into the washroom, everyone,' Woods snapped.

Stenersen moved immediately, and it was probably his unquestioning obedience which caused the others to follow without protest. In the washroom they stood hesitating, looking bewildered. While Inge kept her pistol trained on them, Woods crossed to the doors leading to the anteroom and bolted these as well. Then he, too, took out his automatic.

'Wash up, quickly,' he said coldly, 'and change your clothing.'

There was a tense silence as the surgical team completed their washing and observed the usual hygiene procedures of the theatre. Inge and Woods themselves took turns to wash and keep guard.

'I'd better explain to them, Inge,' Stenersen said after they had finished.

Inge nodded.

'My friends,' Stenersen turned to his colleagues. 'This is my niece Inge, and some of you may remember Doctor Woods, who used to work here some years ago. They have come from England.'

The surgical team continued to stare in bewildered silence.

'There is no need to explain to you what is happening in our country. I have heard that our forces in the north cannot hold out much longer, even with the aid of the Allies. Soon poor Norway will be under total occupation. I have been contacted by

London. It seems my presence, and indeed your presence, is needed to perform an operation which will benefit the Allied war effort and help achieve ultimate freedom for our country. On this basis I have agreed to accompany my niece and Doctor Woods to England. What is more . . . I have promised that you will accompany me so that we can continue our work in a free country.'

'This is insanity, Herr Professor!'

A small, dark man with a flushed, excitable face pushed forward.

'Doctor Hersleb,' Stenersen said, as if to introduce the anaesthetist. 'I have given the matter much thought. The situation is quite simple . . .' He took a piece of paper from his pocket. 'This is an order from the new Reichskommissar. It gives me until tomorrow to pack my bags and be ready to leave for Berlin where I am ordered to serve the Third Reich.'

Stenersen gazed at each of his team in turn.

'Which is it to be, my friends? Serve our conquerors in Germany or serve Norway in England until such time as we can return, free people in a free country?'

There was a hesitant shuffle and then one of the other doctors said, 'I'll go with you, Professor.' One after another, the rest of the team joined in a chorus of agreement. Only the little man, Hersleb, shook his head in disapproval.

'The entire scheme is madness. Of course the Germans won't remove us to Berlin if we do not want to go. The Germans are civilized people and we are not soldiers. They came to Norway to protect us from the imperial policies of the Allies . . .'

Inge stared at the little man in disgust.

'I don't know what world you are living in, Doctor,' she said softly, 'but it certainly is not this one. The Germans are removing the Czechs and Poles, men, women and children, to act as slave labour in order to free their young men for the fighting forces. If you think that the Germans will treat Norwegians any differently from the other peoples they have conquered, then you are a fool or worse.'

Hersleb flushed.

'I don't have to put up with insults. We Norwegians are a Nordic-Germanic people. Aryans. We are not like the mongrel mixes of Poland and Czechoslovakia!'

Woods moved forward and thrust the point of his automatic hard into the little doctor's midriff. Hersleb grunted in pain.

'Like it or not, you are coming with us,' he said coldly. He

[148]

glanced at the others. 'I'm afraid that is enough discussion on this matter. There is no time for debate. The two SS guards will start wondering about the delay and they'll be breaking in here in a moment. We must move.'

Stenersen nodded agreement.

Inge moved across to the firedoor in the corner of the washroom, threw the bolts and pulled it open.

'Down the firestairs into the basement,' she ordered. 'Keep close and no talking.'

Hersleb scowled.

'I refuse to take part in this madness,' he snarled.

'Like it or not,' Woods repeated grimly, 'it's too dangerous to leave you behind to chat with your Nazi friends.'

'This is abduction. I protest!' Hersleb was white faced.

'You'll be able to make an official protest to the Norwegian authorities . . . in London. Now get a move on. I would hate to use this . . .'

He gestured with the Webley and suddenly remembered that he had not slipped off the safety catch which Commander Wallace had shown him. He doubted whether Hersleb knew enough about firearms to have perceived his mistake.

Inge was already leading the way down the spiral iron staircase which led down three floors into the large basement area. The heat was fairly powerful and the distant hum and throb of the dynamos created an oppressive atmosphere. At the foot of the stairs Inge halted until Woods caught up.

'Through the walkway to those metal doors,' he called to her. While his attention was momentarily distracted, the little anaesthetist, Hersleb, suddenly darted away across the boiler room, yelling 'Help! Help! I'm being abducted!' The man ran like a rabbit down the walkway. Woods let out a curse and raised his Webley automatically, but found himself hesitating.

'I'll get him!' he yelled to Inge. 'You take them through the passage.'

Woods started after Hersleb and found one of the doctors coming with him. The man smiled. 'It's our necks as well. I'll help you.'

Hersleb had disappeared among the mass of pipes and boilers. Woods halted, listening. There was nothing to be heard above the hum of the machinery and the sigh of escaping steam. He bit his lip. Then there was a sudden scurry, shoe leather slapping on iron. Hersleb had doubled back to make a dash up the firesteps.

Woods rushed forward and reached the foot of the stairs as Hersleb was scrambling upwards. He lunged up and grasped the man by the bottom of one trouser leg and heaved. Hersleb was not holding the rail. He tottered, tried to regain his balance and came tumbling down on top of Woods. For a moment Woods lay winded while Hersleb sought to scramble away, but the young doctor who had followed Woods grabbed the anaesthetist and caught his arm in a vice-like grip. Hersleb swore violently and tried to struggle.

'Now, now, Doctor,' hissed the young man, 'this is for your own good as well as ours.'

Woods climbed to his feet, retrieved his automatic and took hold of Hersleb's free arm.

'Thanks, Doctor . . ?'

'Jan Birkenes.'

'You'll not get away with this,' hissed Hersleb. 'Terrorists! Bandits!'

Woods pocketed his gun and tore off his tie and the tie Hersleb was wearing. He deftly twisted them round the man's wrists and, with the help of Birkenes, trussed the man's hands behind him.

'Swine!' yelled Hersleb.

Birkenes smiled thinly as he reached into the little man's pocket, drew out a handkerchief and tied it across the anaesthetist's mouth to form a gag.

'Things will be much better if you are quiet for a while, Doctor,' he said gently.

Woods pushed Hersleb before him and proceeded along the walkway toward the iron doors to the passage. Inge and the others were standing anxiously by the doors. She looked relieved as they came up.

'I thought I told you to go on up the passage,' Woods frowned.

The girl bit her lip.

'Allright,' said Woods, 'let's not lose any more time.'

He bent to the bolts. The assistant janitor had not obeyed Sweeny's instruction to oil the bolts. They were very rusty and it took the combined strength of Woods and Birkenes to free them. The men had barely forced open one of the doors when a sound rang out, vibrating across the expanse of the boiler room. '*Halt! Hände hoch!*'

Woods spun round. He was so tense that the action was automatic. Maybe if he had thought about it he would have obeyed the order. Instead, his finger squeezed on the trigger of the Webley. The gun bucked in his hand and the shot went whining across the basement.

'Get going! Get going!' he yelled.

Inge dived through the door, pulling her uncle with her. The others followed as a couple of pistol shots rang out. Luckily the equipment, the boilers and dynamos and the mass of pipes, were obstructing the aim of the German guards and their shots went wide and ricocheted. Woods pointed the gun in the direction of the shots and squeezed the trigger twice more. Never having fired a gun in his life, he found it extraordinary how the metal object jumped in his hand. Birkenes had dragged Hersleb through the door in the wake of the others and now Woods followed. The passage was about six feet wide and ten feet in height, with an arched roof. It smelt musty and damp. Ahead of him, Inge was lighting the way with a torch and the dim glow revealed that the brick walls were covered with green mould and dripping water. The atmosphere was putrid.

'Get them to the other end!' cried Woods. 'I'll try to hold off the guards from here.'

'But . . .' Inge began to argue.

'Christ! Get going!'

The girl turned, the doctors and nurses behind her, Birkenes prodding the reluctant Hersleb, forcing him to stumble along. Woods glanced out into the basement and let off another shot. The whine of the bullet suddenly stopped when it hit a pipe and then there was a sudden scream as steam escaped at high pressure. He glanced across his shoulder. The glow of Inge's torchlight was fading away along the passageway. He turned and scrambled after it.

The passage curved after a short distance and he halted. Looking back, he could see the light of the boiler room coming through the open iron doorway. If the Germans came that way they would be silhouetted. If only he was a marksman. They would be sitting targets to someone who knew about guns. Behind him he was suddenly aware of some light. Then he heard Sweeny's voice.

'Come on, man! Run! I'll cover you.'

He rose and pounded along the rest of the passageway towards the faint light coming from Sweeny's end.

Sweeny had opened the door of the mausoleum and moved the group through into the cemetery.

'Come on, Woods,' he called. 'I'll hold them up for a while.

You get everyone across the cemetery to Branting's coach.'

Woods moved out of the mausoleum into the cemetery. Inge and the others were waiting there. He led them away through the gravestones, helping Birkenes haul the still reluctant Hersleb along.

In the passageway, Sweeny saw a figure outlined in the doorway at the far end. He aimed carefully and fired. The figure gave a cry and crumpled. Sweeny let off two more shots. Then he reached into his pocket and took out a grenade – one of two which he had acquired from Arne Branting. He pulled the pin and counted the seconds before lobbing it down the passageway. Almost immediately there was a roar and a blast of heat before acrid black smoke trickled from the entrance. Sweeny did not look back. He was already running after the rest of the party.

He moved swiftly around a tall memorial and nearly collided with one of the nurses, who was kneeling on one knee. She glanced up, startled for the moment, with fear in her grey eyes.

'I fell,' she muttered, rubbing her ankle. 'Twisted it, I think.'

Sweeny bent down and felt it with some expertise. Years at sea had qualified him with some degree of first aid experience.

'Can you put weight on it?' he grunted.

'I don't think so,' she replied hesitantly.

The girl suddenly gave a gasp of astonishment as the tall red-haired man swung her suddenly across his shoulder without apparent effort. He held her in an easy fireman's lift and hurried on along the path.

Branting had eased the old motor bus into the entrance to the cemetery and sat behind the wheel, engine running. Inge had already managed to get the whole party aboard. She was standing at the door with Woods. Pistols in hand, they were staring anxiously across the cemetery to the mausoleum, from which black smoke was rising like a signal. Sweeny lumbered into sight with the girl across his shoulder. He simply brushed by them onto the bus and dumped the girl unceremoniously into the nearest unoccupied seat. Stenersen moved over to the girl with an anxious face to see if she was all right.

'I just stumbled over a root or something,' the girl muttered. 'I'll be fine, Professor.'

Sweeny had gone forward to Branting's side while Inge and Woods had climbed aboard and slammed the door shut.

Branting put the coach in gear immediately and drove swiftly out of the cemetery. Once outside, though, he did not drive very fast because there were several German military vehicles on the roads. He hoped they would mistake the coach for a regular bus. Within a few turns he had left the main streets behind and increased his speed a little through the narrow streets of the city's eastern quarter, moving along the wharves fronting the Akerselva river until he came to a warehouse whose doors stood open. He drove in and halted. Sweeny and Woods immediately jumped down and swung the large doors shut behind them and threw the bolts. Only then did Sweeny grin and take out a packet of cigarettes.

'So far, so good,' he said softly.

# CHAPTER EIGHTEEN

Hauptmann Eschig arrived at the Riks-Hospitalet in answer to the alarm call which had been forwarded to his office. Feldwebel Weiss drove the staff car to the hospital entrance, where a number of SS guards and green-uniformed *Feld Polizei* stood in uncertain groups. They snapped to attention when Eschig climbed out of the car.

'Who's in charge here?' he demanded.

A black-uniformed SS man answered him. 'Sturmbannführer Knesebeck, Herr Hauptmann.'

At that moment Knesebeck came down the hospital steps. Eschig frowned.

'Herr Sturmbannführer.' He gave a punctilious military salute.

The Gestapo man frowned.

'Eschig. What are you doing here?'

'My office was informed of some attack on the hospital. An exchange of gunfire. Naturally, security in the city . . .'

'There is no need for your office to worry about this affair. It is a Gestapo matter.'

'I appreciate that, of course, Herr Sturmbannführer.' Eschig kept his voice purposefully even. 'Still, I have to make a report to my superiors.'

Knesebeck scowled.

'One of my men has been killed by terrorists. Another has been seriously wounded.'

'How did it happen?'

'The men were guarding Professor Stenersen, who was due to leave for the Reich tomorrow. Stenersen and his entire team appear to have been spirited out of the hospital by a gang of terrorists. They removed them from the operating theatre, down a fire escape into the basement and then along an underground tunnel into the cemetery across the way there. They had transport waiting on the far side of the cemetery and have disappeared.'

Eschig pursed his lips.

'Stenersen? Isn't he a well-known surgeon?'

Knesebeck glowered. 'Yes. He was one of those who had been ordered to work in the Reich.'

'Any idea who these terrorists were?'

'No. A soldier in front of the hospital managed to catch sight of one of them as he fled through the cemetery. The *dumkopf* didn't fire because the man was carrying a woman over his shoulder. He said that the man he saw was tall, well-built and had red hair.'

Eschig's jaw dropped in surprise.

'Where is this soldier?'

Knesebeck turned and pointed at one of the *Feld Polizei*.

'Repeat your description of the man you saw in the cemetery,' snapped the Gestapo officer.

'*Zum Befehl*, Herr Sturmbannführer. He was a tall man. He had red hair, very bright red hair, and he was extremely well built.'

Lars Sweeny? It seemed impossible. Yet it had to be him.

'These terrorists, they managed to abduct the entire surgical team of Professor Stenersen?'

Knesebeck nodded.

'Why would they want to do so?'

'To prevent them going to work in the Reich, why else?' snapped the Gestapo man. 'I am putting the other Norwegians on my list into protective custody until they are flown off tomorrow. I have established roadblocks throughout the city. The swine will not be able to get out of Oslo.'

Eschig nodded, saluted politely and turned back to his car. His mind was a kaleidoscope of racing thoughts. What was Sweeny's purpose in Oslo? To seek out the killer of Freya and Erik Hartvig or to spirit prominent Norwegian citizens out of German hands? Was he acting on his own out of some desire for personal vengeance or did he have some definite mission to accomplish? The captain climbed into his car and snapped at his sergeant, 'General von Falkenhorst's headquarters, Weiss. Make it fast.' Eschig had an idea – only a hazy idea at this point, but enough to decide him on a definite course of action.

When everyone had disembarked from the bus, Branting took charge.

'Please follow me,' he said shortly.

Sweeny went to the nurse who was limping. She smiled at him.
'I can manage,' she asked in answer to his unasked question.
'It's not as bad as I thought at first.'

Branting led the group through a side door and past a series of
deserted warehouses which stretched along an entire section of
the river. After a short distance Branting entered another
warehouse, in which stood an ambulance.

'Courtesy of the Didemark Mental Asylum again?' smiled
Woods.

Branting grinned.

'Different vehicle but the same principle. Inge will ride up
front with me. There's a nurse's uniform on the seat. The rest of
you will have to cram yourselves into the back as best you can.'

Professor Stenersen examined the ambulance thoughtfully.

'You have thought things out well, Inge.'

Inge grimaced. 'Not me, Uncle. This is Lars Sweeny; he is in
charge.'

The professor extended his hand.

'I'm afraid there isn't much time to get acquainted, Professor,'
Sweeny said. 'We must move off immediately.'

'Where are we making for?' asked Stenersen.

'Across the border, eventually.'

Stenersen nodded and turned to Woods. He smiled as he
shook the younger man's hand.

'I haven't said that it is good to see you again, Michael. I'm
very glad to see you, although I wish it was in better
circumstances.'

Woods grinned as he returned the handshake.

'We'll have a long chat when we get back to London, sir.'

Stenersen nodded and then turned to where Hersleb was
standing, hands still secured behind his back, red in the face, the
gag still in his mouth.

'Can't we leave him behind?'

Sweeny shook his head.

'We do not want him to pass on information to his Nazi friends
and, besides, we promised London to deliver the full medical
team.'

Inge had already changed into the nurse's cap and cloak and
Sweeny left it to Woods to get everyone into the back of the
ambulance while he had a quiet word with Branting.

'What road do you plan to take?'

'I thought we'd head to Lillestrom and then northwards.'

Sweeny nodded approval and joined Woods in the back with the others. It was crowded inside and everyone clung to whatever handholds they could find. Hersleb had been dumped unceremoniously in a corner.

Branting eased the vehicle out of the warehouse and along the deserted industrial roadway, turning through several narrow streets until they exited along the Nordregate. Almost as soon as they turned onto the northern road they met a roadblock. A German armoured car was swung across the roadway, effectively closing it. Half-a-dozen soldiers under an efficient looking *unteroffizier* stood with machine pistols at the ready. Branting had no choice but to brake gently and lean out of the window with a grin.

'Keep calm and back me,' he hissed to Inge, as he smiled at the *unteroffizier*. '*Guten tag.*'

The German ran his eyes suspiciously over the ambulance. '*Haben Sie Ihren Führerschein bei sich?*'

'Of course,' Branting continued to smile, reaching forward for some papers. The *unteroffizier* glanced through them.

'What vehicle is this?'

'Ambulance from the Didemark Mental Asylum,' Branting smiled confidentially. 'We are transporting some loonies to the hospital. Special assignment this one. Couple of violent ones.'

The German stared at him in disgust.

'I wish to inspect inside.'

Branting shrugged.

'Be it on your head. They're locked in and you'll need your soldiers there to control them. As for me, well, my job is to drive this thing, not handle dangerous patients.'

Inside the ambulance, Sweeny had broken out in a cold sweat. There was only one thing for it. When the Germans came to open the doors he would have to come out shooting and hope that he managed to incapacitate all of them before they were able to recover from their surprise. He glanced at Woods, wishing the man knew more about firearms. With the two of them . . .

Hersleb started yelling. 'Help me! Help me . . .'

Sweeny swung round. The red-faced little man had managed to work his gag loose. The young doctor, Birkenes, swung round and threw the anaesthetist a punch which snapped his head back. Then he hurried to draw the gag back on, but it had been too late to smother the sounds.

Woods started to howl like a wolf. The others stared at him in shocked amazement for a moment.

In the driver's cab, Branting forced a grin and jerked his thumb back.

'See what I mean?' he said to the *unteroffizier*. 'Crazy as coots, dangerous loonies. I only get paid for driving them, not controlling them.'

The German had taken a quick step backwards at the howling. He frowned and handed Branting back his papers.

'Get moving,' he said. 'At least you wouldn't have any terrorists hiding among that lot.'

'Terrorists?' Branting chuckled, rolling his eyes. 'What an idea!'

Branting was still chuckling with genuine mirth as he put the ambulance in gear and began to move forward. He said nothing to Inge as he drove northwards, passing the outskirts of Oslo. It was not until they were well on their way along the Lillestrom road that he pulled over and slid open the connecting hatch which linked the driver's cab to the interior of the ambulance.

'What in hell happened back there?'

Sweeny's voice came through. 'The little fellow, Hersleb, started yelling for help. We couldn't get to him in time, so Woods started howling. We hoped it would fool the Germans.'

Branting grimaced.

'It was pretty effective. What's happened to Hersleb now?'

'He's having a little sleep,' grinned Sweeny viciously.

Branting nodded.

'We'll be passing through Lillestrom shortly. After that I shall go flat out for Klofta. It might be wise to dump the ambulance soon after, just in case the Germans do some checking after that last roadblock. They can be pretty thorough.'

'Let's get to Klofta first,' Sweeny advised.

The back of the vehicle was becoming unbearable. There were nine adults squeezed into an area which had been meant for two stretchers and two attendants at most. It was made more uncomfortable by the fact that Hersleb was still unconscious from the blow given him by Birkenes. It was Stenersen who suggested that they should try to bring the anaesthetist round. When they had done so, he leant close to the man and spoke to him quietly and firmly.

'You have worked with me for several years, Hersleb. You are an expert in your profession, which is why I have accepted you onto my team even though I disagree violently with your politics. I have never inflicted my political views on you. It is our fate to be thrown together in this rather unpleasant fashion. If it was left to me I would let you out here and now and have done with you. However, I must accept the view that once at liberty you would run off to your Nasjonal Samling friends and their Nazi comrades and get us captured. So here you are and here you will remain. Do you understand this, Hersleb? Please don't cause trouble, because I cannot be responsible for the consequences.'

The little anaesthetist scowled back, but his rage was tempered by fear as his eyes rested on the impassive face of Stenersen.

'You will never get away with this, Professor. Never.'

'That's our concern,' snapped Sweeny. 'Now sit back and take it easy. I haven't sworn any Hippocratic Oath, so I'll have no compunctions about shooting you if you endanger us again. Understand?'

The journey seemed to go on for hours and hours. The cramped ambulance became stifling and humid. Finally it stopped. Branting came back and opened the door.

'We'll stay here for a few moments; no one is to get out. I just thought you might like to have the door open for some fresh air for a few minutes before we press on.'

'Where are we?' asked Sweeny.

'North of Klofta,' replied Branting. 'Seriously, I think we should dump the ambulance as soon as possible.'

'Is it far to the border?'

'Too far to walk with all this lot. I have a contact near Arnes, which is not too far from here. He might be able to help with another type of vehicle.'

'Allright Branting, you're the transport chief.'

After a minute or two the ambulance moved off again along the hilly road.

Sweeny found himself gazing around at the strange group in the back of the ambulance, trying to weigh their characters. Professor Didrik Stenersen was as he had expected; an intelligent man of sixty with a thoughtful and compassionate face, now lined with anxiety. He was quiet and yet decisive. A man of few words but well chosen when they were wanted. He had a soft humour and an inner vitality. He was the sort of man Sweeny could trust.

Hersleb was the problem; a little, excitable, florid-faced man who was, apparently, a staunch supporter of Major Vidkun Quisling and his Norwegian fascists. He was a petulant, spoilt

[159]

child of a man, and he would have to be watched carefully until they were on friendly soil.

Stenersen's two surgical colleagues, Doctors Jan Birkenes and Arendt, were young men. Birkenes appeared quick-thinking and capable. He had certainly reacted swiftly and decisively when Hersleb began to shout. Both men appeared able to follow orders without wasting time on stupid questions.

The three nurses were different. The younger two – he had learnt that their names were Kristine and Hilde – appeared to have come along because everyone else had done so. They followed rather than made their own decisions. They were young and pretty, and obviously competent at their jobs or Stenersen would not have chosen them as theatre nurses. It was the chief nurse who attracted Sweeny, Trina Lanstrad, the one who had fallen in the cemetery. Her face was browned by the winter sun; its healthy tan spoke of the outdoors. Her eyes were wide-set and grey, her mouth full and red. Her hair was silver-blonde and well-groomed. He put her age around thirty, not much more. Her gaze was direct and capable and her whole attitude spoke of calm practicality, yet Sweeny found himself stirred by an unmistakable animal magnetism that she possessed. He suddenly realized that she was returning his stare, her eyes lightened by some inward humour.

It was a strange cargo that this ambulance carried. Sweeny grimaced. A damned strange cargo.

# CHAPTER NINETEEN

'Are you absolutely certain?' Sweeny was staring at the elderly man to whom Branting had introduced him. 'Is there no transport at all?'

They had arrived in a small hamlet set next to a broad river which Branting had identified as the Glomma. The area had been a centre where iron ore was stored before being shipped by barge northwards along the river to towns like Skarnes, Kongsvinger and Kirkenaer. The hamlet was no more than a collection of boathouses along the river banks with a few ancient dwellings and disused storehouses. Branting had parked the ambulance in one of the deserted warehouses on the river bank and taken Sweeny to an old cottage to introduce him to the old man who was one of his contacts in Paal Berg's infant resistance movement.

The old man shrugged.

'There are no vehicles left in the area. The Germans confiscated everything that can move.'

'But there must be *something*, surely?' pressed Sweeny.

'I can make some enquiries but I doubt it.'

Branting smiled encouragingly at the man. 'We'd appreciate it if you would. And the sooner the better.'

'I'll cycle over to Holtedahl's place,' the old man said.

In a few moments he was wobbling off on an ancient bicycle while Branting and Sweeny returned to the warehouse.

'This was a busy place a few years ago,' said Branting as he saw Sweeny's gaze take in the derelict quays and numerous warehouses along the stretch of river. There were several ancient, decaying barges tied up along the banks.

'There used to be some open cast mining here at the turn of the century, and the barges used to make regular trips. Then the seams ran out . . .' he sighed. 'Well, you know how it is.'

Sweeny nodded, his eyes moving over the rotting wood of the barges until they stopped on an old barge which was tied up against the wooden quay nearby. It was old, decaying, but unlike the others, it was still afloat in the waters of the broad river. The wood was not in good condition and the paint was peeling, but it was not in the advanced stages of decay that the other vessels were in. Sweeny pursed his lips thoughtfully.

'If the old man is right, Branting, and there is no motor transport here, how far upriver is there a decent pass into Sweden?'

Branting frowned, trying to follow Sweeny's line of thought. 'The river runs more or less parallel to the border,' he said reflectively. 'Then it moves eastwards a few kilometres. I suppose Kongsvinger is about the closest place on the river to the border, and then the river follows parallel to it again as far as Flisa. I don't think the river is navigable that far up. I believe there are too many waterfalls and cataracts along that stretch. What have you in mind? I don't believe you'll find any decent boats around here, not big enough to carry us upriver.'

Sweeny grinned slightly and Branting followed his gaze to the ancient barge.

'You are joking!' Branting protested.

'You've forgotten that I've spent most of my life around boats. If her timbers are sound and she isn't weighed down with river water, which I don't think she is by the way she sits there, she'll carry us.'

'By what power?'

'We might be able to work something out.'

'I think you are crazy. Even if that damned lump of wood can float you would have to move it upriver. The Glomma has a pretty strong current and you'll be going against it.'

'These old barges were making that trip before we were born, Branting,' Sweeny said. 'If they could do it then, they can do it now.'

He turned and walked over to the barge.

The telephone shrilled in Sturmbannführer Knesebeck's office. He reached for the instrument and grunted into the mouthpiece. He paused for a few moments, his eyes wide, and then he smiled, nodding slowly.

'Ah yes. Since one of your colleagues of the Nasjonal Samling pointed out that you were one of Professor Stenersen's staff I had presumed that you would be in contact with this office. Where are you and what is happening?'

He paused. The voice on the other end of the line was breathless and a little rapid.

Knesebeck's eyes widened a little further.

'To England? *Grüss Gott*! We must prevent this by all means. Exactly where are you? Hello? Hello?'

He stared at the telephone in disgust before replacing the silent receiver.

He drew a map towards him and peered at the area between Oslo and the Swedish border. The border crossings directly to the east were sealed tight. It was logical that the British agents who had Stenersen and his team were moving them north before trying to cross the border.

Knesebeck bit his lip. Now he had an ace up his sleeve. The British agents did not know that there was a Nasjonal Samling agent among them – one working for the Gestapo. He had not believed his luck when the Hird officer had indicated the name among Stenersen's surgical team. It was just a question of warning the Nasjonal Samling to immediately switch any call that came in from the agent to his office. It would not be long before the agent was able to contact him again and give him a precise location. It was merely a matter of waiting.

Sweeny gave a long sigh and shook his head. He had seen many types of vessel during his years at sea but this one was fairly unique. Branting had been right; the vessel was unseaworthy, if the term could be applied to its status on a river. In normal circumstances he would not attempt to float it to the far bank. Not only was the paint peeling from its timbers, but he could stick his finger into the wet decaying pulp of the deck planking. As for the engine . . . it was an old Kelvin two-cylinder, a lump of rusting metal which might have been the last word in marine engineering when the *Lusitania* went down, but that was a long, long, time ago. He had been a little over-optimistic. Nevertheless, it floated, and if the engine could be made to work, even for a little while, it might get them far enough upriver. He heard a noise on the ladder behind him.

Trina Lanstrad was leaning against it, smiling. She held a cup of coffee in her hand.

'I thought you might need this,' she said.

Sweeny wiped his oily hands on a rag and moved through the gloom of the narrow engine room to take the coffee.

The girl nodded towards the rusting metal of the engine

casing. 'Can you get it running?' she asked.

Sweeny grimaced.

'I can make it go,' he said without any false modesty. 'The trouble is that I don't know how far it will go.'

The girl gazed round the smelly little engine room. To her it looked as if a hurricane had hit it, with its tangle of strange-looking metal piping, odd machinery and thick layers of oil and grease. She turned to regard him quizzically.

'Are you a sailor?'

'I used to be,' Sweeny admitted with a shrug. Two weeks ago? Before the invasion? he asked himself. No, several lifetimes ago. Before Freya's death.

'And now?' She saw the momentary pain in his eyes.

'Now I am playing Sir Percy Blakeney.'

'Who?'

'A character in a novel who went round organizing the escape of people threatened by the guillotine during the French Revolution. He was known as the Scarlet Pimpernel.'

Trina Lanstrad chuckled.

'I suppose I see the parallel.'

Sweeny sipped his coffee. The girl had an infectious smile.

'Where are the others?' he asked.

'In the boathouse.'

'How's our friend Hersleb? Is he creating any trouble?'

Trina pouted.

'He is being very quiet. I don't think you should take him too seriously. He is a bore, very self-opinionated. But he's not dangerous.'

Sweeny shook his head in disagreement.

'I'll have to be the judge of that.'

The girl changed the subject as if Hersleb did not really interest her.

'The Professor said that we are going to London to perform an operation on some important person. Do you know who it is?'

Sweeny shook his head. 'All I know is that I must deliver Stenersen and his team to London as soon as possible.'

'It sounds very mysterious and intriguing,' the girl replied, disappointment in her voice.

Sweeny finished his coffee. He glanced at his watch. It was close to midnight now, too late to move before dawn.

'Are we really going to take this old barge?'

Sweeny nodded. 'We really are. Besides, it'll be the best

method of moving, with the roads crawling with Nazis.'

He turned for a second, standing very close to the girl, sharply aware of her scent, of her warm seductiveness. He frowned, trying hard to ignore the curious animal magnetism which he had felt in the ambulance. She regarded him for a moment with wide captivating eyes, her lips parted in a secret smile as if she was aware of the attraction which he felt for her. Then she turned and climbed up the ladder to the deck.

Sweeny was walking with her back to the warehouse when Branting and the old man loomed out of the darkness.

'I have made some enquiries among those who can be trusted,' the old man said. 'There are simply no motor vehicles available.'

Sweeny shrugged. He had been expecting as much.

'In that case, who owns this barge?'

The old man looked bemused.

'The old *Glomma IV*? Why, no one has moved her since she retired from the river run about eighteen months ago. She's just been sitting there rotting away. The yard owner, who lives in Oslo, was waiting to sell up all the yards and equipment. Why do you ask?'

'If we borrow the barge will anyone get into trouble?'

The old man stared at him in the darkness.

'The owner is in Oslo and these are very uncertain times.' There was a veiled amusement in his voice.

Branting said, 'We shall leave the ambulance here. It would be best if it were disguised and moved as soon as possible.'

'We will see to it.'

Sweeny turned and stepped into the warehouse. Everyone was lying or sitting around a fire where Inge was cooking some food. He glanced round and then frowned.

'Where's Hersleb?' he snapped.

Woods started guiltily.

'I untied him a few moments ago so that he could go to the toilet . . .'

'A little man?' enquired the old man at Sweeny's shoulder. 'I thought he was of your party. I saw him slipping up to my house a moment ago.'

'Damn it!' swore Sweeny, turning, pushing by them and running to the house. He saw Hersleb walking around the side of the building and grabbed him. Woods and Branting were hard on his heels.

'What the hell . . .?' screamed the little anaesthetist.

[165]

'What are you playing at?' demanded Sweeny.

'I came up here to use the old man's lavatory,' Hersleb replied indignantly.

'I have a telephone in the house,' explained the old man, catching them up.

'I used the lavatory,' insisted Hersleb. 'I didn't see the telephone. I wish I had. I wish I . . .'

'Shut up!' Sweeny cuffed him across the mouth.

The excitable little man stared at Sweeny, his face a comic mask of fear.

'It's my fault,' muttered Woods. 'I thought we were so far out in the wilds here that he would not try to get away. I hadn't thought about a telephone.'

Sweeny's eyes blazed in the darkness.

'Yes, it is your damned fault, Woods. Take the little bastard and don't let him out of your sight again.'

Branting laid a restraining hand on Sweeny's arm.

'It was a mistake any one of us could have made.'

'We can't afford to make mistakes,' growled Sweeny. 'I want everyone aboard the barge. I'm going to start working on the engine now and hope to have it ready by first light.'

It was well after dawn when they were woken by the protesting roar of the ancient engine. Branting came from the wheelhouse where he had been drowsing and peered down into the engine room to where Sweeny had been working most of the night with the aid of an electric torch.

'How is it?'

Sweeny grinned up at Branting, tired but with an air of excitement about him.

'She's a little erratic but she might do us. Get ready to cast off for'ard and aft.'

Branting nodded. Woods came out of the for'ard cabin, blinking in the early light. The noise of the engine was rousing everyone.

'What is it?'

Sweeny emerged from the engine room.

'Get back to the cabin and keep an eye on everyone, Woods,' he said sourly. 'Especially Hersleb. I don't want to be forced to shoot him.'

Woods stared at Sweeny, momentarily angry, and then shrugged and turned back.

The wheelhouse was situated at the stern of the long barge,

[166]

just in front of the engine room. Sweeny moved into it and tested the instruments. Branting had already heaved off the stern line and now went forward. Sweeny waved his hand and swung hard at the wheel as Branting cast off for'ard. The erratic stroke of the ageing engine caused the barge to vibrate. The rusty pistons ground slowly up and down. The water began to churn in a thick creamy foam at the stern. The bow swung, agonizingly slowly, but it moved nevertheless toward midstream. Incredibly, the barge made headway upriver against the current.

Branting came back smiling.

'Well, you did it,' he said.

Sweeny shook his head.

'We're moving, but that's about all. There's only one drum of fuel down there and the engine could seize up at any time. In fact, I'd say the odds are totally against us.'

# CHAPTER TWENTY

The *Glomma IV*, in spite of her age and antiquated Kelvin engine, made fairly good headway upriver. Sweeny's initial nervousness began to ebb and he started to feel a new confidence as they passed the River Ulleren on their left, feeding into the Glomma, and came to Skarnes. There the river curved and moved in a slightly south-easterly direction towards Kongsvinger and the Swedish border. Branting took the wheel for a few hours while Sweeny dozed but, after a catnap, he insisted on taking the wheel again. It was good to be back at the wheel of a boat, even a river boat like the ancient barge. He found himself relaxing with his hands on the wheel and that relaxation meant more to him than eight hours of sleep. He told Branting to get below and see if someone could rustle up some coffee.

Trina Lanstrad came to the wheelhouse fifteen minutes later with coffee and some *flatbrod* and cheese.

'We've made ourselves quite comfortable down in the cabins,' she said cheerfully. 'Doctor Birkenes has managed to get the cooker in the galley alight and boil some water, and the Englishman – Doctor Woods? Yes? Well, he has found an old radio. It works by turning a hand-cranked dynamo. He's managed to get it going.'

'Did he pick up anything on it?'

'Only some official newscasts from Oslo put out by the Germans. They are boasting that they have driven the Allies out of central Norway. They say the British Royal Navy have evacuated all the Allied troops from Andalsnes.'

'Do you think it is true?' Sweeny asked.

The nurse shrugged.

'The newscast said that King Haakon and Crown Prince Olav have fled on a British warship and the Germans have appealed to all Norwegian forces to lay down their arms and surrender because the British have betrayed them.'

Sweeny grimaced and sipped his coffee. As he stood with one

hand on the wheel, eyes carefully examining the banks on either side as he kept the ancient vessel in midstream, he was aware of her grey eyes appraising him.

'Why are you doing this?' she suddenly asked.

He frowned.

'To get you and Stenersen and the others to London . . .'

'No,' she interrupted. 'I mean, you weren't in the army or in the Royal Norwegian Navy. You were a civilian . . .'

'War changes people,' Sweeny said shortly. He hesitated. 'Where do you come from? Oslo?'

She shook her head.

'No. Romedal, a sleepy little place near Hamar, just to the north of here. I went to Oslo as soon as I left school and began my nurse's training at the Riks-Hospitalet. I specialized as a theatre nurse. I've been with Professor Stenersen for three years now.'

'A life dedicated to nursing?'

Trina chuckled softly.

'Not exactly. I was married to an officer in the merchant marine. We were three years together and then his ship went down in mid-Atlantic. No survivors.'

'I'm sorry.'

'Don't be. It happened a long time ago and . . .' She shrugged and added, 'There has been another man since then.'

'Oh?'

'Yes,' the girl grimaced. 'All very improper. Does that shock you?'

Sweeny shook his head.

'You don't have to tell me.'

'Why not?' Trina sighed. 'I'm not ashamed of it. He was married, that's all, and had a position . . . well, I wasn't asking for much.'

Sweeny glanced at her, trying to read her expression.

'It's ended?'

She gave a short laugh. She sounded bitter.

'The war has put a new perspective on things. It ages you.'

'You can't be more than thirty.'

'Thirty-two. I suppose you are married?'

She saw the muscles around Sweeny's jaw tighten a little.

'No. Not married.'

'I'm sorry. Maybe I shouldn't be so inquisitive.' The girl began to turn away from the wheelhouse but Sweeny held out a

[169]

hand, restraining her without actually touching her. He suddenly felt an urge to tell her, to tell someone. She made a solemn and sympathetic audience, listening in silence while he told her of his childhood in Boston, the death of his parents and his decision to move to Norway. He told her how Uncle Tenvig had accepted him into the family and how he had developed a passion for Freya, his cousin, which had not been returned. And then he told her how Freya and her husband had been killed during the invasion. He did not go into details. It was sufficient to tell her that Freya had been killed.

'It was . . . is . . . a bad time for Norwegians,' she said softly. 'Let us hope that all this, this nonsense, will soon be ended.'

She reached out and laid a cool hand on his as he held the wheel.

Branting came bursting into the wheelhouse with his face flushed.

'We've managed to pick up Radio Free Norway,' he said. 'They've confirmed what the Germans have said. The Allies have evacuated the entire central area of Norway. The last ships pulled out of Andalsnes this morning. The King and Crown Prince went as well. But the newscast says that the King is remaining on Norwegian soil and that new Allied lines have been set up in the north.'

Sweeny bit his lip. 'It is lucky we weren't planning to head for Andalsnes,' he said sourly. Then he put his head to one side. Above the chugging of the barge's engine he heard another sound – the high-pitched whine of an aero engine.

Branting moved forward and squinted through the wheelhouse for'ard windows. A speck was moving towards them, following the course of the river.

'Messerschmidt 109,' yelled Branting. 'Coming directly for us.'

The German fighter aircraft swooped across them almost at tree-top height, causing them to duck instinctively.

'It's turning,' gasped Branting, following the line of its flight. 'Surely it can't be looking for this barge?'

'It shouldn't be,' Sweeny grunted. 'Let's hope it isn't some trigger-happy young idiot who wants to start shooting things up. Quick, Branting, get out on the for'ard deck and start waving to it like mad. Look friendly.'

'I'll go,' Trina volunteered, pushing by Branting. 'They are less likely to fire when they see a young woman.'

Before the two men could protest, she had left the wheelhouse and run forward, tearing off her jumper. She took a pose on top of the for'ard hatch as if sunbathing.

As the German fighter came sweeping back, still very low, she began to wave fiercely with her jumper. The fighter buzzed over, began to climb and disappeared over the hills. It did not come back.

Sweeny relaxed at the wheel.

'Just curious, I suppose,' he muttered.

Branting inclined his head. 'Let's hope so.'

The girl returned to the wheelhouse, smiling.

'He's gone,' she said. 'I think he was just sight-seeing.'

'We'd better be prepared,' returned Sweeny. 'How much of this river do you know, Branting?'

'The Glomma? I've sailed her a few times from Skarnes.'

'You said Kongsvinger is the nearest point to the Swedish border?'

'From Kongsvinger northwards the river runs fairly parallel, but it is still quite a hike to the border and that's across the mountains.'

'How big is Kongsvinger?'

'It's a fair-sized town. I am under the impression there are quite a few German troops there. I heard that there has been a lot of hard fighting in the area. The Germans had to take it because of the fortifications there as well as the rail link to Sweden. I think the Germans have put a strong garrison in the castle there which overlooks the river.'

'Is it best to leave the river before Kongsvinger to trek to the border?'

Branting shook his head emphatically.

'No. We ought to stay on the river until we are north of Kongsvinger. Maybe up as far as Nor or Grinder, where we can leave the barge and push east over the hills.'

'And what of our chances of getting through Kongsvinger without being intercepted?'

'That's an unknown quantity.'

Sweeny hesitated for a moment.

'Well, we'll just have to try it,' he said finally.

Hauptman Eschig had finally found time to finish his letter to his wife, Liselotte. Her last letter to him had been full of inconsequential news and her worries about their eldest son, Joachim. He was only eighteen and apparently had a girl friend, Annaliese, which worried Eschig's wife. Reading between the lines, Eschig discerned that Liselotte was more concerned by the boy's acceptance into the Luftwaffe. His papers had come through and he had been posted to No. 11 Flying Training Regiment at Schönwalde, near Berlin. Eschig made a note to write the boy a long letter of encouragement. He must also drop a note to his younger son, Heine, who had been promoted to command of a *Fahnlein* or troop of the *Hitler Jugend Streifendienst*, the boys' police section of the Hitler Youth. Heine, observed Eschig's wife, was following his father's example. He would make an excellent policeman.

Eschig folded his letter and put it to one side as the telephone buzzed.

'This is Knesebeck here, Eschig.'

Eschig sighed.

'How can I be of help to you, Herr Sturmbannführer?'

'I have been told by General von Falkenhorst's headquarters that you have requested to be placed in charge of the matter of Stenersen's disappearance from the Riks-Hospitalet. You know that this is a matter directly concerning the Gestapo, and therefore I must ask you why you have taken this course of action.'

Eschig suppressed a further sigh.

'The matter involves a case on which we were already working.'

'May I remind you, Herr Hauptmann, that I am responsible for the removal of Stenersen and his staff to Berlin?'

'I certainly do not propose to interfere in that matter, Herr Sturmbannführer,' smiled Eschig. 'Naturally, when the Abwehr have picked up Stenersen and his colleagues we shall hand them over to you. We are more concerned with those who have . . . abducted, shall we say? . . . the professsor and his staff.'

'Oh? When we capture these people we shall simply shoot them,' snapped Knesebeck.

'I hope not. We need them for interrogation, especially their leader, who is a man named Lars Sweeny, or so we believe. I have Herr General von Falkenhorst's authority to pursue this matter.'

There was a brief silence from Knesebeck's end of the line.

'I shall expect your office to keep me informed.'

'Naturally.' Eschig put the telephone down and swore softly. Knesebeck could take a running jump at himself. He could have Stenersen and his team, but otherwise this affair was between

Eschig and Sweeny. Eschig felt almost as if he knew Sweeny. He felt oddly protective towards him. He was going to meet the tall, red-haired man soon, he had little doubt. So far he could only move his pieces on this chess board in answer to the way Sweeny had moved his. Soon, however – soon Sweeny was bound to make a mistake, a tiny slip. Eschig would be waiting. It would not be long now.

Sweeny stood at the wheel of the old barge, his eyes moving ceaselessly along the banks of the river as they moved towards Kongsvinger. Sweeny knew little about the city except that it had initially been a fortress during the border war with Sweden in the mid-17th century and that the castle had been raised as a permanent garrison some time afterwards. After the Swedish invasion during the Napoleonic period, the city had begun to grow quickly and its future as a regional centre had been assured with the coming of the railway from Lillestrom in 1862. By 1865 the railway line had been completed all the way into Sweden. Branting had told him that the city lay on the north side of the river, although the railway had been laid on the south side and some suburbs had sprung up there. With the arrival of electricity in 1901 the city had prospered, and a new military fortress had been raised in 1926 to house the permanent garrison.

As the barge slowly fought its way upstream against the current, Sweeny caught sight of the railway tracks along the southern bank. Ahead of the barge, the city came into sight; isolated buildings at first and then a few tall ones in the distance, dominated by a castle on a hill. Branting came up from below where he had been warning everyone to keep under cover while they made their way through the centre of Kongsvinger.

'All set?' Branting muttered.

Sweeny would not admit to himself that his forearms ached. It had been a while now since he had held a ship's wheel in his hands and he tried to relax, but he felt the tension increase as they drew nearer to the town. His knuckles whitened on the wheel and his muscles bunched as if they were receiving orders from someone else.

'Kongsvinger Bridge coming up, Sweeny,' Branting said. 'The town centre and quays are just beyond it.'

Sweeny's lips were a thin grim line and his mouth was dry.

The Kongsvinger Bridge was the only one which spanned the Glomma, connecting the town proper on the north bank to the suburbs on the southern side. If they were to be stopped by the Germans it would probably be here.

'Stand by,' he whispered, realizing that there was an odd metallic taste in his mouth. He felt dry from tension.

He kept the old barge well out in mid-river. He was aware that there were people on the shore, some of whom were examining the old vessel curiously as it chugged by. Sweeny prayed that the ageing Kelvin engine would not act up, that the erratic drop-fed lubrication system would not choose this moment to choke up.

As they chugged under the span of the bridge Sweeny could see the city park to their larboard side. Beyond the park and the houses was a hill from which the frowning walls of a castle dominated the area. Sweeny felt a chill as he imagined the field guns at the enplacements which might be trained on them. To the starboard side, the railway line ran beyond the imposing edifice of a large building, which Branting identified as the Grand Hotel, and into the railway station.

'Jornbanestasjon,' murmured Branting.

They could see a train stopped there, spilling out streams of grey-coated figures.

'Jesus!' whispered Sweeny. 'Looks like the entire German army are arriving.'

Some of the grey-coated figures were pointing at the barge and several began to wave. But it was not a menacing gesture.

'Friendly bastards, aren't they?' Branting grinned as he waved back.

'Let's hope that they are not overly friendly and request us to stop and visit with them,' replied Sweeny dryly.

The river was beginning to sweep round in a sharp curve towards the north now, turning around a sort of headland and broadening considerably. The current was stronger here and Sweeny had to increase the power – but not too much because the Kelvin started to make belligerent noises.

'If we get beyond the reach of the town it should be a clear run up beyond Glamstad,' Branting grunted in satisfaction.

Sweeny was just beginning to relax when a low grey hull suddenly shot out of a small rivulet a few hundred yards ahead. It was a speedboat which turned its razor-sharp bow towards them. On its for'ard casing was mounted a heavy Spandau machine-gun with two men in naval uniforms and steel helmets crouching behind it. There were uniformed figures in the wheelhouse and two sailors at the rear carrying Schmeisser machine-pistols. From the stern a red, white and black Swastika fluttered. The frothing bow wave indicated the speed of the vessel.

Sweeny ceased to feel tense. He moved coldly and deliberately. 'No half measures, Branting,' he muttered. 'We can't survive an inspection. It's us or them. Let Woods know!'

Branting moved with studied casualness out of the wheelhouse and went to the hatchway which led down into the crew's cabins.

'German patrol boat coming at us,' he called softly to Woods. 'Either they go under or we do. Right?'

He turned back without waiting to hear Woods's reaction.

Three metres away the *motorbarkasse* had slowed, the roar of its heavy diesel engine muted to a soft purring. It began to ease alongside. The gunner behind the vicious-looking Spandau on the foredeck was professional. The muzzle of his machine gun made a lateral sweep extending fore and aft of the barge. Sweeny could see that the two sailors at the rear held their Schmeissers at the ready. They were expecting trouble. There were three men in the wheelhouse. A rating at the wheel, a petty officer and a lieutenant. They were all regular German navy. Seven men in all. Sweeny eased back the throttle.

The officer, a young, fair-haired youth, came out of the wheel-house.

'Stop your vessel at once. I wish to come aboard.'

His Norwegian was perfect and idiomatic.

Sweeny glanced at Branting. 'Stand by!' he hissed.

The diesel engine of the *motorbarkasse* increased in volume as the helmsman eased the wheel to bring the patrol vessel rubbing alongside the old barge. The two sailors jumped from the stern of their ship and went forward, taking up positions with levelled machine pistols. Sweeny found he had time to admire their professionalism and precision.

'Spandau first, Schmeissers next,' Sweeny said, knowing that against the automatics they did not stand a chance.

The young lieutenant was beginning his leap for the deck of the barge.

'Now!' yelled Sweeny. He brought his Webley up through the open wheelhouse and fired. His first bullet smashed into the head of the gunner. It was a lucky shot and sent the man spinning from his position behind the machine-gun. He cannoned into his companion, who was waiting to feed the ammunition belt. The man recovered in an instant and dived towards the handgrips.

Branting's shot caught the man in the chest.

The young lieutenant, halfway between the two vessels, was doomed. Sweeny wheeled round and fired twice more. The shots dropped him into the water in the gap separating the two vessels. If there had been any chance of him surviving the bullets, a sudden surge of water, which brought the *motorbarkasse* smashing into the side of the barge, finished him.

Even then, those on the barge did not really stand much of a chance. One of the men with the Schmeisser machine pistols had opened up, sending a stream of bullets into the wheelhouse and causing both Sweeny and Branting to hit the deck as glass smashed and wood splintered above them.

Then one of the sailors seemed to throw up his machine pistol into the air and pivot, arms above his head, before falling to the deck. There was a moment in which the man's companion stood bewildered. Even as he turned to bring his gun back into action, Sweeny was up and fired again, sending the man crashing to the deck. Beyond him, Woods emerged from the for'ard hatch, his face curiously white, his Webley in his hand.

Sweeny was scrambling out of the wheelhouse now, hearing the increasing roar of the *motorbarkasse* diesels.

'Don't let the bastards get away!' he cried, fumbling in his pocket. He brought out the second of the two grenades which Branting had given him. The German vessel was drawing away now, the petty officer shouting instructions at the rating, who was hunched over his wheel. Sweeny ran down the length of the deck to where the German sailors lay and threw the grenade in an arc towards the *motorbarkasse*. Even before it reached the apex, Sweeny had grabbed one of the dead sailors' Schmeisser machine-pistols and was sending a spray of bullets towards the stern of the craft. There was a brief moment and then the patrol vessel erupted in a roar of flames and smoke and flying debris. It sounded like a tremendous thunderclap whose echoes reverberated over the river.

Sweeny was knocked back by the blast from the explosion but recovered swiftly. The German vessel was sinking very fast, what little was left to sink. The grenade had simply torn her apart like matchwood. Her timbers and plywood hull, tinder dry and resinous, burnt immediately. There came a second explosion from the fuel tanks and then only a whirlpool of creamy, yellow foam, with oil bubbling in it, marked the spot where the *motorbarkasse* had been.

He turned around slowly. Branting was already heaving the bodies of the two German sailors over the side. Woods had come up on deck, still white-faced and trembling slightly.

'Welcome to the club,' said Sweeny grimly, with a smile that seemed strangely fixed. 'You have learnt just in time how to fire a gun with accuracy.'

From the direction of the fortress on the hill they could hear the whine of an alarm, sounding like a ship's klaxon.

Sweeny began to move for the wheelhouse.

'Let's get out of here,' he yelled.

'Where?' demanded Branting. 'We're done if we stick to the river now. They must have another patrol boat, or they can send a fighter plane to shoot us up.'

'Who's sticking to the river?' demanded Sweeny, swinging the wheel and opening up the throttles of the old Kelvin again.

'Where can we go?' Woods asked, joining them.

'Around the next bend. As soon as we're out of sight of the castle, I intend to beach her. It will be dark in less than an hour and we can take to the hills. There's still a good chance we can elude the Germans and get through those mountains to Sweden. I'm not giving up now.'

# CHAPTER TWENTY-ONE

They sheltered in a thicket, watching the German scout plane as it circled overhead, swooping close to the old barge which had dug her bow into the soft mud of the embankment about fifty feet below them. They had abandoned the vessel and scrambled up the banks toward the lower slopes of the hills, which were covered in thick forest. The pine woodland, interspersed with birches, alders and elms, carpeted the hills and valleys for miles in every direction from Kongsvinger, which was one of the centres of Norwegian forestry. They kept low as the aircraft moved aimlessly around obviously searching for them.

Sweeny and Branting now carried the Schmeisser machine-pistols which they had recovered from the dead sailors. Woods, more confident now of his ability to use his Webley, was covering Hersleb.

'We'd better start moving, because they'll soon have troops here,' Branting advised as Sweeny stared up at the aircraft.

'You know this area, Branting,' Sweeny nodded. 'What route do you suggest?'

Branting thought a moment before replying. 'It's best to head due east over the hills, but night will fall in an hour or so and it wouldn't be wise to be out on the hills in these clothes. We'll suffer exposure.'

'Is there an alternative?'

Branting made an affirmative gesture.

'I remember a small village, maybe five miles away. There's an hotel there. It'll probably be shut now, but it was a tourist centre for winter sports, climbing, ski-ing and mountain trekking. When I was there about a year ago they kept supplies of equipment for their guests. If we could equip ourselves there, we could head up into the high mountains and be across the border within twenty-four hours.'

'All right,' Sweeny nodded. 'It seems like the only game in town. We'll try it.'

Feldwebel Weiss stood respectfully silent while Hauptmann Eschig took the telephone call from the officer in charge of the *Geheime Feld Polizei* in Kongsvinger. Weiss watched his superior's face pale and his mouth tighten.

'Are you telling me that seven men and a patrol vessel were simply wiped out, almost under the guns of the fortress of Kongsvinger?' Eschig said slowly.

Weiss frowned, trying to understand the message by reading Eschig's features.

'I see. I see.' Eschig was nodding. 'They ran the barge aground exactly where? How about your search aircraft? What direction? Glambergel . . . what's that? Ah, through the mountain passes.' He listened for a few moments, then nodded again, vigorously. '*Das is sehr gut!* The *Wurttembergische Gebirgsbataillon*? First rate mountain troops. Good. Yes, I'll be coming up to direct operations personally.'

Eschig replaced the receiver, picked it up again and jangled the rest impatiently.

'Put me through to the field commander of the Kongsvinger area,' he demanded. Then, with a hand over the receiver, he glanced up at the impassive Weiss. 'Sweeny is quite a man. He's just written off a *motorbarkasse* and seven men at Kongsvinger and still managed to get his party away into the mountains. Get me a large-scale map of the Glambergel region, just east of Kongsvinger.'

Weiss turned to a file, found the map and spread it in front of Eschig, who drummed his fingers as he waited for his call to go through.

A moment later the Abwehr captain straightened in his seat.

'Good evening, Herr Generalmajor. Yes, I have been informed. Herr General von Falkenhorst has placed me in charge of the matter. I understand that you have several companies of the *Wurttembergische Gebirgsbataillon* in your command area. May I suggest, Herr Generalmajor, that you send two companies of these troops into the mountains to head off these people before they get to the Swedish frontier? The Wurttembergers are the best equipped mountain troops we have and they should be able to cut them off without difficulty.'

Eschig listened to the brief reply with his head to one side.

'I appreciate this, Herr Generalmajor. How soon can they leave? Within half an hour? That is good. I shall be flying up to Kongsvinger in the morning. Thank you, Herr Generalmajor.'

It was dark by the time Sweeny's party reached the outskirts of the village. It had taken them nearly three hours of hard walking and some climbing to reach the valley in which the picture-postcard buildings stood, half sheltered by the forest and surrounding a small lakelet. Dominating the buildings was a large wooden construction looking like an overgrown Swiss chalet. It had a wooden veranda on its lower floor and balconies running all round the building on the first and second floor level.

'That's it,' Branting sighed. 'The Hotel Vinger.'

They halted on the edge of the pine forest while Sweeny examined the terrain.

'There doesn't seem to be anyone about,' he mused. 'Everything is in darkness.'

'Who would come for a holiday in the mountains now?' Branting asked. 'The hotel was probably shut up as soon as the news of the invasion came.'

Sweeny and Branting went forward, leaving the others waiting silently among the trees. They scrambled onto the veranda and walked carefully round, peering into the windows, most of which were shuttered so that the interior was inaccessible to prying eyes. Sweeny found a side window which yielded to a few expert twists of his knife.

'I'll go and open the main doors, Branting. You bring the others up.'

He slipped over the sill and found himself in the gloom of the grand foyer. The atmosphere was still and slightly musty. He made his way to the main doors and withdrew the bolts. Branting had brought everyone up and they stumbled in, exhausted and cold, as soon as he opened the doors.

'Well,' said Woods, smiling round in the gloom, 'it looks as if we have this place to ourselves. Who's for a drink?'

He turned to the deserted bar just as a voice snapped: 'Who are you?'

They froze. Sweeny recovered first, turning slowly in the direction of the voice and cursing himself for not spotting the obvious. The main doors had been bolted from the inside and no lock had been turned from the outside. Any simpleton should have realized that whoever had closed the doors would still be within the hotel.

On the far side of the foyer a door had been thrown open and an elderly man stood there. He was clad in an old-fashioned dressing gown and he carried a stick. Just behind him an old woman was peering in consternation over his shoulder.

'The hotel is closed,' said the man slowly, the nervousness in his voice becoming obvious. 'How did you get in? What do you want?'

It was Inge who broke the tension by stepping forward, hands outstretched as if pleading.

'My friends, I believe I am speaking to loyal Norwegians. We badly need your help. We are in trouble with the Germans for we, too, are loyal Norwegians.'

The old man's face was stony in the semi-gloom. He made no reply.

'We need to rest for the night. We need food and something warm to drink. And we need clothes and skis in order to cross the mountains.'

'Anna, get a light,' said the old man slowly, not moving, the stick still in his hand. They could have easily overpowered him but Sweeny decided it was best to do things by persuasion rather than force. The old woman disappeared behind the bar and emerged a moment later with an old kerosene lamp which she lit, spreading a warm glow through the foyer.

'I am the janitor here,' the old man said grimly, as he examined each of them in the light. 'It is my job to protect this hotel and its possessions until the owner returns.' He thrust out his chin defiantly. 'You are all strangers here. We do not know you.'

Arne Branting took a step forwards.

'I have stayed at this hotel many times while I have skied and climbed in these mountains, my friend. Strangers? No, we are Norwegians. If it is strangers that you want to see then you will soon see Germans. They will be coming here soon to take this hotel, and they will not leave when you ask them to.'

The old man frowned. 'I have a duty to the owner,' he said stubbornly.

Inge reached out a hand to him.

'But if you are a loyal subject of our King then you must help us.'

The old man pulled himself up, looking at her indignantly.

'I'm as loyal a subject as any,' he retorted. 'But I know my duty.'

'There is no duty greater than the protection of His Majesty's subjects against the invaders,' replied Inge.

The old man's shoulders suddenly slumped in resignation.

'What can I do against so many?' he mumbled, half to himself.

[181]

It seemed that he had somehow given his permission, for his wife moved forward, smiling nervously.

'Come,' she said, her glance encompassing them all. 'I will show you to rooms where you may rest. There is food if someone assists me.'

Inge took her arm and smiled warmly.

'You are very kind.'

The old woman shrugged and gestured towards her husband, who was standing with bowed head.

'Take no notice of Ottar. It is hard for him to adjust to these troubled times. But we must all do what we can to save our country, is this not so?'

While the old woman led the others up to the rooms, with Woods making sure that Hersleb was locked in a small room by himself, Sweeny and Branting prevailed on the old man, Ottar, to show them to the hotel's storerooms in the basement. They were a veritable Aladdin's Cave of clothing and sports equipment which the hotel maintained for the use of its guests. There was all manner of warm clothing and ski-ing equipment. There was even a pair of field-glasses. Branting, who had some expertise here, was set to the task of sorting out suitable materials for the morning's trek.

After supper, Sweeny gathered Inge, Woods and Branting together and spread a map of the district, taken from the hotel stocks, on the table before them.

'It's up to you, Branting, to suggest a route,' he said.

Branting grimaced. 'We could be in Sweden on Sunday if we follow these passes through the *fjells*. That way we could avoid any German search.'

Sweeny bent forward, frowning over the map as Branting traced a line on it with his finger.

'That's fairly high up,' he observed. 'Surely it would mean retracing our steps almost back to the river and coming up through this valley near the main road? The Germans would certainly have patrols in this area.'

Branting shook his head.

'There is an alternative route which I've climbed on two occasions. Up this *kliev*.'

Woods pursed his lips.

'Climb a rock face?'

'Yes,' Branting acknowledged. 'But it would put twenty-four hours onto the journey if we went down through the valleys.'

'But there are eleven of us, including a reluctant man, and what about Trina Lanstrad's ankle? Didn't she sprain it in the cemetery?' Inge asked.

'I checked her ankle,' Woods intervened. 'It's perfectly OK now. She must have wrenched it on a root or something but she didn't sprain it.'

'There we are then,' Branting smiled. 'Most of us have done some climbing and ski-ing before. I've asked the others. The *kliev* will bring us to a path on the mountain which leads onto a small plateau. We cross that and then its fairly straightforward until we come to the glacier . . .'

'The glacier?' queried Sweeny.

'The Svabensverk glacier. We cut across it and we are in Sweden. It's not difficult.'

'We'll take your word for it,' Sweeny said without humour. 'Just where do we find this *kliev*?'

'Not far from here. We head out along the road at the back of the hotel. About a mile out the path divides . . . the right-hand one goes off into the valley. That's where we can pretend to the old couple that we are going in case the Germans arrive and question them. However, we'll actually take the left-hand path up to the *kliev*. If we start at first light it shouldn't be a difficult climb.'

Woods sighed.

'And we'll soon be in Sweden and then . . . then England, home and beauty. Do you know that tomorrow is Saturday? We shall have been in Norway for a week. It seems like years since I tumbled out of that damned aircraft. Odin's Moon. Remember? The luck of the Vikings. Let's hope it continues to be with us.'

# CHAPTER TWENTY-TWO

Hauptmann Eschig grabbed the telephone as it shrilled on his desk. He had only just entered his office.

'Hauptmann Eschig? *Feld Polizei* commander at Kongsvinger here. The Herr Generalmajor's compliments. He thought that you might like to know that a Sturmbannführer of the Gestapo arrived from Oslo first thing this morning with instructions from the Reichskommissar to take charge of the Stenersen fugitives.'

Eschig swore loudly, cursing Knesebeck.

'Herr Hauptmann?' came the worried voice from Kongsvinger.

'Would you remind the Herr Generalmajor that my orders come directly from Herr General von Falkenhorst who is in supreme command in Norway?'

'The Herr Generalmajor is aware of that but finds himself in difficulty because he has also received a direct order from the Reichskommissar. The Gestapo are claiming jurisdiction over this matter.'

Eschig stared angrily at the receiver for a moment and then placed his hand across the mouthpiece and yelled for Feldwebel Weiss. The sergeant opened the door a moment later.

'Get through to Fornebu airfield,' snapped Eschig. 'I want an aircraft to take me to Kongsvinger immediately. At once! Do you hear?'

'*Zum Befehl, Herr Hauptmann!*'

Weiss hesitated on the threshold.

'Does the Herr Hauptmann wish me to come with him?'

Eschig replied savagely, 'Yes, the Herr Hauptmann does!'

'*Jawohl!*' acknowledged Weiss stoically, his face still impassive.

Eschig became aware of noises from the other end of the receiver.

'Yes? Sorry, I couldn't hear you for the moment. Tell me, have the mountain troops been sent in pursuit yet?'

'No, Herr Hauptmann. It was too dark to send them out last night. However, we have a Storch spotting the area. As soon as we see any sign of the fugitives we have two companies of *Gebirgsjäger* standing by. We should be able to drop these near enough to pick them up without problems.'

'Very well. I shall be in Kongsvinger as soon as I can.'

He slammed down the telephone and strode to the door. Weiss was already waiting for him.

'There is an aircraft ready at Fornebu, Herr Hauptmann.'

'Then the sooner we get there the better,' Eschig said between clenched teeth. 'I don't know what Knesebeck is playing at, but the Gestapo are not going to get their hands on Sweeny. He's mine.'

Arne Branting led the ascent. Under his instructions they had roped themselves into three teams. Branting led the first one, followed by Doctor Birkenes, Inge and Professor Stenersen. The second team was to be led by Sweeny, with the recalcitrant Hersleb next, followed by the nurse Hilde and then by Trina Lanstrad. The third and last team was led by Woods, with the nurse Kristine next and Doctor Arendt bringing up the rear.

As Branting scrambled up the rock face, Sweeny reflected that he appeared to be a man utterly at one with his surroundings. With slow methodical movements he moved upwards, feeling carefully each hold and surface before he eased forward, using his axe to make indentations bigger. He seemed catlike on the shelving rockface. When he was twenty feet up, Birkenes began climbing, then Inge and finally Stenersen. It had been arranged that the first team should pass the halfway mark up the rockface before Sweeny led the second team up. The face rose a sheer six hundred feet and the wait seemed endless before Sweeny judged that the halfway stage had been reached.

It was a long while since he had done any real climbing, so Sweeny moved cautiously. As Branting had warned him, the first seventy feet were tough going. In fact Sweeny thought several times that he would have to stop and turn back, although Branting had assured him that after the initial stage the climb was fairly easy. He continued, but it was nightmarish. One thing he was thankful for was the fact that there was no wind to clutch with icy fingers at his precarious holds. He paused now and then to peer down. Below him was the gasping face of Hersleb, who had remained morose and monosyllabic ever since the incident at the warehouse. He obeyed when ordered but had withdrawn into himself. The little man was moaning with exertion. Sweeny

[185]

wished he would shut up.

Sweeny paused to rest his aching, exhausted limbs and leant out a little to see if he could catch a glimpse of the two nurses, Hilde and Trina. They seemed to be making good progress. He spared a moment to think about Trina Lanstrad. She was so calm and capable. Without pretensions. He wondered why he felt such an almost violent attraction towards her. Then he felt guilty when he thought of Freya. He bit his lip in perplexity. He had not thought of Freya for quite a while. Why was it that her memory no longer stirred him to the same sharp and bitter feeling of despair?

Deliberately he forced his mind back to the task before him and tried to ignore the fact that his body was a mass of agonized pain-torn muscles. He began to move upwards again. He presumed that Branting must have reached the top already. There was surely no more than twenty or thirty feet now which separated him from the top of the climb. There was a slight overhang which obscured his forward vision.

It was while he was reaching for a new hold that he felt the tug at his waist. A small tug, no more. Then came a high pitched scream which echoed away among the surrounding mountains. His blood went cold, his heart pounded and he clung trembling to the rock face, bracing himself for the jerk which would wrench him backwards into oblivion. He stayed still, eyes shut tight, for several seconds.

It was only seconds, but it seemed hours before he opened them and peered down. Not far below him was the gibbering face of Hersleb, eyes round and white, mouth half open, moving and making strange animal sounds.

'What the hell has happened?' yelled Sweeny, his own fear making him angry.

Hersleb was incapable of replying.

Branting's voice came down to him from above the overhang.

'Sweeny? What's going on?'

'I don't know,' Sweeny called. 'Hilde? Trina?'

'It's Hilde!' came Trina's voice, tight with shock. 'She . . . she fell. The rope came away from her safety belt . . .'

'For Christ's sake!' swore Sweeny.

'We must go back for her!' Trina wailed.

'It's no use. It's nearly six hundred feet down. Come on. We must get to the top before we freeze here.'

Sweeny turned, rage and guilt surging through him at the loss of the young nurse. It was his fault. His fault. He had checked the rope, he had made sure it was connected. How could it have happened? He began to scramble upwards automatically but found that the rope at his waist was tight, holding him back. He turned down with a scowl.

'Hersleb! Start climbing or else I'll cut you loose myself.'

He jerked on the rope, causing the pale-faced anaesthetist to start moving instinctively.

Branting's voice called from above: 'Twenty feet, Sweeny. You're coming to a crevice which will act like a chimney. You should be able to walk up it without any problems.'

Sweeny grunted but did not reply. It took all his self-control to stop himself shivering and becoming frozen with fear at the thought of the young girl falling off the rockface. Again he went over the preparations in his mind. He had ensured that they were all roped securely together, so how the hell had it happened? The equipment which they had taken from the hotel was good and fairly new. Branting had checked it as well. And Hilde had been roped between Hersleb and Trina. How *could* she have fallen? He climbed automatically now, hand over hand, his anger and fear driving him on so that he subconsciously called upon resources that he did not know he had.

He was in the chimney now, placing his palms and back against the cold rock, his feet braced against the far side. Slowly he began to push upwards. Below him, Hersleb was sobbing in exertion and terror. He could hear Trina's voice chiding him, pushing him. Long minutes passed until he finally saw Branting's face above him. He reached forward, feeling with infinite caution for the edge of the rock face. Then he felt strong arms pulling him upwards and he was lying on a ledge with Branting and Birkenes beside him. Beyond them Inge Stenersen and her uncle were standing with pale, horrified expressions on their faces.

Branting and Birkenes were swinging Hersleb over now, hauling him up, a frightened sobbing mess of a man. They pushed him none too gently along the ledge and then were reaching down for Trina Lanstrad. Sweeny bent to help them but was not needed. The girl came up the chimney and onto the ledge like a professional.

'What happened?' demanded Sweeny as soon as she had recovered her breath.

'Her safety belt must have broken, I can't think of any other explanation. One minute poor Hilde was climbing above me and then she slipped. The rope should have held her but there was a snapping sound and she was gone. Only the rope was there. It was over in a moment.'

The girl shivered and Sweeny put his arm around her, drawing her away from the ledge toward shelter.

She raised a tear-stained face to him.

'We must go back to see if poor Hilde is alive. There must be a chance . . .'

Sweeny patted her arm firmly.

'There's no way Hilde could have survived that fall. We have to go on, Trina.'

'You mean just leave her?' she gasped.

'If there's to be any meaning to her death, we must go on.' Sweeny's voice was adamant.

'The others are coming up the chimney now,' Branting called from the other side of the ledge.

Sweeny moved to join him, and as he knelt down Branting pressed a small metal clasp into his hand.

'It was still attached to the rope,' he whispered. 'The hooks were in place, but someone has taken the pin out of the clasp. Run a rope through the clasp and it looks fine. Put a sudden pressure on it and the clasp just flies off the safety belt.'

Sweeny stared at Branting, trying to understand the import of what he was being told.

'Are you saying that this was done on purpose?'

Branting returned his gaze evenly.

'I'm saying that the pin was taken out of the clasp so that it would not hold when a sudden weight was put on it.'

'But who would do such a thing?'

Branting momentarily glanced in the direction of Hersleb. Then he shrugged. 'Who knows?' he said, then reached forward to help Woods negotiate the end of the climb.

Branting and Sweeny allowed the group half an hour to recover from the exhaustion of the climb and the shock of Hilde's death. They were into the snow belt now, and the peaks all around them were capped with a fine powdery snow. Branting had ensured that each of them had carried from the hotel warm ski-ing clothes, boots, a rucksack with provisions and skis, sticks, ropes and axes. It was well to be prepared for any problem, although Branting felt that the most difficult part of the journey had been overcome with the climbing of the *kliev*. As soon as the rest period was up, he and Sweeny forced the party to move onwards. Branting took the lead, with Sweeny and Woods bringing up the rear. They trudged along a path which wound round the side of the mountain and across a narrow shoulder onto a white plain. Before them was a line of dark jagged peaks, the last obstacle which separated them from neutral Sweden.

As Branting had foretold, the way was fairly easy. Only at one spot did they have to be extra careful, a place where a broad ribbon of icy-cold water cascaded over the path; a raging white torrent that fell from higher up the mountain. However, Branting knew the safe way past the waterfall. Without hesitation he stepped behind the curtain of water. It was cold, wet and fairly slippery, but the path continued behind the waterfall and rejoined the dry ledge a little further on.

They turned sharply, went through a narrow pass and emerged on the far side of the peak overlooking a *dal* or softly curving valley of snow which was extremely wide, maybe a couple of miles across, with other high peaks all round it. Across the centre of this valley was a discernible path.

'That's the path we would have taken had we gone back along the lowlands,' Branting observed, pointing with his ski-stick.

'How far to the Swedish border?' demanded Woods.

'If we don't have to make any detours, we'll probably cross sometime tomorrow. There is a *turisthytten* up in the mountains where we can spend the night.'

'*Se op!*' Professor Stenersen suddenly yelled, throwing himself into the snow. The others heard the sound of an aero engine a few moments later and followed his example. A Storch, flying fairly high, swept down the valley.

They picked themselves up self-consciously and began to brush themselves down.

'Did it see us?' asked Stenersen.

'I shouldn't think so, Professor,' Woods replied. 'It would have circled back.'

Sweeny's face was grim.

'Nevertheless, it's better not to take chances. We'll press on as quickly as possible.'

Ahead he could see that the mountains were sentinels to a grey-white world obscured by mist. The air was cold and damp. They moved forward now in silence. There were no possibilities of using their skis yet, for the path Branting was taking was a narrow ledge of snow following the contours of the valley but keeping high above it. Hersleb was the only one who seemed to be suffering from the trek, moaning now and again so that Stenersen had to speak sharply to him more than once. Sweeny kept his eyes on the little man. He could not bring himself to accept Branting's statement entirely. Surely the excitable little anaesthetist was not capable of such a cold-blooded murder? And for what? Simply to slow their pace? To force them to halt? That would be so cold and calculated that . . . he shivered involuntarily.

At midday they stopped and ate a snack of *flatbrod* and goat's cheese, with a mouthful of *aquavit* apiece to help keep out the cold. Trina Lanstrad brought Sweeny his ration and seated herself next to him. He sat a little apart from the others, keeping a watch on the valley.

'Are you all right?' she asked.

Sweeny smiled. 'I should be asking you that.'

'Poor Hilde,' the girl bit her lip. 'It is still a shock. I have never seen an accident happen like that.'

Sweeny did not reply. He decided not to tell anyone else about the clasp Branting had taken from the rope. He was hoping that at some stage Hersleb would say or do something to incriminate himself.

'Did you know her well?' he asked after a few moments' silence.

It seemed a silly thing to say, but he was just making conversation.

'Well? She joined the professor's team two years ago. I suppose I knew her as well as anyone. She had a young man that she was going to marry in June. He was called up with the general mobilization. She hadn't heard from him since then.'

'This bloody war,' Sweeny sighed.

'Yes!' The girl said fervently. 'This bloody war!'

Branting was looking at his wrist watch and signalled to Sweeny. They began moving again. The path grew steeper, winding upwards now, with broad zig-zags toward the *hammer*, the sharp shoulder of the mountain.

Sweeny heard the noise without realizing what it was for several seconds. Then he yelled: 'Aircraft!'

They were high on the white slopes of the mountainside, barren snow-painted slopes. He searched desperately for cover of any kind but there was none. The snow was not even thick enough to attempt to dig in and camouflage themselves.

The grotesque, gigantic shape of an aircraft soared suddenly over the spur of the peak behind them and roared over them at no more than a few hundred feet. They all flung themselves down, expecting the rattle of machine guns. Then the aircraft was climbing away from them.

Sweeny followed it with his eyes. It was a large aircraft, its metal fuselage oddly corrugated.

'It's a Junkers troop carrier,' Branting called.

The aircraft climbed in a lazy spiral and then moved back down the valley towards them. There was nothing they could do. Sweeny realized that they had been seen.

Once again the large aircraft flew over them and once again they braced themselves for machine-gun fire. But the aircraft passed over them again without attacking and this time it climbed high into the cloudy sky and went along the line of the valley. Little black dots began to detach themselves from the rear of the aircraft, tumbling out one after the other. Sweeny stared in bewilderment, and then the black dots were suddenly halted and hung under gently swaying mushroom shapes.

'*Fallsschirmjäger!*' swore Branting.

'What?' frowned Stenersen.

'Parachute troops,' replied the young Norwegian officer.

They watched as about twenty or thirty parachutes descended down to the valley floor below them. Branting had taken the pair of field glasses from their case and was focusing down the valley.

'How far do you reckon they are?' asked Sweeny, moving to Branting's side.

'Not far enough,' he muttered. 'Maybe five miles across the valley. At least the Junkers's pilot was unable to put them down any closer to us.'

'Will they be able to catch us up?' asked Woods.

'It depends on how well they know the terrain. If they move up-valley they may be able to pick up some time. If they attempt to come straight for us then we'll have a good head start.'

Branting was focusing carefully. He watched the parachutists landing, observing the way they dealt with their 'chutes and equipment.

'I'll tell you one thing. These boys are no novices in the mountains. They're carrying skis and climbing equipment. I'd say they are a company of *Gebirgsjäger.*'

'What are those?' asked Inge.

'Specially trained mountain troops,' Branting grunted. 'The Germans have been using a lot of Austrian troops in Norway, troops trained in the Alps who know how to handle themselves in high mountains.'

The drone of the Junkers faded away while far below them, across the valley floor, they could just make out a line of black dots moving rapidly along the floor of the valley.

'We'd better get moving,' Sweeny said. 'We want to keep as far ahead of them as possible.'

He turned to catch Hersleb's dark, smouldering eyes, looking down the slope of the mountain towards the valley with a speculative gaze. Sweeny moved across to him and jerked the safety catch of his Schmeisser machine-pistol.

'Don't even think about it, Hersleb,' he said softly. 'I'd shoot even before you reached for your skis.'

The little anaesthetist's pale face turned toward his, a mask of hate and fear. He said nothing.

Woods joined Sweeny and prodded the doctor with his Webley.

'Let's get going,' he said with a thin smile. 'I'm looking forward to having dinner tomorrow night in the Ritz and I don't want you to make me late for it.'

# CHAPTER TWENTY-THREE

It was mid-afternoon now. Thin clouds were streaking the pale sky while behind them, to the west, they could see the tip of a red, angry-looking disc descending into a pink glow over the snow-capped hills. Dusk was coming early; the light was already beginning to fade and the atmosphere was cold and misty. Branting halted the exhausted party on the shoulder of a hill and leaned back wearily.

'We'll rest here for ten minutes,' he called.

Sweeny went forward to join him.

'How far now?'

Branting drew out the map and compass.

'About four hours and we should come to the *turisthytten*. We can spend the night there unless there are Germans about. There is an alternative . . . a cave further up this valley, about two miles from the *turisthytten*.' He jabbed at the map with his finger. 'The cave is just here on this peak called Tindfjell. Tomorrow morning we can move up to the Svabensverk Glacier and then . . . Sweden!' He smiled.

Sweeny was looking at the terrain before them. Branting had indicated a path across a long, low sweeping valley.

'Can we ski across?'

Branting inclined his head. 'If we get a good impetus on the downward slope we should be able to get quite a way up the far slope.'

Sweeny glanced at Hersleb.

'We'll ski across three at a time. I'll bring Hersleb last.'

The exercise was an easy one. The impetus of the run brought them quite a way up the far slope, and here they took off their skis and started to climb again. They were nearing a spur when Branting, who was leading, suddenly dropped down, frantically waving the others to follow suit. Sweeny scrambled quickly to his side.

'Germans, half-a-mile ahead,' muttered Branting. 'It can't be the same troops we saw before. They must have dropped another company ahead of us, hoping to catch us in between.'

Sweeny realized that the terrain around them was hopeless. His eyes met Branting's. The question was obvious without him asking it.

'There's no way we can avoid them,' Branting said simply. 'If we move back we are liable to fall into the hands of their comrades.'

'Can we shoot it out?'

Branting suppressed a harsh laugh.

'Two Schmeissers and three handguns against thirty fully-armed *Gebirgsjäger*?'

'Well, it's a damned sight better than surrendering to the bastards.'

Branting bit his lip. He hesitated and then pushed the map and compass towards Sweeny.

'Can you make your way to the cave at Tindfjell and then across the Svabensverk Glacier?'

'I think so,' replied Sweeny.

'Good. Remember this: hole up in the cave tonight. You should be able to reach it within two or three hours. At first light move out and take the path directly behind the cave. It's a tough ascent for the last quarter of a mile, but it will lead you onto a high plateau where you will find an easy path across the top of the glacier. Once across the glacier you are in Sweden. Just keep going and you'll come to Rottnedal or Torsby.'

Sweeny pushed the map into his pocket.

Branting stood up and fastened on his skis. Suddenly he chucked the Schmeisser to Sweeny.

'Woods will probably have more use for this than I will. Good luck. Maybe see you again someday.'

Before Sweeny realized what the young Norwegian was doing, the man had dug his ski-sticks into the snow and shot forward down the slope in full view of the *Gebirgsjäger*.

The Storch came to a wobbly halt on the Travbane, the old race course, underneath the shadow of the castle hill. The Luftwaffe had converted the field for light aircraft and the Storch managed to put down without problems. An Opel staff car was waiting to take Hauptmann Eschig and Feldwebel Weiss up to battalion headquarters at the castle. The vehicle moved swiftly through the town, passing tramping squads of armed men and sullen townspeople on its way to the former Norwegian military base. A staff captain came forward, saluted and conducted Eschig through to the commander's office, where Weiss was left outside at uneasy attention.

A harassed Generalmajor glanced up from a desk and nodded.

'A glass of schnapps, Herr Hauptmann?'

Eschig responded with formality and declined.

'Is there any word from your troops regarding the fugitives?'

The Generalmajor pulled a sheet of paper toward himself and glanced over it. 'They were spotted some hours ago, and we have air-dropped two companies of *Gebirgsjäger*, one in front and one behind them. Oberleutnant Gerhardt is in command and is in contact by radio with headquarters. They'll soon have your fugitives. They are the finest mountain troops in Europe.'

'I don't doubt it. I want to join them as soon as I can. Is it possible to supply me and my sergeant with parachutes and a plane and pilot to take me to the area?'

The Generalmajor frowned.

'You have, of course, received parachute training and are able to survive in the mountains?'

'I have had training in the Tyrol. Don't worry, Herr Generalmajor, I'll keep up with your men.'

The Generalmajor gazed thoughtfully at Eschig.

'You must want these people very badly, Herr Hauptmann. I'll do my best. In the meantime Sturmbannführer Knesebeck is very keen to interrogate the fugitives when they are caught. He has set up a Gestapo headquarters in the local police station in the town.'

Sweeny and the others watched Branting swerving down the mountain slope in astonishment. There was nothing they could say or do. They heard a distant shout and the crack of a rifle shot, but the young Norwegian continued zig-zagging rapidly down towards the valley.

'The damned fool!' cried Woods.

Sweeny turned angrily and threw the Schmeisser at him.

'That damned fool is sacrificing himself for you!' he shot back. 'For all of us. The least you can do is accept it.'

'You callous bastard!' Woods cried. 'I'm going . . .'

Sweeny took a step forward and slapped Woods hard across the face. He staggered back in shock. Before he could recover his senses, Stenersen had intervened, grasping Woods's arm.

'Sweeny is right, my boy,' he said quietly. 'Branting is drawing the Germans away from us so that we can stand a chance of getting away. He is a brave young man.'

'A stupid young man,' snapped Hersleb, speaking for the first time in a long while.

Sweeny whirled in his temper and punched him, catching the little man squarely in the mouth.

'I'm going to scatter your guts all over the snow!' he cried, his teeth grinding in hate.

Stenersen moved forward and restrained him.

'No, you're not, Sweeny. You are going to lead us into Sweden. We'll see what has to be done with him there.'

Sweeny hesitated, suddenly calmed by the soft authoritative tone of the professor. He sighed and gestured toward Hersleb.

'Birkenes, Arendt, pick that little swine up and keep him out of my way.'

He gave one backward glance down the mountain. A cluster of black specks were streaking down the slope after Branting, the Norwegian himself no more than a tiny dot far below. The Germans had taken the bait. It would be hours before they caught up again. Branting had bought them valuable time. The damned fool. The poor damned fool!

Far below, crouching over his skis, Arne Branting bent his body forward into the wind, ski-sticks tucked under his arms. It was beginning to snow, at first only a few flakes driven by the wind, but then it grew thicker and began to come in rapid gusts so that he was suddenly engulfed in a world of grey and white, hardly able to see a few yards in front of him. He could hear the hoarse shouts of the German soldiers behind him in spite of the hiss of his skis and the wind against his ears. He realized that the wind was veering from one direction to another, which did not augur well.

He dipped and turned, praying that the driving snow would hide his tracks as well as his body. But even as the hope entered his head, the snow began to ease and finally stop. His one hope now lay in speed. The slope was steepening and he was beginning to travel faster, still zig-zagging though the soft fresh snow.

A rifle shot cracked and something struck the snow in front of him. They were good troops, these German mountain troops. Like the Norwegian border troops, they could fire while balanced on their skis on a downward run. He zig-zagged again and bent further into the wind, making his body as small as possible to increase his speed.

The snowfall which he had hoped would be a blessing now became a problem. Ski-ing over fresh snow was not the same as moving over a hardened snow surface. Adjusting one's speed on fresh snow was difficult; it could only be maintained by the steepness of the run. If the slope was too steep then the only course was to engage in a series of diagonal runs to maintain a level speed.

Branting reckoned that he was coming down the slope a little too fast, perhaps about thirty miles an hour. He had to keep his balance for it would be fatal if he ran out of track now. Then an idea came into his mind. Perhaps he could buy time by changing direction. Branting had skied often before the war. Damn it. That was only a couple of weeks ago, yet 'before the war' seemed a pre-historic time. Before him he could see where the shoulder of the mountain split. If he could build on more speed and make his pursuers believe he was heading directly for the valley floor, but instead he could reach the spot where the shoulder split, then turn and head off down the steeper slope, he might be able to outrun them. The only way to make the turn so that his pursuers missed it was to make a 'Christiana'. The Christiana turn or Christi, as it was sometimes called, was the most difficult of all turns on skis. It involved a jump to bring the skis and skier clear from his tracks in order to make a right-angle turn in mid-air.

Branting dug his ski sticks in, pushing hard in an effort to increase his pace, his eyes peering forward now to the spot where the shoulder of the mountain divided. The run to that point was long, clear and very steep. He put his head down, still building up speed. The wind was pressing ice-cold against his face.

He waited until he judged the moment right and then leapt. His heart came into his throat. He knew even as he urged himself forward into space that he had misjudged. The points of his skis lifted forward into the air and he braced himself for the inevitable consequence of his misjudgement. The snow of the slope flung itself at him like a large white blanket and enveloped him.

For several seconds he was drowned in blackness before coming to and struggling against the icy smothering wetness. His mouth and nostrils and eyes were blocked by snow. His legs were numbed and seemed to be twisting under him. He scrambled forward with his hands and sobbed for air. Then someone was brushing the snow from his face.

A fair-haired young man with blue eyes and a sunburnt face was gazing at him solicitously.

'*Das ist Pech für Sie,*' he said genuinely, hesitated and added in Norwegian, 'That is bad luck.'

Two soldiers were lifting him upright.

'Are you injured?' the young officer was asking.

Branting shook his head. 'I don't think so.'

'Good. *Namen?*'

Branting told him.

'*So? Sind Sie Soldat gewesen?*'

'I am a soldier of the Royal Norwegian Army.'

'*Ach so? Welches ist Ihr Dienstgrad?*'

'Captain.'

'You have had bad luck,' the officer said again, smiling. 'If you had brought off your Christi we might not have been able to stop you. Ah, but we will never know.'

'Am I a prisoner-of-war?'

'Of course. What else?' The German offered him a cigarette. 'We are in touch with Kongsvinger. Two of my men will take you to the valley. A Storch can land there comfortably and you will be flown back to headquarters.'

Branting exhaled deeply and gazed up the mountain.

The young German saw his glance and smiled thinly.

'You were quite clever. I did not realize your plan until we were well in pursuit of you. By then it was too late. But you have only bought a temporary respite for your comrades. We will soon catch them up. I, too, have spent much time in these mountains, captain.'

He turned and snapped some orders at his men and then turned back with a polite salute.

'It was a good try. The fortunes of war, eh?'

He turned and waved to the rest of his command and they began to move at a quick pace up the mountain, leaving Branting between two burly soldiers. One of them tapped him on the shoulder sympathetically.

'*Kommen.*'

Branting threw down the cigarette and nodded.

[198]

# CHAPTER TWENTY-FOUR

Hauptmann Eschig came awake to find someone shaking him by the shoulders. He had dozed off while sitting in the brigade adjutant's office in the castle, waiting for an aircraft to fly him and Weiss to the mountains.

'What is it?' he demanded as his bleary eyes focused on the impassive face of Feldwebel Weiss.

'I beg to report, Herr Hauptmann, that I have learnt that the *Gebirgsjäger* have captured one of the fugitives . . .'

'Sweeny?' Eschig started forward hopefully.

'No, Herr Hauptmann. A Norwegian officer named Branting. Apparently the man laid a false trail to lead our troops away from the rest of the party. Oberleutnant Gerhardt had the prisoner flown out in the Storch which can now take us back into the mountains to rendezvous with the Oberleutnant's men.'

'Has the prisoner been brought back to Kongsvinger, then?'

Weiss nodded.

'Excellent. I would like to question him before we go.'

'Sturmbannführer Knesebeck has used the Reichskommissar's authority to take the prisoner to the local police station for interrogation.'

'*Verdammt!*' swore Eschig. 'Let's find this police station.'

'Herr Hauptmann, may I remind you that it will be dark soon. If the Herr Hauptmann wishes to rendezvous . . .'

'I know what I'm doing,' replied Eschig. 'I just hope that butcher hasn't killed the poor Norwegian swine!'

Knesebeck leant forward and slapped Branting across the face. It was a hard slap and Branting was nearly thrown from the chair. He was unable to protect himself because his hands were cuffed behind him.

'*Scheisskerl! Schweinehund!*'

Branting stared woodenly at the Gestapo officer. His face felt as if it were on fire.

'You *will* talk, terrorist. Who are your companions? Why did they take Stenersen? Do you belong to an organization?'

Branting did not speak. His mind was working rapidly. He had to buy his comrades time. Knesebeck's gnarled hand crashed against Branting's nose.

'You will talk to me,' he said softly. 'If you do so, you will have nothing to fear.'

Branting shrugged, feeling the blood dripping into his mouth.

'Rudi!' snapped Knesebeck, rising.

Branting felt a pair of strong hands lever him up out of the chair and propel him towards the door of the room. He stumbled from weakness and pain. The hands caught him and slammed him against the corridor wall after the door was opened and then he was pushed along the corridor. At the end of it a door opened into a small tiled bathroom. Knesebeck moved forward while his companion held Branting and opened the window so that the icy cold wind blew into the room. Then he bent over the bath and turned on the cold tap after inserting the plug. Now his companion was ripping off Branting's shirt and trousers.

'Are you going to talk? Yes or no?' snapped Knesebeck.

Branting shook his head, wondering what ordeal he was going to face, standing there naked and shivering in the icy cold. The second man was kneeling at his feet and tying his ankles together with a rope. Then Branting was pushed roughly into a sitting position on the side of the bath.

'Tell us what we want to know, terrorist!'

Branting stared up at Knesebeck.

The man nodded to his companion, who reached forward and wrenched at the rope around his ankles in one easy movement. Branting went crashing back into the bath so that his head was completely immersed in the water. With his hands cuffed behind him and his feet held up above his body he was entirely helpless. He felt the wave of panic that was inevitable. He tried to twist and turn but the hands that held his feet out of the bath were powerful. He tried to kick. Then his mouth opened, the lungs craving air, and he began to swallow water. His mind began to go black as consciousness left him. He was drowning and he knew it.

When he came to there was a terrible pain in his chest. He was lying on the cold tiles of the bathroom floor and Knesebeck's face was gazing down at him in disgust. Branting felt sick and then vomited water onto the floor.

'Will you talk?'

Branting gasped, his lungs straining for air.

Again came Knesebeck's voice: 'Talk!'

Branting could only shake his head.

The second man lifted him easily and threw him back into the bath again. Once more he tried to kick and struggle but it was no use. He passed out again and came to on the tiled floor after an eternity. This time he felt a rushing in his ears.

He could no longer make out what Knesebeck was saying. The man's voice was one long scream.

He lost count of how many times he was thrown back in the bath.

He recovered consciousness again to find that he was being dragged along the corridor. He was pushed onto a chair, cold, wet and semi-conscious. He was aware that Knesebeck was striking him across the face. He tried to laugh because he could no longer feel a thing. His face was too numb.

'You are a fool,' Knesebeck assured him. 'You will die anyway.'

Branting found himself strangely detached, as if he were merely an observer of this grotesque scene.

'We will try one more time.' Knesebeck grinned. He rose lazily, sauntered to the stove in the corner and, opening the door, prodded the coals inside with a poker.

'You are cold, aren't you? Well, we will warm you up a little.' He thrust the poker into the fire, turning it slowly. Branting tried to shut his mind, tried to isolate himself from the pain which he knew was inevitable.

'Sturmbannführer Knesebeck!'

The voice was sharp and authoritative. It cracked across the room. Branting's eyes, almost closed from the pain, tried to focus. He was aware of an officer in field grey entering the room.

Hauptmann Eschig stared from Knesebeck to the huddled naked man on the chair. His face was a mask of disgust and anger.

'You cannot interfere with the *Geheime Staats Polizei*, Hauptmann Eschig,' returned Knesebeck, angry at the interruption.

'No? With the Herr Sturmbannführer's permission, I can and will.'

'You are treading on dangerous ground,' warned Knesebeck.

'Be it so. This is a military affair, not a police matter, and it is under the jurisdiction of the commander of the land, sea and air forces, Herr General von Falkenhorst. He has placed me in charge.'

[201]

'My authority . . .'

'Your authority,' snapped Eschig, 'if I may point out, Herr Sturmbannführer, is vested in the Reichskommissar who is in charge of civil administration in the occupied zones of Norway.'

Knesebeck hesitated. He knew that technically Eschig was right.

'I want Stenersen,' he said defiantly.

'You will get him, Herr Sturmbannführer. But I will get him for you. In the meantime, I suggest that you cease to interrogate this prisoner as he is now in my custody.'

Knesebeck stared at Eschig a moment and then nodded. He smiled thinly.

'I shan't forget this, Herr Hauptmann. I hope that you will not have cause to regret this decision.'

The Gestapo officer slammed the door as he left the room. Feldwebel Weiss, standing by the door, regarded his superior officer with his usual impassivity. Only his eyes showed that he was troubled.

'If I may be so bold, Herr Hauptmann . . .' Weiss hesitated. He was slightly awed by his own temerity at breaching military protocol. 'The Gestapo can be a powerful enemy.'

Eschig turned to his sergeant and actually smiled, wryly.

'I know it, Feldwebel,' he said. 'But occasionally one has to listen to conscience and honour. Also it is a matter of practicalities. Knesebeck would never have made this man speak with his methods.'

He stared down at Branting and sighed.

'It is useless to try to question the man now. Get him to a cell and get him attended to. I want to be able to speak with him when we come back.'

Branting had slipped into unconsciousness again and when he came to he was in the cell. For the first time in his life he felt utterly alone. His agony was atrocious, and the circulation in his arms was almost nil because of the handcuffs. But someone had removed them now. His wrists felt swollen, for the metal had bit deeply into them. He also felt the blood clotting on his face and beginning to draw the skin. His face was hurting terribly now and his mouth was full of the salt taste of his own blood. He lay in the darkness of the cell, his breath rasping. One thought registered strongly with him. He would like a few moments alone, on equal terms, with the vicious Gestapo officer. A few moments . . . that was all it would take.

The Luftwaffe navigator turned and clutched at Hauptmann Eschig's arm.

'It's too dark to land now, Herr Hauptmann,' he yelled. 'Are you really sure you want to make the jump?'

'Of course!' returned Eschig, raising his voice above the roar of the Storch's engine.

'Well, we have a radio fix on the *Gerbirgsjäger*.' He turned and peered forward. Then he jabbed a gloved finger downwards. 'There they are.' Eschig could see the flashing of a torch from below. 'Get ready to jump.'

The Storch was flying through the white-peaked mountains which separated Norway from Sweden. For nearly one hundred years Norway and Sweden had been united into one country and this natural barrier had not meant a thing politically. Eschig smiled. It was one of those inconsequential facts that he had learnt when he had been informed that he was to serve in Norway. The union between Sweden and Norway had been dissolved on 7 June 1905 and on November 18 the Norwegians had elected their own king, Prince Carl of Denmark, who had taken the name of Haakon VII. Norway had become the model democratic kingdom. One of the weak democracies which the Führer had declared to be an impediment to progress. Eschig smiled cynically and turned to Weiss.

'Ready, Feldwebel?'

Weiss nodded impassively.

The Storch pilot was circling round now. Below on the white slopes of the mountain, the torch was flashing out its signal. The navigator moved back and opened the side door, letting in a blast of cold air.

'On this run, Herr Hauptmann,' he yelled. 'On my signal.'

Eschig stood ready at the door, braced for the jump.

The navigator yelled and slapped him on the back.

Eschig launched himself into space. The white of the mountains and the valley floor seemed to merge in the darkness of evening. For some time he was not sure whether he was falling to the ground or miraculously spinning upwards to the sky. Then his 'chute opened, and a few moments later white-clad figures were emerging to help him as he landed. Eschig noticed the dark shadow of Weiss coming down a few yards away. A young man clad in white coveralls, carrying a rucksack and a Schmeisser slung across his shoulder, had moved towards him.

'Hauptmann Eschig?'

Eschig nodded.

'I am Oberleutnant Gerhardt.'

'Any sign of the fugitives?' asked Eschig.

'They've gone to ground for the night, as we should do. There is a *turisthytten*, a hut where tourists in the mountains stay. It's about a mile away at the head of the next valley. I plan to bivouac there and then move on in the morning.'

Eschig bit his lip, hiding his disappointment.

'Are we far behind?'

Gerhardt shook his head.

'I know this country, Herr Hauptmann. I spent many hours climbing and ski-ing here before the war. From the route the fugitives are taking, it seems that they plan to cross the Svabensverk Glacier. There is no other pass ahead. We should be able to cut them off quite easily.'

Eschig felt a sudden elation.

'Are you sure?'

The young oberleutnant smiled.

'I'll wager a bottle of schnapps, Herr Hauptmann. I know these mountains like the back of my hand. We'll get them tomorrow, no question of it.'

# CHAPTER TWENTY-FIVE

The fugitives reached the cave just after dark.

Sweeny was feeling a sense of loss. There was always the chance that Branting might have been able to avoid the Germans, but he felt it was hardly likely. Sweeny realized just how attached he had become to the young Norwegian officer during these last few days; how much he had relied on the man's knowledge and organizing ability. The map he had left behind had been easy to follow, and the only delay had been when Doctor Birkenes had missed his footing, slipped and fallen, knocking his head.

He was a little dazed, but able to keep up with them after a short rest. Trina Lanstrad had dressed the abrasion and the doctor himself had diagnosed a slight concussion. His sense of humour had not been affected, because he grinned at Sweeny and said, 'It's no problem when I have the best medical brains in Norway to look after me. Two nurses and five doctors! At least I've chosen the right time for needing medical attention.'

In spite of his humour it was clear that the blow had been a severe one and Professor Stenersen ordered his colleague to rest immediately. Trina made the doctor comfortable in the back of the cave while the others lit a fire within its confines, so that its flames could not be detected from outside. They were able to prepare some hot soup to have with the *flatbrod* and goat's cheese they carried.

Afterwards, Sweeny organized a watch system just in case the Germans tried to track them under cover of darkness. Woods was placed on watch first while the others were told to get some rest.

Woods took the Schmeisser left by Branting, wrapped a blanket around his shoulders for warmth and went to the mouth of the cave, perching himself on a rock. Outside it was quite light, the pale moon reflecting on the white carpet of snow.

'Okay?' asked Sweeny, making a final check.

Woods was about to affirm that he was fine when he caught sight of a flicker far away across the valley. He thought for a moment it was a reflection.

'What is it?' Sweeny asked, seeing Woods's eyes narrow.

'There! See it?'

Sweeny followed his outstretched hand.

'That's the direction of the *turisthytten*. It must be the Germans. That's about two miles away. We'd better make sure we are up before dawn and well on our way.'

'Sweeny.' Woods was hesitant. 'I'm sorry for what I said earlier about Branting. Do you think they got him?'

'It seems likely, otherwise they wouldn't have come on after us so quickly.'

'The poor bastard,' breathed Woods. 'I really liked the man.'

About half an hour later Inge came to join him with a mug containing a shot of aquavit.

'I couldn't sleep,' she said, sitting down beside him.

'It'll be a long day tomorrow,' Woods warned her, although he was pleased to have the girl's company.

'What will you do when we get back to London, Michael?'

Woods thought a moment.

'Commander Wallace promised that my job at the hospital will be waiting for me. There's no decision.'

The girl had half expected him to say that.

'Seeing the way you've been during these last few days I was wondering whether you might join up?'

Woods stared at her incredulously.

'Join up? You mean join the army or something? Good God, no! There are plenty of people about who like pulling the triggers of these things,' he gestured to the Schmeisser. 'It doesn't take much intellect to destroy men, but it requires some skill to put them together. I wasn't raised to destroy people. I was trained to heal them. That's what I know.'

'I'm going to volunteer to join the Norwegian forces when I get back,' Inge said quietly.

Woods looked at her in astonishment.

'Norway needs everyone she can get to help her during the months ahead,' the girl went on, pretending not to notice the shock in his eyes. 'It may even be years before she is finally liberated.'

'Come on, Inge,' Woods said, 'you are a biochemist. You are trained and people need your training. Any fool can run around in uniform with a gun. Leave fighting wars to men like Sweeny.'

'I've made a choice, Michael.'

'But . . . but what about us?'

Inge smiled at him softly.

'I see no problem. But my first duty is to Norway.'

'That's patriotic emotionalism . . .'

A shrill scream came from the far end of the cave.

Woods leapt to his feet and went hurrying in. Everyone was stirring from where they had been sleeping. Sweeny was already on his feet.

At the back of the cave Trina Lanstrad was standing beside Jan Birkenes, hand to her mouth. Birkenes was stretched on his back, one hand flung out in careless fashion in front of him. His eyes were open and there was a shadow across his neck and chest. It was only when Sweeny moved forward with a burning brand from the fire that they saw that the shadow was bright red. Birkenes had had his throat cut.

Trina Lanstrad began to shiver.

Woods brushed Sweeny aside and felt for Birkenes' pulse, although he knew from the wound it was obviously a futile gesture.

'He's dead.'

Sweeny was staring fixedly at the wound. He kept seeing the wound across his cousin Freya's throat. For a moment Birkenes' face and that of Freya became one. It was a wound that seemed so similar. Sweeny dragged his eyes away and stared up at Trina.

'What happened?'

The girl tried to control her shaking limbs.

'I was just coming to check on him when . . . when I saw . . .'

Sweeny nodded, his eyes seeking out the pale face of Hersleb.

The little man backed away, fear in his eyes.

'Sweeny,' Stenersen said, frowning, 'who killed Birkenes and why?'

'The same person who killed the nurse, Hilde,' Sweeny replied tightly.

'But that was an accident!' protested the professor.

'No. Her safety clasp had been tampered with. The pin was removed so that the clasp broke away from the safety rope the moment pressure was put on it.'

Sweeny took the clasp from his pocket and threw it on the floor.

'See for yourself.'

Stenersen bent forward and recovered it.

Woods was staring in horror.

'Are you saying that one of us is a murderer?'

Sweeny nodded.

'That's obvious.' His eyes were on the excitable little anaesthetist, who began to back away before his accusing stare.

'I did not do it. I did not do it!' The little man began to moan as the others saw Sweeny's gaze and followed it. 'You hate me because I believe in the New Order. I know that. But I did not kill Birkenes. I did not kill Hilde. What kind of man do you think I am?'

'It's monstrous, Sweeny,' Stenersen said quietly. 'We've worked with Hersleb for years. I know he has a loud mouth and is a pain about politics, but . . .'

'I am responsible for your safety, professor, and it appears that I am not doing a good job,' replied Sweeny.

'It's a terrible accusation, Lars,' Trina Lanstrad said. 'The professor is right. We cannot condemn a man just because of his politics.'

'No, Sweeny is right,' Woods said. 'There's no one else other than Hersleb who would want to delay or stop us. Hersleb is the obvious suspect.'

'It is not true,' the little man cried. 'It is not me.'

Sweeny took a step towards Hersleb, but Stenersen intervened.

'If Hersleb is the killer then he deserves to be killed. But I say that we must be sure. We shall be in Sweden tomorrow. Let the authorities deal with it.'

Sweeny hesitated.

'Very well. Doctor Arendt, you will relieve Woods on guard duty. Hersleb, you will sit over here, and Woods . . . you will watch him until I relieve you.'

Stenersen nodded toward Birkenes's body. 'What about . . . We ought to bury Jan.'

Sweeny bit his lip.

'Hersleb, you take the shoulders,' he ordered, while bending to pick up the feet. They moved the body as far as they could into the rear of the cave. It was as good a grave as any, and without spades they could not make a proper grave in the hard snow of the mountain.

Sweeny was dreaming. He was swimming away from the *Gunnlöd*, leaving Uncle Tenvig's bloodstained body lying on the deck. The German E Boat was closing in. Before him was Freya, standing on the shore with outstretched hands . . . only Freya's face kept fading and he saw only the face of Trina Lanstrad. The hands gripped his and started to shake him.

'Sweeny!'

He sat up abruptly. It was Woods' voice.

'Hersleb's gone.'

Sweeny was wide awake.

'How?' he snapped coldly.

'It was my fault . . .' Woods hesitated, looking away. 'I dozed off. Only a few moments, I suppose. It was a grunt that woke me. Hersleb was gone. I went to the cave entrance. He'd knocked Arendt unconscious. It was Arendt's grunt that I heard.'

Sweeny was making for the cave entrance before Woods finished. 'Hersleb's on skis,' Woods said behind him. 'He can't have more than a few minutes' start.'

Sweeny was already strapping on his own skis.

'I should have made sure of the bastard when I had the chance,' he said bitterly. He stood up and grabbed his sticks, swinging the Schmeisser over his shoulder. 'I may be able to cut him off before he reaches his Nazi friends.' He reached into his pocket and threw Branting's map and compass towards Woods. 'Don't wait for dawn. Start moving everyone towards the glacier pass as soon as you can. Don't stop for anything until you are in Sweden.'

Before Woods could utter a protest, Sweeny had pivoted on his skis and pushed himself off down the slope, following the tracks of Hersleb's skis. The moon was still up, throwing the serried ranks of surrounding mountaintops into black silhouette. The snow beneath Sweeny's skis was hard white crystal and it whistled as he crouched down, head bent into the wind. His eyes peered forward into the white wilderness.

The moon on the white snow lit the countryside as if it were day-light rather than the silent hours before dawn. Somewhere among the shadows before him was the treacherous figure of Hersleb. With his skis humming along on the frost-covered snow, Sweeny descended into the valley in a series of sudden rushes, feeling the icy freshness of the air on his cheeks.

Hersleb, in spite of his unathletic appearance, must be a good skier, Sweeny reflected as he followed the tracks. They showed that he had run down the steepest inclines and manoeuvred dangerous bends in order to create short cuts. Once the tracks leapt over a small stream by a tiny waterfall which gushed with white crystal water.

Sweeny felt a terrible sense of impatience as he came to the end of the incline and his forward movement slowed. Now it seemed that Hersleb had been climbing; the snow was a tumble and mess. Sweeny had to turn sideways and shuffle upwards in order to keep his balance. The lonely howl of a dog echoed amidst the mountains. Sweeny stopped and peered into the gloom. Then he went on climbing, following the churned snow where Hersleb had scrambled upwards. He topped the ridge of the hill and looked into the valley

[209]

before him.

At the far end he could see the flickering light from the *turisthytten*. The Germans would be there. He swore aloud, for he saw no sign of Hersleb. For a moment he panicked, but then he saw the black shape moving swiftly down the hill, crouching over its skis, zig-zagging towards the valley floor.

The moon was beginning to race now behind the grey scudding clouds which had begun to sweep low over the mountain peaks. Some of the clouds entangled themselves on the jostling thrusts of rock which battled with each other in an attempt to pierce the dark night-sky with their sharply pointed fingers.

With his lips compressed in a thin line of determination, Sweeny crouched forward and thrust with his ski-sticks. He bent double on the skis, the sticks now firmly tucked under his arms as he sought to make himself as small an object as he could while he hurtled down the hillside.

The pale moon bathed the figure before him in its weird pastel glow. It was Hersleb right enough, racing towards the distant *turisthytten* where the Germans were encamped.

Snow began to fall, as it had done off and on since nightfall. It fell steadily, thrusting its cold fingers against Sweeny's face. Sweeny blinked, trying to keep his focus on the dark form. With the snow falling he could easily lose sight of the man and the snow would quickly obliterate his ski tracks. Sweeny pushed the snow from his eyes with a quick movement of one hand. He let out a gasp of satisfaction. He was gaining. Very slowly, it was true, but gaining nonetheless.

Now he plunged his sticks into the snow in an effort to increase his pace. His eyes saw a steep slope to his left, and in a split-second decision he pushed himself across to it, sweeping round in a semi-circle. Even though he was initially pulling away from his quarry, the steeper slope lent him added speed and by the time he reached the apex of the semi-circle he was travelling swiftly on an interception course.

Hersleb saw him coming and, in the still night air, Sweeny heard his curious cry of fear. In trying to alter his course to avoid the moment of interception, the little anaesthetist turned awkwardly and went tumbling headlong into the snow. There was a sharp crack, a sound like a pistol shot.

Sweeny, bringing himself to a halt by the use of his sticks, thought for a moment that the little man had a pistol. Then he saw that Hersleb had broken a ski. The crack of the wood had been amazingly loud. The little man had not hurt himself. He was scrambling up in the snow. His fear had spurred him to fury now, and he seized one of the sharp pointed ski-sticks and stumbled towards Sweeny, screaming in an inarticulate rage.

Sweeny hesitated a moment and then swung his Schmeisser from his shoulder. Hersleb either didn't see the gun or it didn't register. He kept coming on, fear and hatred blazing in his eyes.

Sweeny squeezed the trigger. The gun jumped in his hand. Hersleb fell forward onto his face. There was something dark staining the snow by his body.

Sweeny came nearer, moving gently on his skis.

The little man raised his head. The fear and rage were gone. There was a curious bewilderment on his face.

'*Det gjør vondt*,' he gasped. 'It hurts. . . *Dette er så dumt*, Sweeny . . . *så dumt* . . .'

His head fell back.

Sweeny became aware of distant shouting. He glanced up. Further up the valley, towards the light of the *turisthytten*, he saw the flicker of torches. The Germans had heard the sound of his shots.

Sweeny bent down and ran his hands rapidly through Hersleb's pockets. There was nothing in them that could give the Germans any information they did not have already. He stood up and began to stride forward on his skis, moving as swiftly as he could further along the valley before attempting to climb the slope in the direction from which he had come.

He felt neither sorrow nor remorse for what he had done, only anger at himself because he had not done it earlier. Perhaps the nurse Hilde and Jan Birkenes would still have been alive.

It was icy cold. Dark, too, for the scudding clouds had now obliterated the moon. There were two more hours to dawn and he hoped to put as much distance as he could between himself and the pursuing Germans. At least, the still-falling snow would obliterate his tracks. It took him quite a while to reach the top of the hill and when he looked back the valley behind him had disappeared in a white mist. He hoped he could remember the direction of the Svabensverk Glacier; hoped that he could catch the others up and not miss them in the dark and snow.

# CHAPTER TWENTY-SIX

Branting recovered consciousness, rather than merely waking from a sleep, with the sun shining brightly through the tiny window of the cell. He was aware of a man standing at the door carrying a tray. Branting screwed up his eyes and groaned as the sensations returned to his aching body.

'Are you all right, son?'

The voice was a rough but not unkind Norwegian voice. Branting focused on an elderly policeman.

'Nothing a few months in hospital won't put right,' he grunted. His voice sounded as if it belonged to someone else.

'I've brought you some coffee. Is there anything else you need?'

Branting swung his legs off the bed.

'Yes. Your revolver and the door of the cell left open.'

The old man grimaced and handed Branting the coffee.

Branting sipped at it and realized that the old man was still standing in the doorway.

'My colleagues and I have been talking,' he said hesitantly. 'We don't like what is being done here.'

Branting sniffed.

'Why do you work for them?'

'I am a policeman. I have been a policeman for twenty-five years. What else can I do?'

'You must fight the Germans. Not work for them. They are the enemies of our country.'

'I'm an old man. I don't like what they are doing . . .' His eyes fell from Branting's swollen and bruised face before he went on. 'But we are told by the authorities in Oslo that we should stand by our jobs, ensure that the country doesn't fall into anarchy.'

'The only anarchists here are the Nazis, my friend,' Branting grunted. The coffee burnt the inside of his raw mouth. 'The only legal authorities are in the north with the King.'

The policeman nodded.

'Many of my colleagues think so. There are six of us. The other five have gone to the top floor to check some files. There are no Germans about. The Gestapo officer and his assistant are across the river at the hotel.'

Branting frowned, suddenly realizing what the old man was implying.

'I must tie you up,' he said, getting to his feet.

'It is understood, young man.'

Branting moved across the cell and took the man's gun from his holster. It took only a moment to secure his willing prisoner with the man's own handcuffs.

'There are German soldiers all over town,' the old policeman said. 'Don't go to the railway station or to the river wharves. It's best to slip through the Byparken and round the castle grounds. The only chance for you is to get away into the country.'

'Thanks,' Branting said.

'Good luck, son. God save the King.'

Branting hesitated at the cell door and smiled.

'Good luck to you, too,' he replied.

He turned down the corridor to the foyer of the police station, checking the revolver as he went. It was an old-fashioned six shot .38 calibre. Better than nothing. He moved cautiously to the main reception office, limping a little as the pain shot through his every limb. The old policeman was right. It was deserted. The Norwegian policemen, appalled at the Gestapo techniques, had agreed to turn a blind eye. Branting's heart warmed towards them. There was an overcoat which had been left conspicuously across the desk. He grabbed it and hauled it on.

He was about to open the door when it swung inwards. For a moment he stood face to face with a young green-uniformed German. The two men gazed at each other in astonishment and then Branting, recovering a split second before the German, smashed his fist into the *Feld Polizei* man's jaw. The young man fell back with a grunt, surprise still on his features.

Branting grabbed the man's machine-pistol even as he fell, tearing open the leather pouches of his webbing and stuffing spare clips of ammunition into his coat pocket.

He stepped over the man and was out of the door into the bright Sunday morning. The police station was situated within the confines of the Radhuset, the town hall, which lay slightly back from the main road that led across the Kongsvinger Bridge through the 'upper city' towards the Kongsvinger Festning, the

[213]

castle which dominated the town. Branting turned and began to limp quickly towards the city park behind the Radhuset.

He had taken only a few steps when the crunch of tyres caused him to glance back toward the police station driveway. A sleek black Opel saloon had turned into the driveway. It halted and his eyes widened as he saw the unmistakable figure of Sturmbannführer Knesebeck climbing out. Fear clutched at his heart and he began to run.

There was a shout behind him as Knesebeck recognised him. A bullet whined over his head. Branting forgot his pain and his throbbing nerves and threw himself towards the meagre shelter offered by some bushes, rolling over and over in the early morning dew which lay wet and cold on the grass.

He clawed at the safety catch of the Schmeisser and sent a burst of gunfire towards the car. Knesebeck threw himself to the ground behind the shelter of the vehicle. Two or three black-uniformed men came sprawling out, fumbling with their guns. A bullet tore into Branting's jacket but it did not graze his skin. He half rose and fired an arc of bullets in the direction of his assailants, grunting with satisfaction as he saw one of them throw up his hands and fall.

Knesebeck was crawling forward towards the front wheel of the Opel to take up a firing position. A sudden revulsion came over Branting, an anger the like of which he had never felt before. Branting took his time, took careful aim and fired a long, low burst. Knesebeck jerked and drew back.

Anger had complete control of Branting now. He rose to his feet, inserted a fresh clip of ammunition into the Schmeisser and began to walk slowly forward, his finger pressing against the trigger. The memory of what Knesebeck had done to him fired him with an overpowering rage.

There came a single crack of a pistol and Branting felt something sear across his forearm. He continued to move forward. The figure of Knesebeck began to wriggle desperately toward the cover of the car. Branting felt a sharp pain in his side now. Then a second pain in his chest. He supposed that he had been hit yet he still managed to move forward, feeling only a dull ache.

There was the figure of Knesebeck squirming on his hands and knees in his raincoat before him. Branting saw the German glance up at his oncoming figure; the man's eyes were round with terror. For the first time Branting felt a sense of satisfaction. He stood there oblivious to everything else, depressing the trigger until the Schmeisser no longer jumped and bucked in his hands.

He felt no sensation as he began to collapse onto the ground. He simply felt as if he were descending into some dark mist, a warm welcoming darkness. He dropped into a kneeling position, unaware of the blood dripping from his mouth. Then he closed his eyes and fell forward onto his face.

It was some time before the group of Norwegian policemen slowly emerged from the police station and examined the scene nervously. Away in the distance they could hear the shouts of German soldiers and a klaxon sounding as the vehicles of the *Feld Polizei* began to race towards the sound of the gunfire.

They saw that Branting lay sprawled on his face. Before him lay the riddled and bloody body of the Gestapo officer. He was clearly dead. Nearby lay two uniformed SS men. One had his eyes open, but a hole in his forehead told where one of the Schmeisser bullets had smashed. The other was also dead. There was a third who still cowered against the car, groaning and holding his stomach. A trickle of red oozed between his fingers.

Two of the Norwegians went and knelt down by Branting and one of them felt for his pulse. He sighed and shook his head.

'He was a very brave man,' he said, glancing up at his comrade.

'He was a Norwegian soldier,' replied the other. 'We must make sure he gets a decent burial. Then, as soon as I am able, I am going to move north.'

The first policeman turned and examined Knesebeck.

'Well, this swine won't be doing any more torturing.' He glanced up at his companion. 'When you go north, I'll be joining you.'

'We all will,' said another. 'All of us will go north.'

It was dawn when Hauptmann Eschig stood looking down at the white, staring face of Doctor Andreas Hersleb.

Oberleutnant Gerhardt shook his head in bewilderment.

'His identification gives his name as Hersleb, Herr Hauptmann. According to the information we have been given, he was one of Stenersen's surgical team. Why would they shoot him?'

Eschig rubbed his chin thoughtfully.

'It would be a logical assumption that the man was on his way to us. Perhaps it would also be logical to assume that they used this means to prevent him.'

'But why?'

'That is what we must discover.'

'Well,' Gerhardt said, squinting into the morning sun, 'they cannot be far in front of us now. If we take the southerly trail it will bring us around to the plateau from which the glacier path crosses into Sweden.'

The Oberleutnant dug the toe of his boot into the snow, describing an arc.

'This is the path they seemed to be following. It curves to avoid the steep valleys and brings them out onto the glacier path at this point,' he jabbed with the heel. 'If we climb this mountain path here,' he indicated again, 'then we can expect to cut them off before they have time to traverse the glacier.'

'It seems that they don't realize the existence of this path which you propose taking,' observed Eschig.

The Oberleutnant shrugged.

'Either that, Herr Hauptmann, or they are hoping that we don't. They could be sticking to the easier path because of the people they are transporting. The route I propose is quite an arduous one . . .'

There was an implied question in the Oberleutnant's voice.

Eschig grinned and said, 'Well, have no worry about Weiss and myself. We will keep up with you and your men.'

'My men are *Gerbirgsjäger*.' There was a pride to the young officer's voice.

'The *Gebirgsjäger* are not the only people to climb mountains.'

'Very well, Herr Hauptmann,' the Oberleutnant said politely as he turned and pointed ahead. At the end of the snowy slopes of the valley rose a tall peak which seemed to dwarf even the giant thrusts around it. Here the mountains seemed to close in on every side. Eschig found it breath-takingly beautiful. He felt like an ant as his eyes rose to the higher slopes and precipitous snowfields, and then even further to bald patches of blue jagged granite where crag balanced upon crag until they vanished among the clouds or simply merged with the sky.

'That's where we have to climb, Herr Hauptmann. That's the Svabensverk Glacier and the pass the fugitives will have to take into Sweden.'

# CHAPTER TWENTY-SEVEN

'That must be the Swedish border,' called Inge, pointing ahead.

Trina Lanstrad, following just behind her, glanced up and grimaced.

'It looks impossible to get across the valley from here.'

The party halted and examined the terrain before them. Sweeny was checking Branting's map.

'There's the glacier between us and Sweden. According to Branting, we have to make our way further up the mountain here to a plateau which gives access onto a path that runs across the top of the glacier into Sweden.'

Stenersen glanced above them. 'We should rest first,' he said.

Sweeny shook his head. 'Plenty of time to rest when we are on the far side of the glacier.'

'I'm exhausted,' Woods protested.

Inge turned with a frown. 'So is Sweeny. He's had a longer night than most of us.'

Sweeny had, in fact, rejoined them just after dawn. No one had asked him about what had happened to Hersleb. They had avoided his face, almost avoided speaking to him until now.

'The Germans can't be that far behind us,' Sweeny said. 'If we rest now we might throw everything away within sight of the border.'

Inge voiced her agreement and reluctantly Woods accepted the logistics of the decision. Sweeny certainly had a point. It would not do to relax if the Germans were as close as Sweeny had reported them to be.

Sweeny was already examining the path which they would have to follow. They had come onto a fairly sheltered shoulder of the mountain which was covered by a forest of birch shrubs; a protected little valley which was nonetheless cold enough for the growth of the shrubs to be stunted. None of them had grown thicker than a man's arm, and it seemed that they had been growing and dying there since primeval times. The ground beneath them was covered by a thick matted tangle of rotten wood, and in most places the trees grew so thickly together that their branches interlaced. Trees that had died still stood, propped up by those that crowded around them. A deceptive covering of snow hid the springy mesh of fallen trees. It would be a difficult ascent to make, for it would be all too easy to break a leg or twist an ankle.

Sweeny examined Branting's map carefully. There was no other path marked on it.

'I'll go first,' Sweeny said as he turned to the others. 'Follow where I go. Professor, you come next; Trina and Kristine will follow. Inge and Doctor Arendt will come next and Woods . . . you form the rear guard.'

He hesitated and looked round.

'Any questions?' No one spoke. 'Right, the sooner we start out the sooner we shall arrive.'

He began to ascend carefully, feeling his way cautiously up through the frozen undergrowth. Several times he slipped and felt his leg go through the rotting wood into dangerous holes, but each time he managed to save himself from injury. The wooded slope rose for about five hundred feet before he finally emerged onto a narrow cleft. To one side of the cleft a small edge ran upwards to a sharp bend which seemed appallingly far above. There was no rest now. Sweeny cursed himself for not being far-sighted enough to rope everyone together. Branting would probably have done so. Nonetheless, they had to press on now. He had thought that once they had made it through the shrubs they would have emerged onto a broader pathway. He moved ahead slowly along the ledge and came around the bend.

His heart lurched. He nearly cried aloud in frustration. The way was suddenly obstructed by a frozen waterfall. The ice hung down across the ledge in a translucent curtain. There was no hope of going on, no hope of turning back. He bit his lip and stared in disgust at the obstruction.

Something caught his eye. He bent forward on the ledge and pushed at the snow in front of him. It gave. The water had frozen as it gushed over the ledge, and he found that there was space within the angle created by the waterflow. It was a small space true enough; about forty by sixty centimetres. He drew out his knife and scraped away the ice and snow which obstructed the aperture. It would take a man.

'We can crawl through here,' he called over his shoulder.

'Wait until I call to you from the far side of the waterfall before you attempt to come through.'

He knelt down and began to push himself into the ice tunnel, trying to fight the terrible feeling of claustrophobia which the encasement produced. It seemed that he had crawled for miles, but it was only about fifteen feet when he emerged through a small blockage of snow at the far end. The ledge here was much broader. He stood up and stamped his feet to regain the circulation. Then he bent to the hole and called back, 'Come through now, one at a time. Don't hurry. Go slowly. It's fairly easy.'

It took some time before they were all through.

Sweeny allowed them ten minutes to recover and then forced them to press on. Ahead, the sun sparkled on the gleaming expanse of the glacier. At this altitude the cold snow was inter-mixed with hard ice crystals, and this caused their movement to be actually easier because it compacted firmly under their weight. The ledge still climbed a little further before passing over a spur. To Sweeny's surprise it opened onto a windswept plateau. It was protected at one end by a little cirque or bowl of snow-covered rocks, while toward the other end it rose in a series of small hillocks to even greater heights where forbidding peaks towered menacingly. The path seemed to run under the peaks and suddenly open out to one side across the very top of the glacier – an unprotected path whose side dropped for hundreds of metres down towards a sprawl of dark conifers that looked like grass from this height.

Sweeny turned to his companions and, for the first time, relaxed his features in a smile of satisfaction.

'Once across there,' he indicated the glacier, 'we are in Sweden, according to the map. From then on it will be downhill all the way, both literally and figuratively.'

'Roll on the British Embassy, a hot bath and a warm bed,' grinned Woods.

Professor Stenersen glanced towards the glacier and shook his head sadly.

'I would not have embarked on this trip had I known it was going to cost so many lives. It should not have cost so much just to get an old man out of Oslo.'

Inge reached forward and squeezed her uncle's arm.

'It is what happens when that old man reaches London that counts, Uncle Didrik,' she smiled firmly. 'Don't forget that there is much work for you to do there.'

Stenersen sighed softly. 'Well, at least it will be good to rest from the tension of the last few days before that work starts.'

Trina Lanstrad nodded agreement.

'Surely we could rest here for an hour or two? I doubt whether the Germans will catch up with us now. They wouldn't be able to make it beyond that last waterfall with their equipment.'

Sweeny shook his head. His eyes were sweeping the plateau and noting the threatening atmosphere of desolation which oppresses people entering places of such barren loneliness. He was aware of the featurelessness of the wilderness, the unimaginable number of silent, ice-bound hills and deserted snow-filled valleys. It was a dead world; a world in which the affairs of the human race were of no account.

'I believe we should move on,' he said finally, turning to the others. 'As well as the Nazis, we mustn't forget that there are Swedish border patrols to be avoided until we are well inside Swedish territory and have made contact with the embassy. And I wouldn't like to be caught up here if a storm blew up. I say, let's move across the border now.'

It was the taciturn Doctor Arendt who first voiced agreement, raising a hand to point across the plateau.

'I don't think we have a choice in the matter,' he said softly.

At the far end of the plateau, from the direction of the cirque of rocks, several figures were moving. They were hard to see in their white coveralls but they could just be made out, moving swiftly on skis.

'Germans! They must have found another way up!' said Sweeny.

Without anyone giving the order, they began to stumble along the path to the point where it opened onto the glacier.

'Inge,' yelled Sweeny as they shuffled forward in a stumbling run, 'you take them across. Woods, you stay with me. We must give the others time to cross.'

Sweeny halted and glanced behind. The tiny figures on skis were moving swiftly across the plateau towards them. They moved professionally. They were well trained, these German *Gebirgsjäger*. Woods had halted, gazing expectantly at Sweeny.

'What do you intend?' he asked.

Sweeny looked to where Inge was leading her uncle and the others onto the glacier path and tried to estimate how long it would be before they were safely across and in the shelter of the snow-covered rocks on the far side. He said, 'Delay them as long as we can.'

He turned back towards the oncoming Germans and unslung his Schmeisser, giving a swift raking burst. He knew they were not in range but he hoped the sound of the weapon would make them cautious and halt their fast forward motion. He heard a harsh shout. The ski-ing figures, almost as one man, came to a halt in a flurry of snow.

Woods grinned lopsidedly.

'Ah well,' he sighed, 'I can't say that it was fun while it lasted.' He unslung his own Schmeisser. 'Even if we hold them back for a while, Sweeny, those bastards aren't going to halt at some invisible border line. They'll move across the border after us as far as they can.'

The skiers were moving forward again. Inge and the others had reached the far side of the glacier path and were running towards the cover of the rocks.

Sweeny looked at Woods. He grinned tightly.

'Do you think that you can fire that thing without killing yourself or me?'

Woods grimaced. 'As Commander Wallace said, it's a matter of pointing it and pulling the trigger, isn't it?'

'The important thing is to make sure the barrel is aimed in the right direction,' Sweeny agreed. 'Wait until they get near enough and give one long burst. Then when I yell, start running across the glacier path.'

Woods frowned. 'What about you?'

'I'll be so hard on your heels you'll feel my breath on your neck.'

The leading skiers were fairly close now. Sweeny could see them unslinging their rifles even as they moved forward. He raised his Schmeisser.

'Fire!'

He and Woods both opened up with a long arcing burst and several of the *Gebirgsjäger* tumbled headlong into the snow. The others halted and took up firing positions.

'Get going, Woods!' cried Sweeny, still firing.

Woods hesitated a moment, then turned and began to run, feeling the wind from bullets whistling past him. The snow in front of him seemed to erupt in a shower of icy particles. He ran on, turning his gaze to avoid the vast open expanse to his right where the glacier fell away hundreds of metres down the slope of the mountain towards the distant valley.

The next moment he was hit in the left shoulder and the powerful, searing impact sent him staggering. He could not recover his footing and sprawled face forward onto the ground. He lay gasping for a moment, feeling his shoulder growing numb. Then a strong arm was heaving him upwards. He could hear Sweeny swearing at him, telling him to get up and move. Automatically he began to do so. Something warm and sticky was oozing down his arm. He lurched forward, Sweeny guiding him.

The sound of gunfire and hoarse cries echoed in their ears.

Then they were across. By some miracle the hail of bullets whined past them on all sides but they weren't hit. Sweeny dragged Woods towards the cover of some boulders and they sprawled behind them in the snow.

Sweeny poked his head up. A soldier was already on the glacier path. He reached forward and sighted his machine-pistol. There was a click. With a curse he wrenched out the empty ammunition clip and inserted another. The delay was fatal. The burst from Sweeny's Schmeisser took the man across the chest, spinning him round and throwing him off the path. His body went sliding and bumping head over heels down the icy glacier and was lost to sight.

Woods was trying to sit up, clutching at his shoulder and wincing from the pain.

Sweeny cast him a sardonic smile.

'It may be some consolation to know that we have just crossed into Sweden.'

Woods forced a grin.

'Do you think we should tell the Germans?'

Sweeny looked at the doctor a moment and smiled.

'You're not such a bad guy, after all.'

Woods grimaced.

'This is a hell of a time and place to reach that conclusion. You're still an overbearing, egocentric, pig-headed . . . Okay, what do we do now?'

Several Germans were making their hesitant way onto the glacier path.

'Can you get across to those rocks and catch up with Inge and the others?' Sweeny asked.

'Let me stay here,' Woods said. 'We can pick them off as they come over and buy more time.'

[222]

Sweeny shook his head.

'They have the advantage of the high ground,' he said, nodding toward some outcrops on the other side of the glacier. 'Once their officer realizes that, he can send snipers up there to pick us off like clay pigeons in a shooting gallery.'

'Then why don't you get going and leave me here?'

The Germans were giving covering fire to some of their comrades who had started to cross. Sweeny frowned suddenly. The ground seemed to tremble momentarily. He heard a soft rumble and peered around. There appeared to be a speck of dust some way up on the glacier above them. His lips formed a thin determined line as he realized what it meant.

'Woods, can you still fire that thing?'

'One-handed Woods they call me, the terror of the West,' quipped the wounded man.

'When I say fire, fire up there, towards the top of the glacier.'

Woods's jaw dropped.

'I don't like to say so, old horse,' he drawled, 'but we don't have much ammunition left to play games with.'

'It's no game,' Sweeny replied grimly, sighting his Schmeisser. 'Now!'

They both fired long bursts towards the glacier. The faint rumble Sweeny had heard began to increase. Now Woods saw what his companion had seen. High up on the peak it seemed that a large cloud was billowing and spreading.

'Jesus! Avalanche!'

He turned and fired again until his ammunition ran out.

The Germans had taken cover, thinking that the gunfire was meant for them. Now they were pushing across the glacier again, apparently unaware of the rolling cloud of white above their heads. They were moving rapidly, but not so rapidly as the rushing mass of snow and rock. It hurtled down with the speed and power of an express train. The soldiers on the path seemed to have no warning of the avalanche before it struck them, sweeping them aside as if they were so many ants. Woods and Sweeny watched in curious fascination as the great white roaring mass of snow came hurtling over the helpless Germans and totally obliterated the path.

It seemed an eternity before silence returned to the mountains, before the cloud of snow finally settled. Sweeny rose slowly to his knees and brushed the white powder from his clothes. He gazed at the desolate expanse before him. There was no trace of the

Germans nor of the glacier path. He turned and hauled Woods to his feet.

'Can you make it?' he asked.

Woods gave him a quick grin.

'Indestructible, that's me. There's nothing wrong with me that a good team of surgeons and nurses can't cure,' he grunted.

Sweeny glanced back at the massive snow pile. 'The sound of the gunfire must have triggered it off. I'm just glad we were on this side of the path when it happened.'

'Poor bastards!' muttered Woods.

'Just bastards,' Sweeny corrected.

Woods stared at him for a moment.

'You're certainly not one for the "forget and forgive" ethic.'

'I believe in the Old Testament, Woods. An eye for an eye.'

Woods's eyes were focused beyond Sweeny, across the glacier. Sweeny saw them widen perceptibly.

'If I were to offer some advice this minute,' Woods said quietly, 'I'd say, start running. You might just make it.'

'What?' Sweeny stared stupidly at him. Then he turned slowly. Across the chasm, about fifty feet above them with a clear field of fire, stood two figures in field grey. One of them was already sighting with a rifle.

Hauptmann Eschig stood on a small outcrop of rock about one hundred and fifty metres from the red-haired man and his companion. Beside him Feldwebel Weiss was sighting with a Mauser rifle. Eschig had watched Oberleutnant Gerhardt lead his men onto the glacier path; had heard the rumble and noise of the avalanche and had seen the best part of an entire company of the *Wurttembergische Gebirgsbataillon* swept to their deaths – *Gerbirgsjäger*, the best mountain troops in Germany. Sweeny had beaten him. He stared down with a grim smile on his face as he examined the tall, well-built red-haired man for the first time. They had never met, never seen each other before, but he felt that he knew this man Lars Sweeny, knew him intimately. Eschig had played the game and he had lost. Sweeny and his comrades had crossed into Sweden and the only path after them was blocked. Eschig sighed deeply. He could not help but admire Sweeny. He was a worthy opponent. And yet – and yet he felt sorry for the man, knowing what he knew now.

Weiss had sighted his Mauser and looked towards his superior.

'I could bring them both down, Herr Hauptmann,' he said quietly.

Eschig shrugged.

'What purpose would it serve, Weiss? You would kill two brave men, that is for sure. But for what purpose? They have already won this game. They have Stenersen and the remnants of his surgical team safely across the frontier, and with or without Sweeny, they'll be in London within a few days.'

'You don't want me to shoot, Herr Hauptmann?'

'Have you ever read Schiller, Weiss?'

The Feldwebel shook his head. He was not even sure who Schiller was.

'No, Herr Hauptmann.'

'Schiller says that in taking revenge a man is but even with his enemy, but in forgoing vengeance he is superior.'

'I don't understand, Herr Hauptmann.'

Eschig nodded to where several of the *Gebirgsjäger*, who had been wounded before the crossing, sat or lay.

'Let's see if we can pick up the pieces.'

Weiss shrugged and shouldered his rifle. At this, one of the men on the far side of the glacier, the one clutching at a wound in his shoulder, began to move away out of range. Only the tall, red-haired man still stood gazing up to the rock where Eschig stood. Eschig smiled thinly, wondering what was passing through the man's mind.

'*Glückliche Reise*, Herr Sweeny!' Eschig suddenly yelled. '*Viel Glück! Auf Wiedersehen!*'

Then he lifted his hand to the peak of his cap in a punctilious military salute, paused in this position for a moment and then turned to follow Weiss.

On the other side of the chasm Woods had paused when he saw that Sweeny wasn't following him. He turned back in time to catch the action of the German's farewell. Then Sweeny had turned and was coming towards him.

'What the hell was that about?' demanded Woods. 'What did he say?'

Sweeny shrugged and glanced back momentarily at the two retreating grey figures.

'The bastard wished us a pleasant journey and good luck.'

# CHAPTER TWENTY-EIGHT

It was evening when they reached a group of *hytte* overlooking a lake among the pine forests of Sweden. They had managed to descend below the snowline into the lush green of spring vegetation. It was still cold but the *hytte*, a collection of some half-a-dozen single room timber structures built for tourists and climbers, were equipped with wood-burning stoves and some paraffin for cooking. In the cupboards were plenty of blankets.

Inge saw to the allocation of the huts. It was agreed that Sweeny would push on to the nearest hàmlet, Rottnedal, first thing in the morning, to make contact with the British Embassy in Stockholm by telephone. He reckoned the place to be a leisurely ten-mile walk away. But he was exhausted. Indeed, everyone was near to the point of collapsing, especially Woods. The bullet had seared across his shoulder, luckily without touching any muscle or bone. But he had lost a lot of blood. Stenersen had personally attended to the wound, and as soon as they reached the *hytte* Trina Lanstrad had given him a new dressing. The party had partaken of a frugal meal and gone immediately to bed.

Sweeny had decided that there was no need to post a guard but, nevertheless, he was the last to retire, making a final round of the *hytte* before entering the room which he was sharing with Woods. There were many things occupying his mind and jostling for attention, but he fell into a deep sleep of exhaustion almost as soon as he lay down.

Something was pressing against his face. It awoke him, causing him to start forward. A soft chuckle came out of the darkness and a cool hand touched his face.

'I'm sorry that I startled you,' Trina Lanstrad's voice was a soft purr above him.

'What's wrong?' Sweeny frowned, trying to ease himself up.

'Wrong? Nothing.' The girl's voice was reassuring. 'I just wanted to be with you, that's all.'

Her voice was deliberately demure, with an undisguised tone of coquettishness in it.

Sweeny felt a tingle of excitement in spite of his exhaustion. Then he frowned.

'Hush. You'll disturb Woods,' he said, gazing across the darkness-shrouded hut towards the other cot.

Trina giggled softly.

'Doctor Woods is not here. That's why I seized the opportunity to come in.'

'Where . . .?' began Sweeny in bewilderment.

'Really,' replied the girl. 'I suppose you don't know that there is anything between Woods and Inge Stenersen? You are supposed to be a perceptive man, Lars Sweeny. He went to her hut half-an-hour ago and he won't be back before dawn, unless I am no judge of character.'

Sweeny heaved a sigh and reached out for his cigarettes.

'What time is it?'

Trina pouted in the darkness.

'Really, Lars Sweeny! A girl, against all her moral upbringing, comes to a man's bed in the middle of the night with no nice moral intention in mind, and all he can ask is – what's the time?'

Sweeny grimaced and reached for the girl's hand.

'I'm not an easy person to be with, Trina,' he said awkwardly.

The girl said nothing, waiting for him to continue.

'I don't know whether I shall ever forget my cousin.'

'One doesn't forget. One adjusts,' she replied. 'I told you of my affair with the married man, didn't I? That's the worst type of affair to have, especially with a man who is prominent in public life. You cannot be seen anywhere together. You sneak into a cheap hotel to snatch a few hours in bed. That's all he has to offer. You cannot go out to a restaurant, to a theatre, or on holiday, just in case . . . Yet I endured it. I endured it for nearly two years.'

Sweeny nodded slowly.

'Perhaps we can help each other.'

The girl leaned forward, her lips moving softly towards his mouth.

'I hope so. I hope so very much.'

Her mouth closed, soft and moist, on his and his arms came up, pressing her slender form against his chest.

Inge Stenersen turned on her side, resting on one elbow and

supporting her head with one hand. She smiled down at Michael Woods.

'What's going to happen to us, Michael?' she asked.

'Marriage, kids, a country practice in some nice rural English village . . .' grinned Woods. 'Or maybe some stipend, a reward from a grateful country for placing myself in peril in their behalf . . . Sir Michael Woods, surgeon by appointment.'

'Stop talking nonsense,' she said, smiling broadly.

'All right,' Woods said. 'Would you settle for the marriage and kids?'

'After the war, perhaps.'

He frowned.

'The hell with the war. It might go on forever. Did you know that in England the marriage rate increased dramatically last autumn, out of all proportion to normal? No one waits until after a war.'

'I told you, Michael, I have to offer myself to the Norwegian service.'

Woods sighed. 'You must do what you consider is right, Inge. But you are a biochemist. That's important work even in wartime. The medical services are just as important as the military. Don't forget, we have to sew back the pieces which men like Sweeny tear apart.'

'That's unfair, Michael,' Inge sniffed. 'Sweeny is a good man. If it hadn't been for him . . .'

'I know. I know. And you're right. Absolutely right. But there is a lack of emotion in Sweeny that I don't like.'

'I think it's merely a cover. I think it's a sign of his having been hurt.'

Woods grinned at her.

'Since when did you qualify in psychiatry?'

'Probably the same time you obtained your certificate in cynicism,' replied the girl, turning onto her back.

'*Touché*!' Woods rolled his eyes. 'Anyway, perhaps Sweeny won't remain in the doldrums for long.'

Inge frowned. 'Doldrums?'

'Those parts of the ocean about the equator where calm and baffling winds prevail,' recited Woods. 'A word used to indicate low spirits.'

'What makes you say that Sweeny might get out of the doldrums?'

'Haven't you noticed how friendly he and your uncle's head

[228]

nurse are becoming?'

'Well, good luck to them.'

'I don't know. I wish I knew what it was about Sweeny. . . . He never seems to drop his guard. There's this coldness . . .'

Inge turned over.

'Ouch,' grunted Woods. 'Mind my shoulder.'

'Damn your shoulder,' whispered the girl. '*I'm* not cold.'

Woods chuckled. 'I can certainly vouch for that,' he replied, taking her in his arms and ignoring the minor spasm of pain from his wound.

It was snowing steadily as Sweeny made his way back from Rottnedal through the pine forest towards the *hytte*. The snow had been falling since early that morning. It fell silently and he was conscious that there were no sounds at all, not even the moaning of the wind through the tall dark conifers which stretched ahead of him.

Everything seemed to be going according to plan. He had telephoned the British Embassy in Stockholm and asked for Captain Jones, giving the codeword 'Valkyrie'. When he gave the message, 'Baldur had risen again', a curt voice had asked him where his party was located, then told him that the embassy would send transport within eight hours. By the next day they would be on their way to London.

Sweeny felt strangely deflated, almost depressed, as if he missed the adrenalin which had been flowing in him so often during the past week. He walked swiftly, head down against the cold. He had expected to be away in Rottnedal most of the day, but as things had turned out, the journey had taken him only half that time. Now there was nothing to do but wait for the transport to arrive from the embassy.

He came within sight of the *hytte* and thought of Trina Lanstrad. His expression lightened a little. The girl was full of surprises. Perhaps . . . perhaps they had some kind of chance, some hope for the future. Two emotionally hurt people made cynical by the weight of experience. It might work out.

He was passing the end hut, which Professor Stenersen had been allocated, intending to go straight to the room which Trina Lanstrad was sharing with the nurse Kristine, when he heard a muffled cry.

Sweeny halted, frowning. Then he turned and hurried to the door of the hut and flung it open without ceremony. He stood

[229]

poised on the threshold, his eyes wide. Just as he had swung open the door he heard the soft 'phutt' of a small-calibre automatic. Professor Stenersen was gazing towards him in bewilderment, one hand outstretched. There was a reddening patch on his shirt front. He opened his mouth to say something and then collapsed slowly to the floor and was still.

Sweeny raised his eyes to the other figure in the room. The one who was still gripping the small automatic and smoking silencer.

Trina Lanstrad stood opposite Sweeny, her face chalky white, the blue eyes hard and cold. The automatic came up swiftly to cover him.

'I'm sorry that you had to come back now,' she said, although there was no softness in her voice. 'You weren't supposed to see this. A pity. We could have been good together.'

Sweeny's face was a brittle mask. His only sign of emotion was a blink of his eyelids.

'Why?'

The word was almost a sigh.

'I am under orders not to let you take Professor Stenersen to London.'

Sweeny shook his head.

'Orders?'

'I am of the Nasjonal Samling. I hold a commission in the Hird. I have been an agent of the *Sicherheitsdienst* for a year now.'

'The *Sicherheitsdienst*?'

'The security service of our allies, the Third Reich.'

A cold realization began to sweep through him.

'Then it was you, you all along, and not Hersleb? Hilde, Birkenes . . .?'

She shrugged as if it were of no importance.

'You pretended to twist your ankle in the cemetery to hold us up. It didn't occur to me even when it appeared to heal so miraculously. Now I can see it.'

Trina Lanstrad nodded.

'And I managed to 'phone my contact so that a patrolboat was waiting for us at Kongsvinger. I slipped up to the old man's house and when I returned, to create confusion, I encouraged that pathetic little man, Hersleb, to slip away so that, if anything went wrong, you would think he was the one making the 'phone call.'

She was not boasting, merely being factual.

'I am actually sorry, Lars Sweeny,' she said as she raised the gun to his chest. The chill had left her eyes now and they were slightly moist and bright.

The blast of the explosion knocked her back with a crash, slamming her against the wall of the hut. Her mouth opened in a small 'o', her eyes widened with shock. The bullet had caught her in mid-chest, just above the heart. The little automatic fell from her nerveless hand with a clatter onto the floor.

'Lars . . .' she gasped.

Sweeny's face was still a cold, brittle mask as he watched her fall. He had not moved from where he stood in the doorway, but now he took his hand from his pocket, still clutching the Webley automatic which he had fired through the cloth of his coat. Coldly and deliberately he raised the gun and fired once more into her prone form. Not a muscle of his face betrayed an emotion.

There were sounds behind him. The others came running from the nearby huts. Woods was the first to reach the door and peer in. He pushed Sweeny aside and bent to the girl. Then he turned, bewildered, to Professor Stenersen. He raised his eyes to meet the horrified gaze of Inge and bit his lip. The girl could tell from his expression that her uncle was beyond help. Behind her, Doctor Arendt and the nurse Kristine could only look on helplessly.

Woods brought his gaze to Sweeny.

'What happened?' He did not recognize his own voice; it was hoarse with emotion.

Sweeny was silent for a moment, his curious mask-like face still directed towards the body of Trina Lanstrad.

Then he looked up and met Woods' gaze.

'The bitch misled us all,' he said. His voice was flat and cold. 'She was a Nazi agent the whole time. Hilde, Birkenes . . . she was responsible. She killed them.'

'But Hersleb?' Woods intervened.

'Hersleb was just a poor stooge.'

Inge was still in shock.

'But why? Why now? We are in Sweden. The British are picking us up soon. Why?'

Sweeny turned to look at the girl and, for the first time, his gaze softened.

'She was under orders, Inge,' he said. 'She had been told to prevent your uncle reaching London. That's why.'

[231]

It was a week later when Hauptmann Karl Eschig made the final entry in the file he had opened on 'The Red Haired Man – Lars Sweeny'. He sat back at his desk and reached for the coffee which Feldwebel Weiss had just brought in. Weiss was standing impassively by the desk. Eschig sipped the coffee and then inclined his head towards the file.

'And that is that, Weiss,' he sighed.

'Herr Hauptmann?'

'What shall we call it? The Stenersen case? The Sweeny case?'

A slight frown passed across the sergeant's bland features.

'There are many things I do not understand, Herr Hauptmann.'

Eschig put the coffee down and looked at his sergeant with a condescending smile.

'Such as?'

'The Lanstrad woman, for example.'

'Ah. Lanstrad. She was an ardent convert of Quisling's Nasjonal Samling. She was an early recruit to a small élite female branch of the Hird. When Quisling took some of the Hird to the Reich last summer for training, she was one of that number. The chief of the SD, the *Sicherheitdienst*, recruited her. She became one of our best agents in Norway. She became the mistress of a very close friend of the Norwegian Crown Prince Olav, an industrialist with a lot of economic and political power. She managed to persuade the man that his hope, the hope for the future, lay with Vidkun Quisling and the Nasjonal Samling. The man then became involved with Quisling's secret plans to take over the Government and welcome our troops into Norway.'

'I see, Herr Hauptmann,' nodded the sergeant. 'It was coincidence, then, that she was Professor Stenersen's chief nurse at the time when the British decided to attempt to get him to London?'

Eschig nodded.

'The biggest coincidence in the whole affair was the fact that the British chose Sweeny to lead this operation. You did say that you were not acquainted with Schiller, didn't you, Weiss?'

Feldwebel Weiss pursed his lips. He had done some research since Eschig had last mentioned the name.

'Schiller, Herr Hauptmann? He was an eighteenth century poet.'

Eschig nodded thoughtfully and recited: ' "What the reason of the ant laboriously drags into a heap, the wind of accident will collect in one breath".'

Weiss stood silently, not sure what kind of comment to make. Eschig raised his head and smiled thinly.

'You see, Weiss, we are ruled by coincidence, by chance. We are its servants and its slaves.'

'I am confused, Herr Hauptmann.'

'The coincidence was in sending Sweeny to the Riks-Hospitalet. You see, Sweeny's cousin, Freya Hartvig, was a journalist on the newspaper *Dagsbladet* . . .'

'I remember, Herr Hauptmann.'

'Good. Under Schanche, the special features editor, Freya Hartvig was working on an exposé of certain prominent people who had connections with the Nasjonal Samling. The plan of Quisling to take over the Government and invite the German Government into Norway to protect the Norwegians was uncovered. But Freya Hartvig had also uncovered something else. The prominent industrialist, the friend of Crown Prince Olav, and his role in the matter had been discovered. Freya Hartvig was about to publish this.

'Trina Lanstrad was not only this man's mistress but an agent of both the Hird and the *Sicherheitdienst*. Her orders were explicit. She was to protect the man at all costs and prevent the *Dagsbladet* from revealing the truth. She went to Stavanger on the night of April 8. She killed Freya Hartvig, killed her very clinically according to the Stavanger police reports. She used her medical skill and cut her throat. She was about to leave Freya Hartvig's apartment with the dossier Freya had collected for her articles when Erik Hartvig came in. Trina Lanstrad reacted quickly and shot him. Then she left.'

'It is hard to believe that a woman could be so cold-blooded, Herr Hauptmann,' Weiss observed.

Eschig grimaced. 'If you have not read Schiller, Weiss, then I do not suppose you will have read the English poet, Rudyard Kipling?'

'No, Herr Hauptmann.'

'There is a poem of his that begins:

*When the Himalayan peasant meets the he-bear in his pride,*
*He shouts to scare the monster, who will often turn aside.*
*But the she-bear thus accosted rends the peasant tooth and nail.*
*For the female of the species is more deadly than the male.*

Eschig paused reflectively.

'A few hours later the invasion started. Trina Lanstrad had not been let into the secret. Had she known, there would have been

[233]

no need for her journey to Stavanger, no need for her to kill Freya Hartvig or her husband or for her to steal the documents relating to her lover. The affairs of man are made up of such "if-onlys", Weiss.

'As it happened, the invasion took place that morning. Sweeny came to find his cousin. The Stavanger police, looking for a motive, still think that Sweeny is the killer they are searching for because it so happened that he had been in love with his cousin. There were enough gossips in Stavanger to make the police think that Sweeny killed her and her husband out of jealousy.'

'But, Herr Hauptmann, according to Schanche, Sweeny found a Nasjonal Samling badge clutched in the dead hand of Freya Hartvig. He, quite rightly it seems, assumed that it came from Freya's killer. How was it that Sweeny, who you have said is a man of exceptional intelligence, did not link that Nasjonal Samling badge with Trina Lanstrad? Nasjonal Samling badges, I have discovered, give the membership number and initials.'

'The badge Sweeny had was 5684 PL,' Eschig said with a wry smile. 'Petrina Lanstrad. The clue was in froht of him the whole time.'

Feldwebel Weiss sighed.

'As you say, Herr Hauptmann, it is a remarkable coincidence that Sweeny, having escaped to England, was returned to Norway to conduct Stenersen's escape and that Stenersen's head nurse was the very person who had killed his cousin. The very person that he sought.'

Eschig brought his gaze back to the closed file.

'I wonder what other ironies there are in the story which we will never know, which will never be placed in the file?'

'Shall I destroy the file, Herr Hauptmann? After all, I suppose it comes under state security secrets.'

Eschig hesitated.

'No. We will keep it. Who knows, the true story of Trina Lanstrad may need to be told one day. What you can do is get me a cognac, though. I feel the need for some stimulation.'

'*Zum Befehl*, Herr Hauptmann.'

Eschig rose to his feet as Weiss went out in search of the cognac, which was 'filed' in the bottom drawer of his desk in the outer office. He turned to the window and gazed down at the green-uniformed *Geheime Feld Polizei* strolling along the sunlit Akersgate, standing by the grand portals of the Storting, the parliament buildings. The May sky was a vivid blue and the pale sun painted the city of Oslo with pastel colours. Yes, he thought, it was right to keep the file secure somewhere. He thought of Sweeny and felt all the more certain of this. The Norwegian police might want to know the truth about the Stavanger murders one day.

'*Amicus Plato, amicus Socrates, sed magis amica veritas,*' he muttered.

Feldwebel Weiss entered with a glass.

'Herr Hauptmann?' he frowned. 'You said something?'

Eschig turned. ' "Plato is dear to me, Socrates is dear but truth is dearer still." It's of no importance, Weiss, just something some Roman said a long, long time ago.'

# EPILOGUE

The conduct of the campaign in Norway brought forth increasing criticism of the British Government in general and of Neville Chamberlain in particular. On May 7, the day Sweeny, Woods and Inge Stenersen arrived back in London, a two-day debate on Norway began in the House of Commons. It was clear that Chamberlain had lost support even within his own party and one of the leading Conservative backbenchers, Leo S. Amery, voiced the opinion of many when he echoed the famous words Oliver Cromwell used to dismiss a Parliament in former times: 'Depart, I say, and let us have done with you. In the name of God, go!' The Labour Party leader, Herbert Morrison, announced that his party intended to divide the House on the issue, and even though Chamberlain and the Government survived the ensuing vote of confidence by 281 to 200, it was clear that several Conservatives had voted with the Opposition. For three days there was a crisis within the British Cabinet and then, on May 10, Chamberlain spoke to the nation on the radio. It was the very day the Germans began their sweep through neutral Holland, Belgium and Luxembourg.

'I had no doubt in my mind,' Chamberlain said, 'that some new and drastic action must be taken if confidence was to be given to the House of Commons, and the war carried on with the energy and vigour essential to victory. . . . In the afternoon of today it was apparent that the essential unity could be secured under another Prime Minister though not myself. In these circumstances my duty was plain.'

Chamberlain resigned at 6.00 pm that Friday. It was well known in Government circles that he wanted to nominate Lord Halifax, a man who shared all his political ideals, as Prime Minister. However, it was Winston Spencer Churchill who emerged as the new leader. On May 12 he told the nation that he had nothing to offer them but 'blood, tears, toil and sweat' but on the following day, speaking in the House of Commons, he promised his total commitment to victory. 'Victory at all costs, victory in spite of all terrors, victory, however long and hard the road may be, for without victory there is no survival.'

Even as Churchill took office, the situation for the Allies in Norway was going from bad to worse. The Supreme Commander of Allied Forces, Admiral of the Fleet, Lord Cork and Orrery, had already decided that the 24,500 men of the Allied command would have to be evacuated. The position in Norway was untenable. Nonetheless, he gave orders for a final attack on the northern town of Narvik, still held by the Germans, and it fell on May 28. Even as the Norwegian town fell, though, the Germans were achieving crushing victories as they swept across a front of 175 miles through neutral Holland, Belgium and Luxembourg to outflank the French defence of the Maginot Line. Soon another, a more fateful evacuation would be beginning – the evacuation of the British Expeditionary Force from Dunkirk.

On June 1 Lord Cork told the Norwegian Government of his decision to pull the Allied troops out of Norway. Commencing on the night of June 6, the British, French and Poles began their embarkation while the Norwegian troops withdrew to specially selected areas where they were given a choice – disband and disperse before being captured by the Germans or, like several other Norwegian units, make a strategic withdrawal over the mountains into neutral Sweden for internment. The third alternative, of course, was to surrender to the Germans. There were not enough troopships to evacuate the remnants of the six divisions of Norway's mainly militia army. On June 7, King Haakon VII and Crown Prince Olav, with members of the Norwegian Government and the Allied Legations, embarked on HMS *Devonshire* from the town of Tromso to go into a bitter exile in England. In the early hours of June 8 the final parties of Royal Engineers and Military Police, in charge of the pierheads, embarked on their transports.

In the withdrawal the Allies took another savage defeat. One of the two aircraft carriers involved in operations, HMS *Glorious*, which had been brought with the *Ark Royal* from the Mediterranean, together with her destroyer escorts, *Ardent* and *Acasta*, was spotted by the German battleship *Gneisenau*. The German ship opened fire with her 11-inch guns from a range of fourteen miles. The *Ardent*, trying to buy time for the carrier, went full steam ahead for the *Gneisenau*, guns blazing. Shells from the German warship tore her apart and capsized her. The *Gneisenau* then hit the *Glorious* and 1,474 officers and men with 41 Royal Air Force pilots and personnel, went to their deaths. The *Acasta* turned on the enemy in fury and made for her but within moments the little destroyer had been blasted out of the water.

Having watched the departure of the Allied forces, the King and the Norwegian Government from Tromso, the commander-in-chief of the Norwegian forces, General Otto Ruge, who had refused to go into exile, preferring to stay and share whatever hardships now befell his defeated army, broadcast to the nation: 'The first chapter in our struggle for freedom is over and we have a dark time to face in a conquered country. But the war continues on other fronts. Norwegians are joining in the struggle there. The day will come when you can raise your heads again.'

Ruge left the makeshift studio to commence negotiations for an armistice with the Germans and to eventually be taken to a prisoner-of-war camp in Germany.

Until April, 1945, Norway was to lie under the conquering heel of the Third Reich. Yet it was to be a double-edged victory for the Führer. Ever fearful that the Allies would invade Norway again, Hitler was forced to maintain a considerable army there. Indeed, the opening of a European front by a flanking movement in Norway occurred to Churchill several times during the war and only the impracticality of the terrain caused the idea to be shelved. Nonetheless, in terms of the tens of thousands of men, the equipment and the German naval forces which were kept tied up in Norway in case of an attack, in addition to the increasing activities of the 'Home Army', the Norwegian resistance, the conquest of Norway became more of a liability than an asset to the Third Reich.

When Churchill formed his Government after the resignation of Neville Chamberlain, he appointed Chamberlain as Lord President of the Council in order to demonstrate that there was no split within the Conservative Party. Yet it was becoming obvious that Chamberlain was ill and that his condition was, in fact, serious. He was examined by his personal physician, Lord Horder, in July and on July 24 he underwent an exploratory operation performed by Mr Edward G. Slesinger, the senior surgeon at Guy's Hospital in London. Slesinger was an expert on abdominal and goitre surgery as well as fractures and was the Hunterian Professor of the Royal College of Surgeons. A major operation was needed and Chamberlain was told frankly that he had an 'even chance' of recovery. The official statement to the public was that the operation was 'for the relief of intestinal symptoms of an obstructive nature'.

On July 29, while recovering at Nuffield House, Chamberlain wrote: 'I understand that I am a model patient. From the professional point of view my progress is entirely satisfactory but my personal opinion is that I have had fair hell.' He was allowed to return home to Highfield Park, Heckfield, near Basingstoke, in mid-August. In September he left his Hampshire home to go to the House of Commons but realized that he was unable to stand the strain of his normal duties. On October 3 he resigned office in Government and in the Conservative Party, although he still remained the Member of Parliament for the Edgbaston constituency of Birmingham, which seat he held with a 21,862 vote over Labour's J. Adshead. But it was clear that Chamberlain would not be able to stand at the next election. On October 9 Winston Churchill, now elected to the leadership of the Conservative Party, remarked that Neville Chamberlain's withdrawal from active public life was a heavy and painful loss. His tone now was a little more respectful than his previous comment on Chamberlain: 'An appeaser is one who feeds a crocodile, hoping that it will eat him last.'

That the operation which Chamberlain had undergone had not been successful was becoming obvious to everyone. On October 14 the King and Queen paid a visit to Chamberlain's home and stayed half-an-hour. On the same day Chamberlain's son Frank, a 2nd Lieutenant in the 69th AA Brigade of the Royal Artillery, was given embarkation leave to visit his father. Chamberlain had written to his friend, the controversial United States ambassador Joseph Kennedy, 'Since my illness makes it impossible for me to be of further service to my country, my great concern is not to be a burden to my wife and family, so perhaps God in His mercy will take me soon.'

On Saturday, November 9, at 5.30 pm, Neville Chamberlain died. The *Daily Telegraph*, in an obituary published on November 11, said:

'Mr Chamberlain was, perhaps, not the ideal war leader, gifted though he was with exceptional and hereditary political aptitudes; but no one could have applied himself more vehemently to the task than he did once the die was cast. Perhaps the Prime Minister's words may be his epitaph: "You did all you could for peace, you did all you could for victory".'

Winston Churchill went on to make a further comment: 'He

met the approach of death with a steady eye. If he grieved at all it was that he could not be a spectator to our victory, but I think he died with the confident knowledge that his country had at last turned the corner.'

On November 14 Neville Chamberlain was buried, with all the pomp and ceremony due to a leader of his country, in the marbled splendour of the vaults of Westminster Abbey.

Yet there is another grave, far away from this famed resting place of great statesmen, of captains and kings, which is equally important. It lies near a bluff shrouded by snow mists on a bleak Swedish mountain, not far from the Norwegian border, where fresh snowfalls and high winds make constant drifts so that the wooden cross that once marked the spot has rotted and blown away. Now there is nothing to mark the grave and the most discerning eye could not spot it, even if there were no whirling snow clouds to obscure the vision and take the breath away.

The scenery here is ever-changing in the gusting snowstorms and strong winds which snatch at anything that is not secure. There is no marker, no solemn inscription, nothing to indicate the grave. Yet that grave exists, somewhere under the drifting snow and winter ice . . . If there was to be an epitaph for that grave it might well be the words of Friedrich von Schiller: 'What the reason of the ant laboriously drags into a heap, the wind of accident will collect in one breath.'